First Light in Morning Star

The *Maidels* of Morning Star

Charlotte Hubbard

ZEBRA BOOKS
KENSINGTON PUBLISHING CORP.
www.kensingtonbooks.com

Why was Lydianne so skittish around him?
Was she becoming more interested in Detweiler?
Was she intimidated because Jeremiah was the
district's bishop, or because he'd been married before?

Jeremiah smiled, hoping his voice didn't hitch like a teenager's. "I, um, was wondering if you'd come to the Shetler reunion with me on Sunday the fifteenth—"

"No! I—I can't do that!"

Startled by the fierce finality of her reply, Jeremiah blurted his response before he thought about it. "Why not? Are you seeing Detweiler?"

Lydianne's eyes widened as she gripped the edge of her desk. "Absolutely not! It's not a *gut* idea to get involved with—this isn't the right time to—"

The deep disappointment on his face must've alerted her to his feelings. "I'm sorry, Jeremiah," she whispered. "Please don't ask me to explain. And please don't ask me again."

Chapter One

Hope fluttered like a butterfly in Lydianne Christner's heart as she parked her rig in the pole barn just north of the new white schoolhouse. It was barely dawn and she was more than an hour early for her interview with the members of Morning Star's Amish school board, but she needed time to collect her thoughts and plan her answers to the questions she anticipated from the five men who would decide her future. It had been a spur-of-the-moment decision when she'd blurted out her wish to apply for the teaching position at the members' meeting after church a week ago—but in the days since, Lydianne's soul had reconfirmed her impulsive outburst.

She *really* wanted this position. The trick would be replying to the school board's questions without hinting at the very personal reason she wished to become Teacher Lydianne.

Did she stand a chance? As she walked toward the new schoolhouse, she pondered the possibilities.

Lydianne had no idea if anyone else had applied for the position in the past several days. Morning Star's previous teacher, Elam Stoltzfus, had already left town to assist his family in the wake of his father's debilitating stroke, so there was no chance he would return. She didn't know of any other married Amish men who'd likely fill the position— nor did she believe any of Morning Star's other single Amish women aspired to teach.

Her close friend, Regina Miller, had just become en-gaged to Gabe Flaud, so she'd be ineligible to teach. Jo Fussner sold the baked goods, canned vegetables, and jel-lies she and her *mamm* made—and she'd taken on the chal-lenge of managing The Marketplace, the renovated stable where local crafters sold their goods. The Helfing twins, Molly and Marietta, ran the noodle factory their mother had begun, and they rented out their *dawdi hauses* to tourists—and they also kept a shop at The Marketplace— so neither of them seemed a likely candidate for the teaching position, either.

Lydianne grimaced when she thought about either of the middle-aged Slabaugh sisters managing a classroom. Esther and Naomi lived on a farm just outside of town, and their main occupation seemed to be sharpening their *maidel* tongues on tidbits of other people's business.

Pity the poor children who had either of them for a teacher! Lydianne thought as she gazed across the large grassy lot between the schoolhouse and the red stable that housed The Marketplace shops.

She warned herself not to assume the school board would hire her, however. After all, she had no teaching experience. She'd taken a job as bookkeeper and stainer at the Flaud Furniture Factory when she'd first come to Morning Star, and she was also the financial manager at The Marketplace, so maybe the men on the board would believe she should remain in her current positions. Martin Flaud, who owned the furniture factory, was the school board president. He hadn't directly challenged her about leaving her job with him to teach school, but his speculative gazes during the past week had given Lydianne plenty to think about while she'd been staining furniture and tallying orders.

But with God's help, I can do this! My heart's in the right place! Lydianne reminded herself fervently. *Just look at what my friends and I have accomplished over the summer. The stable across the way was falling in on itself, and now it's full of successful shops that attract hundreds of shoppers to Morning Star every Saturday—and its commissions have funded the new schoolhouse.*

Lydianne and her *maidel* friends felt extremely pleased about the businesses that now thrived because they had believed in the power of their positive intentions—and because the Old Order church district had bought the property as both a place to hold its auctions and where a new schoolhouse could be built on higher ground. In the first light of this August morning, the white geraniums, purple petunias, bright green sweet potato vines, and yellow marigolds filling The Marketplace's window boxes glowed in the rays of the rising sun. The stable's deep red walls shone with the care she and her friends had lavished upon the building.

Inspired by the sight, Lydianne firmly believed that her ability to manage money, solve problems, and deal effectively with people would be her finest assets as she took on the challenges of teaching Morning Star's Amish scholars. It was her deepest desire to share her love of learning—to share the best of herself—with the children who'd be charged to her care . . . even if one child in particular was the reason she craved the position.

Sighing nervously, Lydianne stepped onto the stoop of

the schoolhouse and opened the front door. Pete Shetler, Bishop Jeremiah's nephew, had built the school on a hillside in the style of a bank barn—which meant the front entrance to the classroom was on flat ground, and the lower level was also accessible without any outside stairs. The pungent aromas of fresh varnish and paint, along with the tang of sawed lumber, made Lydianne throw open the windows to let in the fresh morning air. She indulged herself in a moment of standing behind the teacher's desk, centered in the front of the large, airy room.

Her heart fluttered at the sight of fresh white walls, low-maintenance tan flooring, and rows of new metal desks and chairs—the front row filled with shorter desks for the youngest scholars. The white board that covered most of the wall behind her awaited whatever instructions she would write with a variety of colored markers. The built-in bookcases at the back of the classroom would soon hold a small library as well as a collection of textbooks. Sturdy tables along the side walls would provide space for class projects. A stairway led to the lower level, where the scholars would hang their coats and store their lunch buckets when they came in each morning.

The prospect of beginning a new job—a new life—in this fresh setting filled Lydianne with an even greater excitement than she recalled from when she was a scholar, buying paper and supplies as she anticipated each new school year. Even at twenty-three, she loved learning new things, and she eagerly looked forward to passing on her enthusiasm for reading, writing, and arithmetic to—

"Ah—*gut* morning, Lydianne." A familiar male voice pulled her from her musings. "Somehow I'm not surprised that you arrived early."

Lydianne pivoted, hoping Bishop Jeremiah Shetler

hadn't caught her with a sappy, day-dreamy expression on her face. "And *gut* morning to you, Bishop," she replied in the firmest voice she could muster. "I couldn't resist the chance to look at all the new desks and equipment before the interview began. Pete did a fabulous job of building our new schoolhouse, ain't so?"

The bishop nodded, stepping into the large classroom to admire it. "My nephew has a few questionable habits, but when I see his carpentry skills and the work he can do in short order—when he puts his mind to it—I believe there's hope for him yet," he said with a fond laugh. He winked teasingly at Lydianne. "And maybe if he found a nice young woman who'd marry him—"

"Ah, but if I married Pete, I couldn't be the new teacher, could I?" she shot back.

Bishop Jeremiah's laughter echoed in the large room. "True enough. And maybe he has a few more things to work out of his system before he's ready to be domesticated," he admitted. "But it's a positive sign, that Pete's quit his job at the pet food factory in favor of taking on more building projects for the church district. And the Helfing twins haven't kicked him out of their *dawdi haus*, so maybe he'll find his way into the church someday soon."

Lydianne smiled as the bishop pulled six chairs from the desks in the back row and the worktable and arranged them in an elongated circle. Pete Shetler and his golden retriever, Riley, were the source of several exasperated stories Molly and Marietta had shared with Lydianne and the other *maidels*—but Jeremiah was right. His nephew had taken on the task of building the schoolhouse after he'd led the work crew that had refurbished the stable in record time before The Marketplace shops had opened in June. Didn't everyone deserve the benefit of the doubt and a second chance, after all?

Even you, her soul whispered. *So pay attention and give it your best effort this morning.*

As the hands of the wall clock above the door approached eight o'clock, the other members of the school board arrived. Preacher Clarence Miller greeted Lydianne, as did the younger board members, Glenn Detweiler and Tim Nissley. As they took a few moments to look at the new classroom and its contents, Lydianne fortified herself with a deep breath. She prayed silently for the right answers to whatever questions they might ask her, because—except for Bishop Jeremiah—they all had children in school.

Each man also had the power to express doubts about her lack of experience, or whatever other flaws he might perceive that would keep her from being a fitting replacement for Elam Stoltzfus.

Martin Flaud paused in the doorway, surveying the classroom. The morning sun glimmered on his silver-shot brown hair and beard as he removed his straw hat and gazed at Lydianne. "Shall we get on with our interview?" he asked in a businesslike tone. "I, for one, am eager to hear what Miss Christner has to say about teaching our children."

Swallowing hard, Lydianne sat down in the chair that Martin indicated as her place. She smoothed the skirt of her lilac cape dress and straightened her apron, hoping she appeared fresh and competent. As the men took seats in the circle, she saw that none of them had brought any notes—and she wondered if she should've scribbled a few reminders on a tablet before she'd come, if only to refer to it in case her mind went blank during the interview.

But now, God, it's in Your hands, she reminded herself.

She put on her best smile as she waited for Martin or one of the other men to speak first. Had they agreed beforehand about how the interview was to proceed, and who would ask certain questions?

Bishop Jeremiah cleared his throat. "Why do you want to be Morning Star's new teacher, Lydianne?" he asked with an encouraging smile.

An answer—the image of a bright young face—immediately came to mind, but Lydianne reminded herself that even though it was the district's bishop asking her this question, she couldn't tell the whole truth. "I've always loved children, and I feel confident that—"

"I'm surprised you're not married with a family of your own," Preacher Clarence interjected. "At your age, surely you've had a serious beau or two—"

"All the years you've worked for me at the factory, I've wondered about that, as well," Martin chimed in earnestly. "Yet, when I see you at church or around town, you're with your *maidel* friends rather than a young man."

Lydianne blinked. She hadn't expected questions of such a personal nature—at least not so early in the interview. She sensed she needed to answer the preacher and her employer without backing down, however, even if—again—she couldn't possibly reveal the whole story of her past. "I—I was engaged before I came to Morning Star, *jah*," she replied softly. "But my fiancé drowned at a family reunion. On the day before we were to be married."

The male faces around the circle sobered. A few moments of uncomfortable silence filled the schoolroom before any of them spoke. Lydianne struggled to keep the tears from her eyes, trying to remain professional despite the emotional timbre of her voice.

"I'm sorry to hear that, Lydianne," Tim Nissley said. His

little daughter would be a first-time scholar this fall, so he'd recently agreed to join the school board. "But you've probably cared for younger brothers and sisters, *jah*?"

Lydianne smiled carefully. "No, I was the last child of fifteen—so much younger than my siblings that Mamm always called me her little miracle," she added with a chuckle.

She sat up taller, reminding herself that because she was a *maidel* with no family in Morning Star, folks around town were naturally curious about her past. So far, her experience with children wasn't stacking up very well, but she hoped to convince these men she was a qualified candidate for their teaching position anyway.

"I was only seventeen when Mamm passed, and Dat had been gone a while by then," she explained. "My sisters and brothers were all married with homes in various places, so I—I came to Morning Star six years ago for a fresh start. I'm grateful to God—and to you, Martin—for the job at the furniture factory, and that I'll soon be able to buy the little house I've been renting for my own."

"I'm also sorry for your losses, Lydianne. We're pleased to have you here amongst us, and pleased that you're interested in teaching our scholars," Bishop Jeremiah put in gently. As though to steer the interview back toward its original direction, he focused purposefully on the other board members. "What do you gentlemen want to know about Miss Christner's goals in the classroom, or how she intends to handle discipline problems, for example?"

Lydianne glanced gratefully at the bishop, sensing his support. She hoped he and the other men present wouldn't realize there were some large gaps in her story.

"What with my two girls and Clarence's daughters being

the oldest scholars, and most of the other children just starting school this year, I doubt our new teacher will have a lot of discipline problems to contend with," Martin remarked as the other men nodded in agreement. He smiled at Lydianne, his stern features softening. "I'm surprised— and sorry, too—that you'd be leaving the furniture factory, but my Kate and Lorena are delighted that you want to be their new teacher."

"*Jah*, my girls are, too," Preacher Clarence put in with a nod. He gazed at her in that stern, purposeful way he had as he phrased his next remark. "I think, after having Teacher Elam all their lives, my Lucy and Linda are looking forward to a change. If you take up teaching, however, I'm wondering if you'll need to quit managing the finances at The Marketplace. What are your thoughts on that?"

Lydianne had anticipated this question, because the Amish shops she and her *maidel* friends had organized last May had become hugely successful since they'd opened on the first of June, and business showed no sign of slowing down as summer came to an end. "I don't run a shop, and The Marketplace is only open on Saturdays," she reminded him. "My accounting duties are very flexible, schedule-wise, so I don't expect them to interfere with my teaching. If they do, however, I'll turn the bookkeeping over to Jo Fussner, who's the other main manager.

"My scholars will always come first," she added emphatically. "I realize that because this is my first year of teaching, I'll need time to prepare lessons, create class projects, and maintain the classroom. I have no qualms at all about giving up my responsibilities at the new shops, if I need to."

As the other men nodded, Glenn Detweiler, who ran a

woodworking shop at The Marketplace—and who'd lost his wife over the summer—came out of the silent isolation that had enveloped him of late. "We have no other applicants, so I think we should offer Lydianne the position," he blurted. "*Gut*ness knows my Billy Jay needs a caring, compassionate woman in his life. He's been lost without his *mamm*."

Lydianne was startled by Glenn's wistful remark—and so were the men seated around her. Martin's flummoxed expression suggested that Glenn had eclipsed the school board's prearranged plan for the interview by saying outright that they should offer her the job. He glanced around the circle of men and then gazed at Lydianne.

"If you'll step outside for a moment, we'll discuss Glenn's suggestion," Martin said diplomatically. "But if there are any other questions—or if you have questions for us— we'll address those first, of course."

Lydianne rose immediately, not wanting to distract the board with questions just for the sake of asking something. Except for differences in their personalities, Amish teachers had been conducting classes the same way for decades— and even the textbooks hadn't changed from one generation to the next. The men watched her go, as though they had no further need to hear her philosophies on education or her plans for handling situations in the classroom.

As she stepped outside and off the front stoop, she welcomed the breeze and the chance to collect her thoughts. Had anyone else interpreted Glenn's remark as a bid for Lydianne's personal attention . . . a hint that he might consider her as much of a candidate for Billy Jay's new *mamm* as for his teacher?

She wasn't sure how to handle that possibility. Glenn Detweiler was a nice fellow—and with his full head of black hair and the matching beard that framed his face, Lydianne considered him attractive, too. No one questioned his devotion to seven-year-old Billy Jay or his infant son, Levi, either, but the idea of stepping in to replace Dorcas as the mother of his two sons intimidated Lydianne far more than taking on the challenges of becoming the district's new schoolteacher.

The school board surely won't encourage such a relationship, either, Lydianne reasoned as she strolled toward the pole barn to check on her horse. *They'll want their new teacher to commit to the classroom at least for an entire school year.*

"Hey there, Polly," she murmured, reaching into her apron pocket for a sugar cube. "How do you like this pole barn? You'll be spending more time here—and out in that nice pasture—if I get this job. You might like that better than hanging around home all by yourself, ain't so? I'm thinking several of the older kids will drive to school each day."

As the mare nuzzled the cube from her hand, Lydianne turned at the sound of footsteps. Bishop Jeremiah was walking toward her, his wide smile suggesting positive news.

"We've reached our decision," he announced. "Not that you had any competition."

Lydianne chuckled, controlling the rush of joy that made her want to whoop out loud. "I suspect Glenn's remark caught a few of you board members off guard."

The bishop nodded. "He's not been himself lately, and understandably so," he remarked as she moved into step beside him for their return to the schoolhouse. "It'll do Billy Jay a world of *gut* to engross himself in school rather than spending his days with his grandparents while Glenn's working in his woodshop. I suspect Elva, his *mammi,* clucks over him like a hen when she's not focused on baby Levi."

"*Jah*, being with other kids will surely brighten Billy Jay's days," Lydianne remarked. "He'll have your nephew Stevie, who's also starting school—"

"And I'm glad he'll have *you*, Lydianne," the bishop said softly as they reached the schoolhouse door. "Glenn had that part right. Your sunny disposition and sense of purpose will do his boy a world of *gut* at this tough time in his young life."

As Bishop Jeremiah opened the door, she didn't allow his compliment to go to her head—certainly not with Glenn and three other men watching them enter the classroom. Martin rose from his chair, as did the others.

"Miss Christner, we're pleased to offer you this teaching position," he said as he grasped her hand. "If you need time to consider your answer—"

"Oh, no, I'll be happy to accept!" Lydianne interrupted gleefully. "*Denki* so much for considering my application. What I lack in experience, I'll make up for with careful preparation and my love of learning. I won't let you down."

"That thought never entered our heads," the bishop put in. "And with Lorena Flaud and Clarence's Lucy being in their final year of school—and with their sisters right behind them—you'll have plenty of assistance as you teach the youngest ones the basics of reading and arithmetic. I anticipate a productive year for our scholars."

"I fully agree," Martin said. "We can figure out when your last day at the furniture factory will be—"

"And I'll report for work as soon as I've been home to change my clothes," Lydianne assured him.

"Sometime soon, you can visit the bookstore on Bates Street to purchase the educational posters and supplies you'll need," Bishop Jeremiah suggested. "We've already ordered new textbooks and other teaching basics, because the ones in the old schoolhouse have served us for a number of years. It seems only fitting to start in our new building with fresh books and wall hangings."

"This is so exciting!" Lydianne said as she shook each man's hand in turn. "Maybe this sounds silly, but I still love the smell of fresh packages of notebook paper and new bottles of glue, and the joy of opening a fresh box of crayons—thinking of all the drawings and reports and projects that lie ahead of us."

As she left the schoolhouse and drove down the road, Lydianne floated on a cloud of euphoria. After she turned off the main county highway to head for home, she paused at the sight of a little blond girl chasing a butterfly on the front lawn of Tim and Julia Nissley's place. With the sunshine shimmering on her golden hair and upturned face, six-year-old Ella Nissley looked for all the world like a little angel. Her laughter rang out as she ran and reached eagerly for the butterfly, followed closely by a little brown puppy that yipped and yapped.

Lydianne's heart overflowed with a wave of emotions. Her dream had come true: she would now be Ella's teacher. But she would have to be very, very careful. Ella was the apple of her adoptive parents' eyes, and Lydianne had no intention of interfering with their happy family.

No one else, including Tim and Julia, knew that Ella was the newborn baby Lydianne had given up when she'd been an unwed mother.

Chapter Two

On the following Saturday morning, Jeremiah stood slightly apart from the large crowd gathered in the field beyond The Marketplace, where the produce auction was in full swing. His younger brother, Jude, stood on a flatbed truck with a microphone, caught up in the auctioneer chant that came as second nature to him—a speed and agility of speech that made Jeremiah's head spin whenever he tried to follow exactly what Jude was saying at any given moment.

"Sold!" Jude cried out. "Two bushel boxes of green beans at thirty-five dollars apiece! Next, we'll be starting on the canning tomatoes, folks, and we've got some beauties today! This first lot comes from the Wengerds' nursery, and you'll not find any finer, firmer tomatoes than the ones our shopkeepers, Nelson and Michael, raise on their farm over by Queen City."

As Jude chatted up the potential buyers, the two Wengerd men were hefting sturdy boxes of deep red tomatoes onto the flatbed so folks could get a better look at them. Glenn Detweiler and Gabe Flaud were working nearby, shifting more boxes of fresh vegetables into place so the auction would continue without any downtime. Jeremiah watched the two younger men work as though they knew each other's rhythms and moves well—because as lifelong friends and owners of shops in The Marketplace, they often helped during the auctions rather than remaining inside to run their shops.

"Here we go, folks! Each box holds half a bushel of tomatoes," Jude called out as he gazed out over the crowd of eager onlookers. "Once we establish the price for the first buyer, he or she can claim additional boxes for the same amount. Then we start again, until we've sold all the tomatoes. We'll start the bidding at ten dollars," he added as he held up a huge, red tomato for everyone to see.

As Jude began to chant and interested buyers' hands shot up, his nephew, Pete, and Michael Wengerd yelped from their spots on opposite ends of the flatbed, pointing at each bidder and keeping track of the rising price Jude was singing out.

Wiping his forehead with his bandanna, Jeremiah slipped away from the auction and headed toward the rustic red stable that housed the shops. It did his heart good to see Pete actively engaged in the business being conducted, helping Jude. Their blond, muscular nephew had been on the slippery slope that led to nowhere, working the night shift with English fellows at the pet food factory near Higher Ground—and then blowing his pay at the pool hall until well past noon most days. After being in charge of renovating the stable into shops and then building the new schoolhouse, Pete seemed to be living a life of more purpose. Jeremiah knew better than to press his nephew about joining the church and settling down, but at least the chances of that happening seemed a lot better now than they had at the beginning of the summer.

The air-conditioned stillness enveloped Jeremiah as he stepped inside The Marketplace, out of the bright sunshine. He paused, allowing his eyes to adjust to the muted light of the gas fixtures. Aromas of coffee and Jo Fussner's fresh-baked goodies made his stomach rumble.

He waved at Jude's redheaded twins, Alice and Adeline, as they cleared dirty dishes and napkins from the tables in The Marketplace's open central commons. It was good to see the girls working for Jo—and enjoying it immensely— after they'd gone through a patch of adolescent trouble when their *dat* had remarried. All in all, Jeremiah felt greatly satisfied about the direction the younger members of the Shetler family were headed these days. God had been good indeed, and the bishop was grateful that He'd helped Pete and the twins put their difficult times behind them.

When he spotted the slender blonde in Glenn's wood shop, Jeremiah's heart thudded faster for a couple of beats. Ever since her interview on Monday, his thoughts had been filled with Lydianne—and he wasn't sure why. She was an attractive woman, to be sure, but she was several years younger than he and of such a different temperament than his dear, deceased Priscilla, that he'd never given her a second thought as marriage material.

There's a lot we don't know about Miss Christner, he mused as he found himself stepping in her direction. It had come as a complete surprise to hear that she'd lost a fiancé as well as her parents before she came to Morning Star— but where had she come *from*? She'd lived here about six years, so why didn't he know more about her family?

Jeremiah told himself this wasn't the time or place to press the new teacher for answers, yet, as he watched Lydianne straightening the wooden toys on Glenn's shelves, his curiosity prickled. She'd been covering Detweiler's shop lately, because Glenn had missed some time at The Marketplace when his wife had fallen ill and then died after Levi's birth had severely depleted her body. Was there more to their relationship than he'd imagined? Had Glenn's outburst about his young son needing a woman in his life been a play for Lydianne's sympathy—a bid for her affection?

Jeremiah frowned as a totally different emotion overcame him. He suddenly didn't *want* Lydianne to be interested in Glenn—and that revelation gave him pause.

"Ah, Bishop, how are you?" Lydianne called out when she spotted him near the shop's doorway. "How's the produce auction going?"

Jeremiah was happy to answer a question that had nothing to do with relationships—his, or Glenn's. He reminded himself that Lydianne often acted as a floater, helping in the various shops when owners had a lot of customers, or when they needed to be away for a bit. Her presence in Detweiler's shop didn't necessarily mean she was interested in the young widower.

"Jude's out there selling beans and tomatoes and zucchinis—you name it—by the bushel boxfuls," he replied with a smile. "And from what I can see, our crowd increases with each auction we hold. It's been a real advantage to have the larger field this property provided us—not to mention the use of the restroom facilities behind the schoolhouse. I'm glad Pete talked us into building those with multiple stalls on each side—and flush toilets."

"And how's Glenn doing out there? Maybe it's my imagination, but he's seemed a lot sadder lately. Really preoccupied," Lydianne remarked.

The sympathy in her voice ratcheted up Jeremiah's envy—and why was that? Everyone in the church district was very concerned about how Glenn was managing to keep up with seven-year-old Billy Jay and dealing with a new baby, even though his parents lived with him. "He's very busy, shifting boxes of produce," he replied carefully. "I suspect he's glad to have work that keeps him moving and engaged, rather than hanging around in his shop when there's a lull in the customers. Grief gets more difficult when you have too much time to think about things."

Lydianne nodded, focusing her clear blue eyes on him. "I would imagine you know a lot about that, even though your Priscilla's been gone for a few years now," she said softly. "They say time heals all wounds, but some folks leave holes in our lives that we have no way to fill again after they pass."

Jeremiah blinked rapidly, his soul crying out with the reality that Lydianne had stated so succinctly. She knew about love and loss, after all, even if she'd never been married.

"I suspect you can give Glenn exactly the kind of comfort and advice he'll be needing, seeing's how you've been down the same road," she continued gently. "Folks who haven't lost a spouse can try, but they don't truly understand the long, lonely silences that haunt the one who survives."

The long, lonely silences that haunt the one who survives.

Jeremiah drew in a long breath to steady his emotions. Somehow, Lydianne had just summed up his entire life since Priscilla's unexpected passing. When he'd returned home from the emergency room without his wife, after an MRI had identified the ruptured brain aneurysm that killed her, it had been the silence in the house that had clawed like a crazed wild animal at his soul.

He pulled himself from the past, searching for words that wouldn't sound maudlin—or miserable. "You make a *gut* point, Lydianne," he said in the firmest voice he could manage. "I should probably offer to spend time with him a couple evenings each week. What with his parents being elderly and his boys demanding a lot of attention, I doubt Glenn has anybody to share his troubles with."

And if he's spending evenings with me, he won't be with you, Lydianne.

The thought, coming totally from out of the blue, startled Jeremiah. Why was he suddenly so determined to keep Glenn and Lydianne from becoming romantically involved? It was only natural—and extremely beneficial—when men and women paired up and lived in the matrimonial state God wanted for His children. Belonging to a warm, loving family was the greatest blessing anyone could ask for.

Once again, he searched for a safer, less emotional subject to discuss. "Have you been to the bookstore yet to buy supplies for the schoolroom?" he asked. "When you go, be sure to put those items on the school board's account. We certainly don't expect you to pay for them out of your own pocket."

Lydianne's face lit up like the summer sun. "I'm going Monday afternoon after I get off work at the factory," she replied brightly. "I haven't had a chance to shop yet, because I suspect Martin's been finding more bookwork than usual—and assigning me more staining—now that he knows I'll be leaving after this week."

Jeremiah chuckled. "The Flauds will miss you and your *gut* work," he said. "And what with Regina leaving soon to marry Gabe, Martin will be hard pressed to replace the

two of you ladies—especially because the company takes
so many orders here at The Marketplace these days."

"*Jah*, each week when I review the accounts with Martin,
he says he needs to hire one or two more carpenters as well
as replacements for us stainers," she agreed. "Who knows?
He might talk to Pete—or Glenn—about signing on, even
if they don't want to work full-time. They're both awfully
gut with wood."

"They are," Jeremiah agreed, suddenly needing to leave
rather than to talk any more about Detweiler with this
attractive young woman. "Well, have a *gut* day, Lydianne.
I've got some errands to run and a few other folks to catch
up with."

Had he sounded rude or abrupt? As he headed toward
the other shops, he hoped the new teacher hadn't picked
up on his mixed feelings about her sympathies for Glenn.
He spoke briefly with Martha Maude and Anne Hartzler
in their quilting shop, accepted a fresh brownie from Jo in
her bakery, and exchanged a few words with Martin in the
Flaud Furniture shop.

When he stepped outside again, Jude's voice was still
ringing above the crowd as he raised the bid on boxes of
green cabbage that the women were probably buying to
make kraut—although some of the folks in the crowd ran
restaurants and cafés in nearby towns, as well. Jeremiah
started toward the corral behind the rustic red stable,
whistling for his dapple-gray Percheron gelding. He felt
strangely restless and uninterested in the goings-on at
The Marketplace, needing to retreat to the stillness of his
porch and the pastures that surrounded his home.

He swung himself up onto his horse's broad bare back.
As Jeremiah rode toward the county highway, he murmured,

"Let's go home, Mitch. Careful now—there are lots of cars out because it's Saturday."

The Percheron's spotted ears stood up as he listened. Mitch followed the white plank fence that surrounded The Marketplace's grounds, remaining in the mowed grass beside it and as far from the traffic as he could walk. When the traffic lights at the intersection of Morning Star's main street turned green, Jeremiah urged Mitch into a trot as they crossed in front of the stopped cars on the highway.

From there, the street became a paved road that cut through the countryside, which was dotted with Amish farms. Jeremiah relaxed. The slower pace of life on this side of town soothed his soul, and the sight of green pastures dotted with trees, where Saul Hartzler's registered Angus cattle stood in the shade, made his world feel right again. Perched upon the next hillside, his white farmhouse shimmered in the August heat and humidity, but rather than ride directly home, Jeremiah guided his horse to the packed dirt trail around the next bend.

As he passed the rows of tall, green, field corn growing between his home and the road, he anticipated a bumper crop this fall. Although he still sold a lot of his corn to the grain elevator in Clearwater, he'd begun having most of it processed into ethanol when he'd taken on the additional duties of being Morning Star's bishop, earning him more money for the same amount of labor. Jeremiah was also pleased as he rode past several acres of alfalfa hay that would soon be ready to cut. Most of this crop would be baled and sold to Plain families in the area to feed their livestock over the winter.

Many of his neighbors could no longer support themselves by farming, but Jeremiah felt blessed. When Jude had married his first wife several years ago, he'd taken over the Shetler family acreage, so Jeremiah had purchased two large adjoining farms from families who were leaving the Morning Star district. Farming allowed him to keep a flexible schedule and tend his congregation's spiritual needs. He'd hired Will Gingerich, the nephew of Bishop Vernon in Cedar Creek, to help with planting and harvesting, which gave Jeremiah more time for his church duties and provided extra income for Will.

Farming also kept him humble and at the mercy of God's weather conditions. It took enormous faith to plant crops in the spring and then deal with badly timed rain, hail, droughts, and sometimes even tornadoes, before harvesting whatever the Lord had provided by fall.

Jeremiah knew exactly what it meant to be dependent upon God. Every farmer did.

Mitch followed the trail toward the woods that grew along the banks of the Missouri River tributary and formed the boundary between Jeremiah's two farms. On hot days, the canopy of trees gave welcome relief from the heat. Large outcroppings of rocks along the riverbank provided a place where Jeremiah loved to sit when he needed time alone. The rush of the water played a tune his soul never tired of hearing. When he felt perplexed or lonely for Priscilla—or needed to think about church matters—he lost himself in watching leaves and bubbles flowing along with the water's current.

Rather than dismounting to sit on his favorite rock, Jeremiah gazed at the river for a bit and then turned Mitch back toward the house. "Mamm says I'm due for a haircut before we have church tomorrow," he remarked. "And you know I always do what my mother tells me!"

The Percheron whickered, as though he were chuckling.

After Jeremiah fed and watered his gelding and the buggy mare in the stable, he headed for the house. As he entered the large kitchen, his *mamm* looked up from the half-gallon pitcher of fresh-brewed tea she'd made. With a quick twist of her wrists, she emptied a plastic tray of ice cubes into the pitcher.

"Too hot in this kitchen to cook tonight, after I spent the day baking bread and frying chicken to take to the common meal tomorrow," she announced. "I've got potato salad to go with a few pieces of that chicken I kept back for us—"

"That's fine," Jeremiah said.

"—unless maybe you have other plans, like treating a lady friend to supper."

His eyebrows shot up. Why had she said *that*?

Mamm laughed. "*Gut* grief, son, do you figure to spend the rest of your life in this house with *me* for company? Surely you can find better entertainment on a Saturday night than snapping green beans on the porch."

He searched for a thread of conversation that would go in a different direction. "You said I needed a haircut—"

"And I can have you clipped and ready for a date in two shakes of a lamb's tail!" she shot back. To show him just how serious she was, she took her sharpest scissors from the kitchen drawer, grabbed a tea towel, and waved him toward the front porch. "Folks are starting to talk, Jeremiah, saying it's time you found another wife. It's been more than three years—"

"I know exactly how long Priscilla's been gone, Mamm." Lydianne's face flickered in the back of his mind, but he blinked the image away. To distract himself further, he poured two glasses of tea before he followed her out the door with them.

"—and it's time for you to move on with your life," Mamm continued with a wag of her finger. She sighed, blotting the moisture from her forehead with the towel. "If it would make things easier for you, I could move back over to Jude's place and help Leah with their new baby when it comes—"

"Leah's *mamm* already lives there with them," he reminded her gently.

"—so you and a new bride could start the family you weren't able to have before," she continued in a tight voice. She waited for Jeremiah to position himself in a chair before draping the towel over the front of his shirt. "It might be easier for a second wife if you didn't have your buttinsky mother around all the time, so I'll relocate. I'll do *anything* if it means you'll be happy again . . . and give me some more grandbabies."

Jeremiah's throat got so tight he couldn't talk. He focused on his flummoxed mother before grasping her hand. Ordinarily, Margaret Shetler was outspoken and totally in control of her emotions, yet she seemed upset as she met his gaze.

"Mamm, what's all this talk about privacy and marriage and babies?" he asked gently. "I appreciate your offer—but what's got you so stirred up about my singular state today? And why would you think I want you to move out? This is your *home*. You're living in the *dawdi haus*, so—come the day I might remarry—my wife and I would have the rest of this huge two-story house to ourselves."

With a sigh, his mother held out her hand. Jeremiah pulled the comb from his pants pocket, and she ran it through his hair before she replied. "I—I suppose it's because Rose Wagler's baby is almost due, and your brother and Leah are expecting their wee one in September, and—"

Jeremiah's heart shriveled at the wistful tone of his *mamm*'s voice. He'd tried not to think too much about those two bundles of joy, because other couples' new babies were another reminder that he and Priscilla had been unable to conceive. In the back of his mind, he'd always wondered if he might be to blame—but he hadn't dared consult a doctor to find out. He'd accepted their childless state as God's will.

"—I don't want you to miss out on the blessings of having a family, Jeremiah," she continued in a hoarse whisper. She positioned her scissors about an inch beneath his ear and clipped in a line that ran around the back of his neck, finishing on the other side. As she fingered his beard where it joined his sideburn, she sucked in her breath. "You're getting gray hair, son! Now you *really* need to get serious about finding a wife!"

"Before I turn into an old goat?" he teased. He'd noticed those little silver streaks earlier, when he'd been shaving his cheeks, but it was one more thing he was trying not to think about.

"While you can still—you know. Father children."

Jeremiah closed his eyes, wondering how to get his mother onto a more uplifting subject. "I'm only forty-one—and who would you have me court, Mamm?" he challenged. "Name me all the women you think would make me a *gut* wife. And I'm telling you right now, Naomi and Esther do *not* fall into that category."

At least his mother had the grace to grimace at the idea

of his marrying either *maidel* Slabaugh sister. She trimmed the hair that fell over his forehead as she considered her response. "We'll have a lot of folks coming to town for the Shetler reunion, middle of next month—"

"And they're all cousins or shirttail relatives of some sort," Jeremiah reminded her firmly. "It's not a *gut* idea for me to swim in such a small gene pool. Try again."

She carefully trimmed a few stray hairs on his left eyebrow. "The Helfing girls are single, and there's Jo—"

"Jo's accustomed to living with her mother—and can you imagine our life if Drusilla came here to live with us?" Jeremiah put in quickly. "Besides, those gals—and Lydianne—are all in their twenties or early thirties. Way too young for me, and maybe not suited to being a bishop's wife, ain't so?"

Mamm trimmed his other eyebrow without answering him.

"It's not as though I'm a first-time husband," he continued, "and my time's not entirely my own. I have to give energy and attention to church members whenever they need it. New—younger—wives might not adjust so well to that. And they might not be ready to walk the higher path folks expect a bishop's wife to follow."

Mamm took the towel from around his neck and shook it out. "You're awfully quick to discount the eligible women in our district, son. Does this mean you need to scout around in other towns?"

Jeremiah let out a short laugh. "Oh, believe me, Vernon in Cedar Creek and Tom in Willow Ridge—and every other bishop I know—have been dropping big hints about the unattached women in their districts," he said with a shake of his head. "They've told me I'm too picky. But I refuse to settle for just anybody to get the matchmakers off my back. I'll never love another woman the way I loved Priscilla—"

"And that's the problem," Mamm interjected softly. "Priscilla's gone, dear. You can't seem to see anyone else in a positive light, because the shine of her halo blinds you to other possibilities."

Jeremiah gazed out toward the lawn. His mother was right—he'd loved his wife with all his heart, and he'd placed her memory on a rather saintly pedestal. In his dreams he still saw Priscilla's flawless face, framed by her pale blond hair; he still heard her gentle voice in his ear, the way she'd sung as she'd worked in the kitchen. These memories were blessings, because they helped him forget the headache she'd complained of for a couple of days before it had suddenly become so unbearable that she'd passed out from extreme pain.

By the time he'd gotten her to the emergency room, it had been too late. The doctor there had suggested that an MRI of Priscilla's head might pinpoint the cause of her death, so Jeremiah had agreed to that procedure. The scan showed that an aneurysm had burst in her brain—but that knowledge hadn't really eased the excruciating pain her passing had caused him. Jeremiah had indeed elevated his wife's memory, enshrining her in his mind, because that was what had kept him sane while he grieved.

As he faced the truth of his mother's statement about the shine of Priscilla's halo, Jeremiah kept looking out past the porch railing—but no matter how long he focused on the huge blue hydrangea in Mamm's flower garden, it didn't suggest a solution to his problem.

"Other men seem to adjust their requirements and find

new mates, Jeremiah—and that's what God intends for you, too, dear," his mother continued in a thin voice. "Maybe it's my imagination, but I think Glenn's already heading in that direction. He's certainly had his eye on Lydianne of late."

Jeremiah sucked in his breath before he could catch himself. Why did Mamm have to start on *that* topic now?

"Of course, Glenn needs a *mamm* for his little boys, so his situation is different from yours," she continued matter-of-factly. "Even so, I'd hate to see him start courting her before *you* tried to win her. Of all the *maidels* in Morning Star, Lydianne impresses me as the most level-headed and open-minded. She's cheerful and generous and intelligent—"

"That's why we hired her as our new schoolteacher," Jeremiah interrupted. "It would be poor timing on my part to court her with intentions to marry her. We'd have to hire another teacher before the school year was out—"

"There you go again, finding excuses not to even take anyone out on a date!" Mamm blurted in exasperation. "You find ways to meet everyone else's needs, yet you're not the least bit imaginative when it comes to pursuing your own happiness. Your brother hitched up with the least likely woman on the planet, but Leah's proven herself to be every bit as wonderful as Jude believed she was. And now they have a nice, happy family."

"Partly because Leah's *mamm* does the cooking and a lot of the household chores so Leah can tend her livestock," Jeremiah pointed out. He remembered quite well how many times he'd tried to dissuade Jude from marrying the woman who'd been more at home in a barn than in a kitchen—but his brother had proven all the naysayers wrong.

And Jeremiah envied Jude and Leah their happiness every time he saw how good they were together.

Mamm sighed. "I can see this conversation's going nowhere. Just think about what I've said, all right? Your clock's ticking, son. It's later than you think."

After Mamm went into the house, Jeremiah remained morosely in the chair with the two untouched glasses of tea on the porch table beside him. Even though he was thirsty, he'd lost his taste for any sort of refreshment.

I'd hate to see him start courting her before you tried to win her.

Mamm's words about Glenn and Lydianne replayed in his mind a couple of times, like a broken record, before he could stop them from repeating. Why had she zeroed in on the possibility of *that* relationship? And why did the thought of Detweiler and the new teacher together irritate him to the core?

Of all the maidels *in Morning Star, Lydianne impresses me as the most level-headed and open-minded. She's cheerful and generous and intelligent . . .*

He sighed and stood up. His mother was probably as right about Lydianne as she was about the fact that he was starting to get some gray hair.

And those two ideas don't go very well together, do they? Miss Christner was indeed a nice young woman—a nice *too*-young woman. There was no denying that she was an attractive blue-eyed blonde, but wouldn't he feel like an old wolf leading an innocent young lamb into his lair on their wedding night?

Why are you even thinking about going to bed with Lydianne? You're her bishop! Jeremiah chided himself.

Disgusted and restless, he went into the mudroom and

grabbed the big basket of green beans his mother had picked during the day. What else did he have to do but snap them into bite-sized pieces so they'd be ready when she wanted to can them?

Sadly enough, Mamm had been right about that, too.

Chapter Three

At church the next morning, Lydianne fanned herself, but found no relief from the heat. The congregation was crammed into the Slabaugh sisters' farmhouse basement—which was theoretically cooler on an August day because it was downstairs—but as the service wore on, she and her *maidel* friends and all the folks around them became clammy with sweat. Esther and Naomi had graciously supplied old pasteboard fans mounted on wooden handles, which Griggs Mortuary, the local funeral home, had disposed of years ago. Even Jesus and the twelve disciples, pictured in the Upper Room, appeared listless and inattentive as Lydianne fanned herself. She didn't think it was terribly uplifting to be reminded of her demise, either, as she read the mortuary's faded ad for pre-planned burial arrangements.

"We must never forget the folks Jesus referred to as 'the least of these,'" Preacher Clarence Miller droned in his reedy monotone. "In this morning's passage from Matthew's twenty-fifth chapter, our Lord tells us that when we assist the widows and orphans amongst us—those who need

our help with food and clothing and emotional support—
we are ministering to Christ Himself."

Beside Lydianne, Regina Miller shifted restlessly on the
pew bench. Lydianne gently patted her best friend's arm,
knowing Regina—as an orphan—always felt uncomfortable when her uncle preached on this passage. Not long
ago, when Regina had been shunned for painting and selling her amazing wildlife watercolors at The Marketplace,
Preacher Clarence had insisted that she had to sell her
home and move into a tiny room in his house. Although it
was the Amish way for a man to take in the unattached
females of his family, Regina had felt more like a prisoner
than a guest while she'd endured living in the windowless
room tucked beneath the Millers' staircase.

Regina flashed Lydianne a smile. These days, her freckled face beamed with the anticipation of her marriage to
Gabe Flaud. The Flaud family had surprised the couple by
buying Regina's quaint little bungalow, freshening its
rooms with paint, and refinishing the hardwood floors.
The bride-to-be had every reason to rejoice in the love that
had redirected her *maidel* life.

Lydianne envied Regina's happiness, even as she realized she, herself, couldn't possibly marry. When she glanced
down the pew bench in front of her, where Julia Nissley
cradled a drowsy little Ella in her lap, Lydianne sighed
inwardly.

Ella would forever be her deepest, darkest secret.

Lydianne couldn't imagine the repercussions if the
Amish congregation in Morning Star found out about her
past. It would upset the Nissley family and get Lydianne
shunned, at the very least.

And what husband would want to discover, when he
took her to the marriage bed, that Lydianne was not the

innocent young woman he'd assumed her to be? Premarital relations were not only frowned upon, they were forbidden by the *Ordnung*. She and Aden had crossed that line only because they were to be married—never guessing he would die the day before their wedding.

When Ella awoke, wiggling her fingers in a wave, Lydianne's heart stood still. As the little girl matured, she resembled Aden Lapp more with each passing day. Ella had inherited her father's nose, eyebrows, and heart-shaped face, and when she focused on Lydianne, it was as though Aden were gazing at her.

Shaken to the core, Lydianne quickly returned Ella's wave and refocused on Preacher Clarence. She would never forget the day she and Aden had attended the Lapp family reunion, so deeply in love as they accepted the congratulations of the far-flung relatives who'd come for their wedding on the following day. Lydianne had suspected she was in the family way, and she'd planned to tell Aden when they found a few moments of privacy.

But when they'd slipped away to cool off in the state park's shaded, secluded pond, he'd drowned.

Aden hadn't been a strong swimmer—Lydianne wasn't, either—yet when he'd playfully boasted that she made him feel like such a man he could cross the pond and come back, she'd encouraged him. Not wanting to get her dress wet, she'd waded in barefoot to cheer him on from the shallows. He'd reached the far shore, but as Aden started back toward her, Lydianne could tell he was struggling. When he'd flailed in the pond's deep center, she'd run to summon help from the other folks at the reunion.

By the time they'd returned to the water, however, Aden was gone.

"Lydianne, what's wrong?" Regina whispered near her ear.

Her friend's low voice pulled Lydianne from her tragic memories. When she blinked, she realized tears were dribbling down her cheeks and hastily swiped at them with the back of her hand. "I'm fine," she murmured. "Just a wandering thought. Nothing to be concerned about."

It took all her effort to regain control of her emotions. At long last, Bishop Jeremiah pronounced the benediction. When he announced that the school board had hired her, Lydianne had to force a smile and acknowledge everyone's congratulations. As the congregation stood up, eager to seek fresh air, she followed the women upstairs to the kitchen. But instead of helping set out the common meal, she hurried outside.

The shade of the old maple trees in the Slabaugh sisters' backyard was an improvement over the stuffiness of the crowded basement. Her relief was cut short, however, when the men began setting up large folding tables. Before she could slip back into the kitchen to avoid questions about her damp, pink face, Billy Jay Detweiler made a beeline for her.

"Teacher Lydianne! Teacher Lydianne!" he cried out. "When Dat told me you were gonna replace Teacher Elam, I was so happy!"

The boy's excitement gratified Lydianne—and what could she do but lean toward him and squeeze the small, strong hands that were gripping hers? "It's going to be a wonderful-*gut* year, Billy Jay," she assured him. "And won't it be fun to start out with new desks and new books and a whole new school building?"

"*Jah*! Dat took me over to see it," he replied with an emphatic nod. "The floors look so shiny and slick, I bet you could slide all the way across the room on your butt if you got a runnin' start at it!"

"And I'd better not hear about you doing that, son," a familiar male voice said behind them. "We've talked about how you're supposed to behave in class, ain't so?"

Lydianne turned to smile at Glenn, who was holding tiny, sleepy Levi against his shoulder. "Those floors are so shiny, I doubt he's the only scholar who'll try that," she said gently.

"*Jah*!" Billy Jay crowed, still gripping her hands. "Me and Stevie have been talkin' about it, and we wanna have a contest to see who can slide the farthest!"

Lydianne burst out laughing before she could catch herself. It probably wasn't wise to let the boy think she would approve of such an activity—officially, anyway—but it was a treat to see him grinning from ear to ear. "I'm glad you're excited about starting the school year, Billy Jay," she said. "You're a year ahead of Stevie, Gracie, and Ella, so you can show them the ropes."

When the boy spotted Stevie Shetler across the yard, he darted off.

Glenn sighed apologetically. "It *is* a fine thing to see Billy Jay smiling again," he remarked, swaying from side to side as he held his other son. "I'm really glad you accepted the position, Lydianne. If there's anything I can do—anything at all—to help you, or to set my son straight when he gets too wild, I want you to come and tell me first thing, all right? And don't think you have to have school discipline on your mind as a reason to visit."

Lydianne blinked. Was Glenn showing interest in her, inviting her to his home?

Before she knew how to respond to his remark, she noticed that Bishop Jeremiah was unfolding a table beneath a nearby tree. His facial expression suggested that he'd caught the gist of Glenn's conversation.

Why is he looking at us that way? Does he think Glenn's out of line while he's still mourning his wife—or is he jealous?

Rather than saying anything the bishop might construe as inappropriate, Lydianne cleared her throat. "Well—I really should help carry out water pitchers and utensils and such. It's *gut* that we're having a picnic today rather than eating inside, ain't so?"

As she entered the farmhouse, she felt like a teenager at a Singing, rejoining her girlfriends to escape from boys whose attention she was trying to avoid. Lydianne shook her head at such a thought. She had no reason to duck away from the bishop or Glenn, because they were both very nice men, each in his own way—

But why let them think you're interested? You'll never get married, remember?

When she met up with Jo and Regina, who were each carrying a big tray of sandwiches, Lydianne held the door for them. "We *maidels* need to sit together today," she said with a pasted-on smile. "We don't have many more common meals before Regina will be married, and then she won't want to spend her time with us after Sunday services."

Her redheaded friend's eyes widened. "Why would you ever think that? It's not as though I'm going to live on a different planet after Gabe and I get hitched!"

"*Jah*, but you'll have other priorities," Jo put in with a chuckle. "As well you should!"

As they reached one of the serving tables and set down their trays, Regina motioned for Lydianne and Jo to come closer. "When I heard that this Friday would be your last day at the factory, Lydianne, I told Martin I'd be leaving then, too," she said softly. "While you're getting the new schoolhouse ready, I need to be helping Aunt Cora and Delores Flaud with wedding preparations, after all. They've insisted on taking charge of the festivities, since I don't have a *mamm* to do that."

"That's very sweet, and I'm not one bit surprised," Lydianne said. She looked around to be sure none of the men were listening to their conversation. "What did Martin say when you wanted to leave earlier than he'd originally figured on?"

"*Jah*, did he fuss—because the wedding's not until October?" Jo asked.

Regina chuckled. "Truth be told, Delores must've already talked to him about the wedding preparations, because he didn't seem all that surprised about my leaving sooner rather than later. Maybe he's already found folks to replace us."

As Molly and Marietta Helfing came out of the house carrying big plastic pitchers of iced tea, Jo waved them over. "We've just learned that Lydianne and Regina are both leaving the Flaud Furniture Factory next Friday," she said. "I think this calls for a party, don't you?"

"Definitely!" Molly replied. "Not that we need an excuse for a party."

"It's been a while since we all got together for some fun—something besides our potluck meetings in the office at The Marketplace," her twin sister put in eagerly. "What with making so many more noodles to keep up with our Saturday sales, I'm ready to *play*!"

Marietta's lighthearted remarks raised Lydianne's spirits. Early in the year, Marietta had finished a brutal round of chemotherapy after having a bilateral mastectomy, so it was good to see her smiling again and regaining her strength. Her cape dress still hung like a sack on her too-skinny frame, and beneath her *kapp*, her hair was barely an inch long—but at least it was growing back.

"You could all come to my house!" Lydianne suggested. "We can also celebrate the fact that I'll soon be a home-owner. I'm signing the contract in a couple of days. And since next week's a visiting Sunday—"

"I'm *gut* with going to your place as long as you let the rest of us bring all the food," Jo insisted. "You shouldn't have to cook for your own party."

"Or we could meet at *my* house," Regina suggested happily. "Now that Gabe and his family have painted all the rooms and redone the floors, it's ready for company!"

"We could have a progressive dinner!" Molly blurted. In her excitement, her white *kapp* shifted, revealing hair as short as her twin's. Amish women were forbidden to cut their hair, but when Marietta had lost her long brown tresses during her chemo, Molly had defied the *Ordnung* and shaved her head in support of her sister. "We could start at our place with appetizers, and then head down the road to Lydianne's for the main course—"

"Because she's got a kitchen that's not stacked with boxes of bagged noodles!" Marietta put in with a laugh.

"—and we could do dessert at Regina's place," Molly finished. "We could be eating and laughing and talking all day long next Sunday! What a great plan!"

Lydianne smiled gratefully at her friends. With these four young women for company—even if Regina was soon getting married—she knew she could get through *anything*.

Chapter Four

As Jeremiah drove his rig toward Books on Bates Monday afternoon, he wondered if his perfectly logical reasons for being there didn't look like flimsy, ill-disguised excuses for catching a glimpse of Lydianne. He'd called ahead to tell Justin Yutzy, the Mennonite storekeeper, that he'd be stopping by to pick up the school's textbooks, yet he wondered if Morning Star's new teacher wasn't astute enough to realize that his timing wasn't a coincidence. After all, he could've stopped by the store at any time to fetch those books.

When he saw Lydianne's horse and buggy at the bookstore's hitching rail, Jeremiah felt like a schoolboy spying on a girl he had a crush on. Shaking his head at such silliness, he pulled in and parked. He was the bishop, after all—and the member of the school board who'd long ago agreed to be in charge of obtaining the new textbooks. Besides, if Lydianne figured out that he wanted to spend time with her, was that such a bad thing?

At least Detweiler won't be here.

As he approached the door, Jeremiah again wondered why he felt such rivalry building between himself and the widowed woodworker. Or was he actually heeding his mother's advice and seeking out the company of an attractive young woman?

When the brass bell above the door seemed loud enough to wake the dead, he cringed—and then he spotted her over the tops of the bookshelves. Lydianne was back in the corner where classroom supplies were displayed. To his relief, she seemed so engrossed in choosing materials that she hadn't even looked up when the bell jangled.

Jeremiah paused, not wanting to break the store's serene silence. In the light from the back window, Lydianne's face took on the soft glow of a golden angel as she focused on a folded pasteboard banner. It was the same green chart with white lines and cursive alphabet letters that had been displayed above every school's blackboard for as long as he could remember, yet she appeared to be on a sacred mission—choosing what her students would look at every day as they practiced their penmanship.

Justin stepped out of the workroom behind the checkout counter with a large box. "*Gut* morning, Jeremiah!" he called out. "Saw you pull up, and I bet you've come for your schoolbooks. I've got a few more boxes to bring out—we appreciate your large order!"

"Need any help with them?" Jeremiah asked, turning toward the storekeeper so Lydianne wouldn't catch him gazing at her.

"Nah, I've got the rest of them on a cart, so we can wheel them out to your rig. You want to check them over before we load them?"

"I'd like to see them—if I may," Lydianne piped up from the back of the store.

When Jeremiah turned, her smile dazzled him. "Teacher Lydianne, it's *gut* to see you," he said, hoping he sounded surprised. "Of course, you can look at our new books. Take a copy of each text home for your own reference, if you'd like. We have plenty."

As she wheeled her shopping cart to the checkout counter, Jeremiah saw that she'd filled it with a number of colorful educational posters, packages of construction paper, and other practical classroom materials.

Justin wheeled his large cart out in front of the counter, smiling at the young woman. "It's always exciting to start a school year with fresh books and supplies, ain't so?" he remarked. "I got your books from the same publisher you've used before, Jeremiah, and these are the most recent editions. Newer illustrations, but the text is pretty much the same."

Jeremiah glanced at Lydianne. "Maybe I should've consulted with you before we ordered these," he said as they watched Justin pop the boxes open with his pocketknife. "I just assumed—but maybe I shouldn't have—"

"It's not as though spelling words or addition facts or the multiplication tables have changed," she pointed out with a lighthearted shrug. "By choosing the school's texts, you've saved me a lot of decisions, truth be told."

"*Jah*," Justin agreed. "Basic book learning is the same as when our parents and grandparents were kids—but I'm happy to have a computer helping me with ordering and inventory these days."

Jeremiah was only vaguely aware of the storekeeper's remarks. Lydianne's smile had made him extremely aware of how attractive she was—and her accepting, practical viewpoint pleased him, too. "Well, I—I'm sure the school's library could use some new titles, so how about if you choose those?" he asked.

She looked up from the math book she was thumbing

through. "I'd be happy to, Bishop," she said, inhaling deeply. "Oh, but there's something magical about the smell of new books—and about opening one for the very first time, don't you think?"

Jeremiah blinked, totally unable to think when she focused on him. Why had he never noticed the lighter flecks in Lydianne's big blue eyes, which made them seem to twinkle at him?

"Magical," he repeated. Magic wasn't something Plain folks put any store in, but he sensed that this woman could effortlessly make him believe in just about anything.

"Here's the student workbooks that go along with the reading and math texts," Justin remarked as he opened the final box. "And the teacher editions are in here, as well. I think everything's accounted for, Jeremiah. Shall I print out your receipt?"

Jeremiah wasn't at all sure what the shopkeeper had asked, but he nodded anyway. "That'll be fine. And when Miss Christner finishes her shopping today, you're to bill her materials to the school board, as well."

"Will do." When Justin tapped a few keys on his computer, the printer started humming. "I'll wheel these out to your rig now."

Jeremiah hoped his smile didn't appear as lopsided and goofy as it felt. "I'll help Justin with the loading while you continue your shopping," he suggested. "I'm driving the books out to the schoolhouse. Shall I, um, wait until you're finished and take your supplies, as well?" he stammered, gesturing toward her shopping cart. "Or would you like to come along and show me where you want your books?"

Why did he *almost* feel as though he was asking her for a date?

"Who am I to refuse when somebody else is willing to do the heavy lifting?" she asked lightly. "Won't take me but a moment to finish here—only a few other items I'd like to choose now, until I see how much more wall space I have. Go on ahead, if you want, and I'll be there shortly."

His heart thumped happily in his chest. He followed Justin out to the parking lot before he said anything that sounded silly or adolescent, wondering why a simple trip to the schoolhouse suddenly felt like a grand adventure . . . time alone with Lydianne.

"Nice gal you've hired," Justin remarked as he stacked the boxes in Jeremiah's rig. "Something to be said for a teacher who's had a little life experience teaching your kids, rather than having one of the girls who's just come up through the eight grades."

"We were all pleased—and a bit surprised—when Lydianne expressed an interest in the position." When Justin climbed into the rig, Jeremiah handed up the remaining boxes. "She's been a bookkeeper at the Flauds' factory, you know, and she's one of the managers out at The Marketplace, too."

"Now *there's* an enterprise we're all happy to see succeeding," Justin put in. "That place is so busy on Saturdays, I'm wondering if I might rent a small space to sell some of our inspirational paintings and those wall plaques with the faith-and-family sayings on them."

"Lydianne can answer that question about space availability for you," he said as the last box went into place. As Justin stepped down to the pavement, Jeremiah extended his hand. "*Denki* for getting our books so quickly. It's always a pleasure doing business with you."

The storekeeper's handshake was firm. "Happy you've

come to us again to keep your school up and running, Jeremiah," he said with the hint of a grin. "We'll see how long your new teacher keeps her position before, um, somebody talks her into getting hitched, *jah*?"

As Justin returned to the store, Jeremiah's jaw dropped. Were his inclinations *that* obvious, to a man he saw only once in a while?

Can Lydianne read me like a book, as well? Does she suspect my feelings for her?

He quickly unhitched his mare, shaking his head at that stray thought. *What feelings? It wasn't as though I could've ignored her presence or refused to talk to her. Ordinary conversation about school business—that's all it was!*

Even so, as he directed his horse toward the county highway, Jeremiah was grinning like a kid who'd just won a prize at the county fair. He was about to spend time helping Lydianne put away books.

No big deal, so don't make it into one.

Jeremiah couldn't help tingling with anticipation. No one else would be around the schoolhouse or The Marketplace, so nobody would know they were there.

Especially Glenn and my mother.

Late on Monday afternoon, Lydianne approached the schoolhouse feeling a bit apprehensive. Morning Star's rush hour traffic was a noisy blend of cars and pickups, as well as horses clip-clopping along the shoulders of the road, until she turned onto the deserted grounds around The Marketplace. The white schoolhouse sat farther down the lane, not far from a narrow band of woods. As she drove past the large red stable that housed the shops, she saw how the window boxes of colorful flowers glowed in the sun's rays. She wondered if Pete could add some window boxes to the schoolhouse to brighten its exterior walls.

Flowers are the least of your concerns, she reminded herself as she pulled up to the school's hitching rail. Bishop Jeremiah's mare grazed in the pasture near the pole barn where his rig sat, as though he planned to stay awhile. The schoolhouse windows and main door were open to allow air circulation, yet Lydianne felt too warm already.

Was it proper for her to be out here alone with Bishop Jeremiah?

She laughed at such a notion—laughed at herself for feeling so nervous. The bishop was the leader of their church district, the man to whom members of the congregation entrusted their very souls. Besides, Jeremiah Shetler had to be nearly forty, and probably considered her very young and inexperienced. He was open and friendly, dedicated to the children she would teach—not a fellow who would risk his reputation, or hers, by engaging in improper behavior just because nobody else was watching.

In his sermons, Bishop Jeremiah often reminded them that God was watching, after all. God would know exactly what went on in the schoolhouse, and Lydianne reminded herself that it was her responsibility to act accordingly. She was Morning Star's new teacher, not a young woman making a play for the bishop just because the opportunity had presented itself.

Tell yourself that the next time he gazes at you with his bottomless brown eyes. Something's changed, and he sees you differently now. Anybody can see that.

Firm in her resolve, Lydianne hopped down from her rig and wrapped her arms around one of the big boxes of materials she'd chosen. When she entered the schoolroom, Bishop Jeremiah immediately stopped unpacking textbooks.

"Let me—you should've told me you had these bulky boxes to—"

The bishop's words stopped short as his arms shot around the sides of the box, gently trapping hers beneath them.

"Um, how about if we set this on the table?" Lydianne suggested, nodding toward the one nearest the door. "You can let go, if you want. It's not heavy."

"Okay—sorry," he mumbled as he released her.

Bishop Jeremiah sounded as nervous as she felt. Had Lydianne's circumstances—her secret past—been different, maybe it would've been all right if he seemed as aware of her as she was of him. She sincerely liked him, but she knew better than to appear interested in his attention. "I suppose you could bring in those other boxes—"

"I'm on it," he blurted, immediately heading outside.

After she set the box on the table, she went over to the textbooks he'd been unpacking. Lydianne selected two copies of each one, and she was carrying them to her big desk in the front when Bishop Jeremiah came inside again.

"You're sure we have enough that I can keep copies of these at home?" she asked when he returned with the final box.

"Yup. I ordered several extras, because over the next few years we'll have more scholars," he replied. "I'll put your teacher's editions and the workbooks right here on this back desk."

Nodding, Lydianne busied herself standing a complete set of the textbooks on edge at the left side of her big wooden desk. It felt wonderful to accomplish the first task of preparing for the new school year. She would bring her favorite bookends from home—a ceramic dog and cat the kids would enjoy—but it seemed like a good idea to return for more setting up when she could do it alone.

"Which of the bookshelves do you want to store these texts in?" Bishop Jeremiah asked.

Lydianne paused, hoping she didn't sound picky. "How about if we put a copy of each beginner book on the small desks in front," she suggested. "We can arrange the older scholars' books on this shelf near the white board, and I'll figure out what each of them needs when they arrive the first day. Let's leave those back bookshelves empty to be the library."

"Sounds like a plan."

Lydianne allowed her guest a wide berth as she carried the other materials to a table near the front of the classroom. It would be perfectly proper to ask the tall, able-bodied bishop to mount the print and cursive alphabet posters above the white board, yet she wanted to do that herself. The schoolroom would feel like her second home if she put things in place the way she wanted them.

"Justin included a couple catalogs of books at various reading levels, suitable for Plain student libraries," he remarked as he emptied one of the boxes. "I'll put them here on this back desk—and then I'll be out of your hair."

She sighed, sorry their exchange felt so stilted . . . sorry she couldn't respond to the attraction she felt for Bishop Jeremiah. It was one of the many opportunities she hadn't known she'd be forfeiting on that lovely, romantic afternoon when she and Aden had—

No gut will come of recalling the special way you loved Aden, or regretting the beautiful baby you made with him. Move on.

"How about if I take these sturdy boxes downstairs?" the bishop asked. "You never know when they might come in handy."

Lydianne nodded. "That'll be fine. *Denki* so much for your help today."

His smile reflected the same sense of regret she was feeling—and perhaps the loneliness that filled her soul, as well. "You're welcome. I'll be on my way now."

His footsteps echoed in the stairwell. A few minutes later the door closed downstairs, and he crossed the lawn to the corral. He drove away with a parting glance at the schoolhouse door.

Lydianne sighed as she watched him. Was it her imagination, or did the bishop feel as wistfully disappointed as she did?

She gathered her books and catalogs and drove home. As much as she loved her small yellow house, nestled among blooming blue hydrangeas and shaded by large old trees, she was acutely aware of how quiet the place was because she lived there all alone.

Chapter Five

Wednesday morning, as Lydianne and Regina were settling into their work in the furniture factory's staining room, the door opened. Gabe Flaud, Martin's son and the shop foreman, smiled at them as he entered. Two familiar young women followed him in, taking in the room with curious gazes.

"Mary Frances and Nettie have agreed to try their hand at being stainers," Gabe said, nodding at the sisters. "They've started work today so you two ladies can show them the ropes before you leave us on Friday."

"What a great idea!" Lydianne nodded encouragingly at the two Umbles, who were daughters of the Flauds' longtime cabinetmaker, Elmer. The sisters were in their late teens and wore their honey-brown hair pulled up beneath dark blue kerchiefs. "It's not a difficult job, but it requires some concentration and careful attention to your brush strokes."

"*Jah*, the biggest challenge is preventing drips—and brushing away stray rivulets of stain before they set and start to dry," Regina put in as she went to a cabinet at the back of the room. "Let's get you each a new brush and a container to hold some stain. You can start on these small tables after you've watched us for a bit."

"You're in *gut* hands, girls," Gabe said to the Umble sisters. "Watch how Regina and Lydianne work and ask them all the questions you can think of."

Lydianne couldn't miss the playful wink Gabe flashed at Regina, his fiancée, before leaving the small room. She sighed to herself. Lydianne knew she could never marry, but she envied her redheaded friend's happiness.

Regina's freckled face turned a becoming shade of pink as she watched Gabe leave. "Truth be told, we're happy you girls have applied for these jobs. We believe women are much more patient and meticulous than men when it comes to staining."

"And we'd advise you to pick out a couple of your oldest, most faded dresses and wear them all the time," Lydianne said, gesturing at the multi-colored smears of stain on her shabby gray dress.

"Figure on having permanently stained cuticles, too," Regina put in as she held up her hands for the girls to see. "You can clean your hands 'til the cows come home—and it's not a *gut* idea to use brush cleaner on your skin, so we use borax soap. As you can see, however, I wear my work wherever I go. I'm hoping the stains will be gone in time for my wedding."

Nettie eagerly grasped her new brush, watching closely as Lydianne poured a small amount of oak stain into the two containers. At eighteen, she was short and stocky, like her *dat*, while Mary Frances was a little taller and a year older. "How do you know what color you're supposed to use? Looks like you've got a lot of big cans of stain in your cabinet."

Lydianne pointed to the order form that was stuck to the

corkboard on the cabinet door. "When an order's pieces are all complete and sanded, one of the men sets them in here with a form like this," she explained. "It tells you exactly what pieces are included, what type of stain to use—"

"As well as when the furniture is supposed to be shipped out," Regina continued. "Depending upon how humid it is, you need to allow at least a couple of days for stain and varnish to dry."

"It's noisy in here because we always have the exhaust fan running," Lydianne said, pointing to the large fan in the building's exterior wall. "But if we left the door open, sawdust and other stray particles from the shop would drift in and stick to the stain. Then the finish would be speckled and imperfect, and we'd have to sand the piece down and start all over."

"Just like when you paint a wall, you begin at the top," Regina said as she deftly brushed stain across the left edge of the bench top she was working on. "You start high and work low on a piece of furniture."

Mary Frances watched closely, nodding. "We do all the painting around home," she remarked. "That's partly because Mamm won't climb a ladder—"

"And Dat doesn't put down a drop cloth or pay attention to where the paint's dripping," Nettie joined in.

"He also painted the windows shut up in Mamm's sewing room, so now she won't let him near a paintbrush," Mary Frances put in with a chuckle. "We think he did it on purpose, because he really hates to paint."

The small room filled with their laughter. As the morning went by, Lydianne felt confident that the Umble sisters would do their very best to produce the top-quality finishing that Martin Flaud demanded—even if it might take them a while to work up to the production speed she and Regina had reached.

When Martin came into the staining room Friday morning to observe the Umble sisters' progress, he studied the end tables and chairs they had completed. Lydianne thought his smile might be hiding a secret as he exchanged pleasantries with the four of them, until he finally cleared his throat.

"You ladies have insisted you don't want any fuss or even a special lunch before you leave us," he said in a voice that quavered a little. He gazed at Lydianne and Regina as he pulled two envelopes from his pocket. "I want you to know again how much I've appreciated your fine workmanship, and I wish you both the best in the new lives you'll soon be taking on.

"Here are your final checks—and I'm turning you loose early," Martin continued as he handed them out. He was keeping his voice light, but his eyes held the telltale shine of sentimental tears. "Neither of you has missed much work over the past few years, so you deserve extra time off today."

Lydianne's eyes widened. "Well, *denki*, Martin! I surely wasn't expecting—"

"Gee, if Lydianne didn't make out these paychecks, who did?" Regina teased as she accepted hers.

Martin laughed. "That would be me," he replied. "Before Lydianne started keeping our books, *I* was the payroll clerk—so now I hope I can keep the factory solvent as I take up that role again. Now scoot on out of here before we get all sentimental about your leaving."

"Put your brushes in the cleaning jar, and we'll take

care of them later," Mary Frances offered as she waved them off.

Nettie nodded, her smile accentuated by little speckles of stain on her chin. "You've been patient teachers, and we'll do our best to keep up your *gut* work and the shop's reputation."

Her boss's wistful remarks had surprised her, but Lydianne didn't question Martin's motives. She and Regina slipped out of the staining room and exited the factory through the back door near the big exhaust fan without any of the men in the shop seeming to notice. The two of them quickly crossed the lawn, until they rounded the corner of the big metal factory building where none of the employees would see them.

"Woo-*hoo*!" Lydianne cried out joyfully as she grabbed Regina's hands. "I feel like a girl who just sneaked out of the schoolroom to play hooky—except we won't be going back!"

"I had no clue that Martin would let us go early!" Regina said as she began to bounce like a pogo stick.

Lydianne joined her, feeling delightfully free as she hopped up and down. After a moment she stopped to peek inside her envelope—and then she gasped. "My stars! This is—well, Martin gave me *quite* a nice bonus. How about you?"

Regina quickly pulled her check out and stared at it. "Who knew he'd be so generous?" she asked in amazement. "Not that long ago, I thought he was becoming a very difficult man to work for, what with his critical remarks—"

"But he's turned over a lot of new leaves since his heart problems were fixed—and since you and Gabe have gotten engaged," Lydianne added emphatically. "I should probably use some of this money for dress fabric. I surely can't wear my grubby old staining clothes in the classroom."

"It's time I upgraded my wardrobe, too," Regina agreed. "I won't want to wear my factory dresses once I'm Gabe's wife, after all. It'll be nice to wear fresh clothes while I tend the house and embroider linens for my customers at The Marketplace."

Lydianne smiled at her best friend, feeling more buoyant than she had in months. What a gift it was to receive unexpected time off, along with extra pay! "What if we walk uptown to the fabric store and choose some colorful fabric right now—and then I'll treat you to a pizza? It's a big day for us, and before long I won't be able to dilly-dally on a weekday, ain't so?"

"That's right, Teacher Lydianne. Better enjoy being a free woman while you can."

"Puh! Same back at *you*, Miss Miller!" Lydianne teased as she slipped her arm through Regina's. "Once you're Mrs. Flaud, you'll be answering to Gabe and keeping your household in order. I say we also deserve ice cream after our pizza, ain't so?"

That evening, Jeremiah closed his eyes as he sang the smooth, sustained bass line of "Precious Lord, Take My Hand" with several men from the congregation who'd gathered on his front porch. He looked forward to these weekly musical gatherings with his friends because they brought the weekdays to a satisfying conclusion with a sense of harmony that came as much from longtime friend-ships as from the songs Gabe chose for them to practice.

As the last chord drifted on the breeze, Gabe made the cut-off sign with his hands. "I think we've got that one down," he remarked with a nod. "What are your thoughts about doing a few of our songs at the Shetler reunion, middle of September, and then at the Flaud family gathering on the twenty-ninth?"

"I think we should go for it!" Glenn piped up. "Who doesn't enjoy listening to uplifting music that's snappier than what we sing in church?"

Jeremiah was pleased to hear Detweiler's upbeat tone of voice and opinion. The young widower had become immersed in the songs they sang during these Friday night sessions, probably because they gave him a break from his woodshop work and the day-to-day routine with his little boys and his elderly parents.

And Glenn had a point. It was hard to ponder problems while they were singing gospel harmonies and interesting rhythms. They learned their selections from songbooks that had full musical notation—which Gabe was adept at teaching them—and the gospel songs were a world apart from the ancient hymns written in the *Ausbund*, which were text on the pages arranged verse by verse, like poetry.

"Delores has been hinting to some of the far-flung relatives that we fellows will be singing at the reunion," Martin said.

With a squeak of the screen door, Jeremiah's *mamm* stepped out to the porch to refill their pitcher of lemonade. "I'm hoping you fellows will perform, too," she put in. "Maybe we could take some time during those reunions to listen to your music, and then you could pass around song sheets and lead us in a sing-along! Everyone would enjoy that."

Deacon Saul laughed. "*Jah*, and it might relieve the tedium of the chit-chat after the reunion meals," he teased.

"With some folks who come, you can run out of things to visit about after a while."

"Some of them talk about the very same aches and pains from one year to the next," Reuben Detweiler remarked with a chuckle. "I'm all for offering a little entertainment at both of those reunions. We practice every week, so we might as well share the ability the *Gut* Lord has given us, ain't so?"

"That's the spirit!" Jeremiah said, nodding at his friends. "Seems to me we have a special gift to offer, thanks to Gabe's ability to teach and direct us. It's also a bonus that such a *gut* and positive activity has come from the musical secret Gabe kept for so many years, and for which he served out his *bann*," he added with a smile for the younger man. "After all, if Gabe hadn't confessed to taking guitar lessons and slipping in to play the Methodist church's piano, we wouldn't be learning so much more about music from him."

Gabe smiled gratefully. "It's settled then. I think we'll be a big hit!" he remarked as he collected the songbooks. "Margaret's been kind enough to bring us more lemonade, and after all our singing, I'm ready for a big glassful."

"I'll pour!" Glenn said as he rose from his porch chair. "I ran across a really *gut* deal this week, and I'm excited about it."

All the men smiled encouragingly at the carpenter as they held out their glasses. "How's that, Glenn?" Jeremiah asked as he accepted a refill. "We're all happy that you've found something that makes *you* happy."

Glenn's dark beard parted with his wide smile. "A friend of mine who builds a lot of decks had a customer cancel, and he can't return the pricey composite boards that're already cut to size," he began. "I snapped up a bunch of the shorter boards, and I've been making picnic tables for the new schoolhouse! They'll pop apart so we can store them in the winter, and they'll stand up to the summer sun and rain without any maintenance. I think Teacher Lydianne's going to be tickled that she and the kids can eat their lunches outside when the weather's nice."

"What a great idea!" Saul exclaimed. "I think the district should reimburse you for those materials. That composite decking isn't cheap."

"I bet you folks that run shops at The Marketplace will be using them for your lunch breaks, too," Matthias Wagler put in as Glenn refilled his glass.

Gabe smiled. "That's another great idea—especially when we get into cooler fall weather," he said. "Awfully nice of you to put your time into such a project, Glenn."

Jeremiah hoped his expression didn't betray his mixed feelings about Detweiler's generous offering to the schoolhouse grounds. He suddenly wished *he* had the talent for crafting something useful and enjoyable, because he wanted to see the look of surprised gratitude on Lydianne's face when he gave it to her.

But he was a farmer, not a carpenter. His building skills enabled him to make basic repairs to barn stalls, fences, and equipment, but he lacked the ability to create anything of true beauty. A lot of woodworkers made their fiancées cedar-lined hope chests or other pieces of fine furniture, but he'd resorted to giving Priscilla a clock—which still sat on the dresser upstairs. She had treasured it, and Jeremiah remembered her lovingly each and every time he looked at it.

Why are you thinking about engagement gifts? Why can't you be pleased that Glenn is so excited about his surprise—which is more for the schoolhouse than for Lydianne, after all?

Despite his prayers and best intentions, Jeremiah sat out on the porch in the darkness long after his friends had gone home. What might he give to the district's new teacher—or do for her—that would convince Lydianne to spend time with him rather than with Detweiler?

Chapter Six

"Now *this* is the way to spend a visiting Sunday!" Regina crowed from the back seat of Jo's family-sized buggy.

"*Jah*, we should quit our jobs more often and have Jo drive us around town for our meals," Lydianne put in with a laugh. She slung her arm around Jo and hugged her as the double rig rolled down the road toward the Helfing place. "This progressive dinner was a fine idea, and it's very sweet of you to do some of the cooking and the driving for us today."

Jo shrugged good-naturedly. "It was easy enough to put together a roasted chicken dinner—I baked two birds and left one for Mamm," she added as she guided the horse onto the next country lane. "It'll be fun to see what Molly and Marietta came up with for appetizers and dessert so you girls didn't have to cook. I wish we'd thought about doing progressive dinners sooner! We'll have a great time today, just us girls."

Lydianne gazed down the road as the Helfing place came into view. It was a glorious August day, cooler because a front had passed through in the night. She was looking forward to celebrating with her close friends without other folks in the congregation making a big fuss about her and Regina leaving the Flauds' factory—and without feeling Bishop Jeremiah's gaze on her.

The horse had just entered the twins' hard-packed dirt driveway when a large golden retriever shot out from behind one of the two *dawdi hauses* that sat slightly behind the main house. His raucous barking shattered the Sunday morning peace.

Molly stepped out of the white two-story house, scowling. "Riley!" she scolded. "Be quiet! Go home!"

As the big dog began to circle her horse and rig, still barking, Jo slowed down. "Makes you wonder if the girls put up with this ruckus every time somebody comes over," she murmured to Lydianne. "It's a *gut* thing Pete and his dog aren't living at our place!"

"Drusilla wouldn't stand for all this noise," Lydianne agreed with a laugh.

By the time the buggy reached the shady rear side of the house where the Helfings' small noodle factory sat, Molly had come outside to grab the big dog's collar. "You girls can go on inside, and I'll be right there. Back you go, you big mutt," she said as she turned him away from the buggy.

"I'll grab your roaster, Jo," Regina called out from the back seat. "You can hold the door for me."

Lydianne stayed behind to unhitch the horse and lead it to the nearby pasture. She'd always liked the Helfing place, because its lush green yard was shaded by a lot of large trees. She couldn't help noticing that the flower beds the twins' *mamm* had always tended appeared trampled— although the lawn was neatly mowed, and the house and outbuildings all boasted a fresh coat of white paint. When she reached the back stoop, Molly was returning from putting Riley into the *dawdi haus* farthest away from them.

"I guess you know our *mamm*'s rolling in her grave because that *dog* has been napping in her flowers," she said with a shake of her head. "The other day I caught him digging in one of the beds, and lo and behold he pulled out a bone he'd buried. Does no *gut* to threaten Pete about it, because he just laughs it off. Says dogs will be dogs."

"Aw, come on, Molly," Pete called through an open *dawdi haus* window. "You know you love Riley, deep down."

Molly rolled her eyes as her twin sister opened the door to let them in. "We have to watch what we say when the windows are open," she murmured. "The bishop has paid Pete's rent through the end of September, so we'll see what the winter brings. When Marietta complained about Riley being such a terror, Jeremiah gave us a bonus rent check for putting up with him."

Marietta laughed as she welcomed Lydianne with a hug. "*Jah*, the bishop thinks we're helping his nephew stay on the straight and narrow," she put in. "I have to say it's been nice having Pete mow the grass, though—and he recently painted all of our buildings, too."

Lydianne chuckled—and let out a gasp. A big hand-lettered banner was stretched across the top of the mud-room wall, with CONGRATULATIONS, REGINA AND LYDIANNE written in bold colors. Balloons were fastened at either end of it, too.

"I feel like I've walked into a birthday party!" Lydianne said. "You girls have really gone all out for us!"

Molly grinned. "Well, it is a birth of sorts, what with both of you going in new directions," she pointed out.

"And it was an excuse to get out our marker sets and

color!" Marietta added. Her face, still very thin after her cancer treatments, brightened. "It was also incentive for us to deep clean the kitchen and set this week's noodle orders out in the factory, too, so it looks like we keep a normal house."

"Ever since we've been selling at The Marketplace," Molly explained, "we've been piling big boxes of bagged noodles wherever we had room for them. Having you girls over for our progressive dinner is a special occasion!"

As they entered the kitchen, Jo was placing her blue graniteware roasting pan in the oven to keep the main course warm for later. Regina was filling the water glasses at the places around the kitchen table, which was covered with a pretty oilcloth in a summer floral pattern that complemented the soft yellow walls. Several plates and bowls filled the center of the table, which was set for five.

"This is a feast!" Lydianne said as she chose a seat. "We could stay here all day eating this stuff you twins have made for us."

Molly waved her off as the rest of them sat down. "It's nothing fancy, but it's food Marietta was hungry for—which means her appetite is finally returning."

"*Jah*, it's been a long while since we made Mamm's pimiento cheese ball and her liverwurst spread," Marietta remarked. "Otherwise, wrapping some pickle spears in thin-sliced ham, putting out some crackers, and dumping ranch-flavored tortilla chips into a bowl alongside some salsa was no big deal. Help yourselves!"

Lydianne grabbed the bowl of chips while her friends all chose the foods closest to their plates. As they passed the appetizers around the table, the kitchen was filled with companionable silence.

"Well, we've filled you in on *our* renter," Molly said in a low voice. "How are things going at your place, Jo, with the Wengerds being in your *dawdi haus* on Friday nights?"

Jo chuckled as she spread a thick layer of pimiento cheese on a cracker. "You'll never get my *mamm* to admit this, but I think she really likes having Nelson and Michael to cook for—and they're staying a lot of Saturday nights that fall before visiting Sundays, as well," she added. "They say that after their busy Saturdays selling flowers at The Marketplace—or helping with the produce auctions— they aren't fired up about making the drive back to Queen City in the evening."

"Could be they like the meals you ladies are cooking for them," Regina remarked before taking a big bite of a wrapped pickle spear. "And if Nelson's wife passed on a while back, maybe they enjoy your company as much as the food."

"And how about *you*, Jo?" Molly asked. "Michael's a really nice guy—"

"And he's got those dreamy blue-gray eyes," Marietta put in with a sigh.

"—and he's *gut* about helping without being asked," her sister continued with a hint of a grin. "Wouldn't surprise me if you two came to be more than just friends—"

"But that will never happen!" Jo blurted. She quickly shoved a corn chip heaped with liverwurst spread into her mouth, as though this would keep her from having to say anything further.

Lydianne noticed the pinkness of Jo's cheeks and the way she was blinking as she looked away. Knowing how awkward it felt when folks assumed there was a romance going on when there wasn't, she considered her words carefully. "Why do you say that?" she asked softly. "Michael would be very blessed if an energetic, well-organized, *compassionate*, young woman like you took an interest in him."

As everyone else around the table nodded, Jo shook her head. "Let's be honest," she muttered. "It's no secret that I'm too tall and big boned and hefty, just like Dat was. Mamm's always telling me I'm my father made over, and she's right. What fellow wants a woman with a face and a body like Big Joe Fussner's?"

Stunned at her friend's blunt self-assessment, Lydianne reached over to grasp Jo's wrist. "Oh, but that's not true—"

"Phooey on that!" Regina insisted from across the table. "Let's not forget that your *mamm*, bless her heart, tends to see things in a negative light—"

"*Not* that there's anything negative about you or your looks, Jo!" Marietta protested. "Why, you're the most wonderful—"

A loud pounding on the front door made them all sit up and look toward the front room. "Hey, what smells so *gut* in there?" Pete called out. "Do you suppose a poor, lonely, *hungry* guy might come in for some company and food on this visiting Sunday?"

Lydianne and her friends exchanged wary glances around the table.

"It's your house, so it's your call," Regina whispered as she gazed at the twins.

"*Jah*, but this is supposed to be a party just for us girls," Marietta protested.

Jo, who seemed glad for the interruption, took a wrapped pickle spear. "He *is* all by himself," she pointed out, "and we have more than we'll eat before we move on to Lydianne's place—"

Molly rolled her eyes, turning toward the door. "Come on in, Pete," she said loudly. "But Riley has to stay outside!"

Pete entered the kitchen with a confident grin as he took in the young women gathered around the table. "Looks like quite a hen party you're having here," he teased as he pulled a spare chair to the head of the table. "You no doubt need me here to establish some proper order, *jah*?"

Absolute silence filled the kitchen.

Molly lifted an eyebrow at him. "If you've interrupted our celebration with *that* attitude, Mr. Shetler, you may as well head back outside with your dog."

Rolling his eyes playfully, Pete studied the platters of food in the center of the table. "Come on now, Moll, this is me you're talking to," he cajoled her. "Didn't I mow the grass yesterday? And didn't I paint your barns and the chicken house last week—without you asking me? Surely, I'm *gut* for a plateful of these munchies," he suggested as he looked around the kitchen. "And whatever you're having for your main meal smells fabulous, too."

Marietta rose to fetch him a plate from the cupboard. "And didn't we pay you for your painting work and thank you profusely for doing it?" she shot back. "Sometimes I think your *mamm* should've named you Pest instead of Pete."

Lydianne exchanged quick glances with Regina and Jo, who seemed as surprised as she was about the nature of the conversation the Helfing sisters were having with their renter. Although their words could've been construed as confrontational, their voices conveyed a completely different picture. She was about to remark on how cozy the twins were sounding when a wail similar to a siren started up near the open kitchen window.

"Riley—quiet!" Pete ordered as he heaped tortilla chips on his plate.

Lydianne stuffed a cheese-covered cracker into her mouth to keep from laughing, although the dog's howling became so loud and insistent that when Jo opened her mouth to make conversation, she gave up.

"Riley!" Pete cried out as he helped himself to a huge serving of the liverwurst spread. "Shut up!"

Molly's resigned sigh suggested that this wasn't the first time the golden had interrupted whatever she and Marietta were doing. "I'll go tell him what's what!" she muttered as she rose from the table.

Pete accepted the plate holding the pimiento cheese ball from Lydianne with a gracious smile. "So, how's life for you and Regina now that you're not at the furniture factory?"

Regina's face lit up. "I'll adjust pretty quickly to not working with that noisy exhaust fan and all those fumes—"

Molly's shriek from the mudroom made them all turn around as Riley burst through the door and shot past her. Before anyone could blink, the excited dog plopped his front paws on the table, snatched the cheese ball from its plate, and escaped to the other end of the kitchen.

"Bad dog! Bad dog!" Molly said sternly as she followed him. "Riley, sit!"

Riley swallowed the cheese ball in one big gulp. Then he sat down obediently, grinning at her with a yellow-smeared tongue lolling from his mouth.

"I really am sorry, girls," Pete said around his mouthful of food. "I wanted to try some of that cheese ball, too."

Lydianne could read the impatience in her friends' faces, so she wasn't surprised when Jo rose from her chair.

"How about if we leave you the rest of these appetizers, Pete, and we'll move along to the next stop on our progressive dinner?" she asked, glancing at the other *maidels* for their answers.

"Let's do it," Marietta muttered. "I'll grab the brownies—"

"I'll fetch the roaster from the oven," Jo put in as she picked up her hot pads.

"I'll bring the ice cream from the freezer," Molly added as they all headed for the door. She turned to Pete, who looked befuddled as he sat alone at the kitchen table. "And meanwhile, if Riley gets sick from eating all that cheese, it's your job to clean it up, Mr. Shetler. Enjoy the rest of your day. We certainly intend to!"

The five of them climbed into the double buggy, with Regina up front beside Jo and the rest of them in the back with the food. Once they were headed toward the road, Molly shook her head. "I'm really sorry our party got derailed. I should've known better than to let Pete—or Riley—spoil the time we'd said was just for us girls."

Lydianne smiled. "You were only being nice, sharing what we were eating."

"*Jah*, but we always fall for Pete's line about being lonely and hungry," Marietta explained dolefully, "and then we kick ourselves. He's a nice guy at heart—"

"But he really needs to grow up," Molly remarked crossly. "We told him when he came here as a renter that we *cannot* allow Riley inside the noodle factory, and twice he's slipped in the door as we were coming out from a morning's work."

"We had to sanitize *everything* before we could continue with the fresh noodles we'd left on the tables to dry," her sister said. "If that dog ever jumps up on a table to grab noodles, we'll lose the entire batch—not to mention the time and ingredients that went into them."

"And *then* we'll give Mr. Shetler the bill for what his dog ruined," Molly stated sternly. "I've mentioned these incidents to Bishop Jeremiah, but he's asked us to be patient—thanking us because Pete is so much more productive and headed in a more positive direction nowadays."

Lydianne, Regina, and Jo nodded sympathetically. The buggy rolled down the road for several moments with only the clip-clop of the horse punctuating their silence.

"How about if we chalk it up to doing Pete a favor—and feeding him—and we look forward to the rest of our dinner?" Regina asked. "It's only eleven-thirty, so we still have the rest of the day together."

"And *denki* for those wrapped pickles and your *mamm*'s special pimiento cheese ball and liverwurst spread," Jo said to the twins. "You got our celebration off to a fine start."

As they passed the next farmstead, Lydianne tried not to be obvious about gazing around the yard. Her whole body thrummed at the sight of Ella riding a miniature pony all by herself. Her *dat* stood back a ways, watching her carefully, but the little blonde appeared quite confident about guiding her mount as she circled the front yard.

"Would you look at that!" Molly crowed. "I wouldn't be a bit surprised if Ella's practicing her horsemanship so she can ride to school one of these days."

Both of the Helfing twins stuck their arms out of the rig's windows and waved. Lydianne's heart took off at a trot, hoping the little horse wouldn't be spooked. When Ella waved back, she felt a pride unlike any she'd ever known.

"Ella's such sweet little girl—and sharp as a tack," Jo remarked over her shoulder. "It'll be a joy to have her in your classroom, Lydianne."

"*Jah*, I think so, too," Lydianne replied carefully. "I don't recall being nearly so brave or so *gut* at sitting a pony when I was only six."

"Who knows? She's always been quiet, but once she spends her days around other kids, she might prove to be a handful," Molly said with a chuckle. "I really came out of my shell when I started school, as I recall."

"Puh!" Marietta teased. "You never had a shell, sister. I've always been the shy, quiet, well-behaved twin. Everyone will tell you so!"

As they all laughed, Lydianne's gaze lingered on the little girl—*her* little girl—and she reminded herself yet again that it was going to be tricky not to show favoritism to Ella Nissley. A teacher was to treat all of her students as though they were special and capable—important members of her class, and worthy of her praise and encouragement.

A few minutes later they turned onto the road that led to Lydianne's place. Marietta held the brownie pan to keep it from sliding across the seat when the rig rounded the corner, while Molly held the lid on Jo's blue roaster.

"Your house always looks nice and cool in the shade of those big old trees," Regina remarked from the front seat. She leaned forward, studying something intently. "Isn't that Bishop Jeremiah's horse at the hitching rail? No one else I know rides a dapple-gray Percheron."

Lydianne's head snapped up. She hoped her friends wouldn't notice that her cheeks were catching fire as she gazed through the buggy's windshield from the back seat.

Why would the bishop be at my house? He surely doesn't intend to talk about school business on a Sunday . . .

Jo chuckled knowingly. "It is a visiting Sunday," she pointed out as she drove up the lane. "So maybe he's come to pay our Lydianne a visit!"

"But we're having a *maidel*'s day—and we've already been interrupted once," Lydianne protested. "Quick—how can we politely move him along, so we girls can enjoy our chicken dinner?"

Jo looked over her shoulder with a short laugh. "That'll be your call, Lydianne. Who am I to tell the bishop he's not welcome?"

Chapter Seven

When Jeremiah spotted the approaching double rig—
with Jo Fussner and Regina Miller gawking at him from its
front seat—he kicked himself. When he'd hinted to Mamm
at breakfast that he might visit Lydianne rather than going
to Jude's place for Sunday dinner, she'd immediately
packed a fresh loaf of bread and some of the casserole she
was taking to his brother's place, for him to share. Despite
his insistence that this was only a *visit*, Mamm was acting
as if he were initiating a courtship. There'd been no acceptable way to back out—not that he'd really wanted to.

But he hadn't counted on the five *maidels* spending the
day together.

"What a nice surprise, Bishop!" Jo called out as she
parked the buggy.

"*Jah*, you're just in time to join us for dinner," Regina
chimed in playfully. "We're celebrating Lydianne's and my
last day at the Flaud factory."

The Helfing twins emerged from the back of the rig
with a big roaster and other pans of food in their hands—
and expectant expressions on their faces. Lydianne's
flustered glance told him that he'd caught her off guard.

Jeremiah's thoughts spun into overdrive, searching for a believable reason for his showing up unannounced . . .

"And aren't you the perfect guest, bringing some food to contribute?" Jo asked breezily. She leaned over the small pan he was holding and inhaled appreciatively. "Smells like Margaret's cheesy potato and ham casserole—one of my favorites!"

"How about if the rest of us go inside and set things on the table so you and Lydianne can have a moment alone?" Molly asked playfully. The contents of the blue roaster she was carrying toward the door smelled heavenly.

"*Jah*, take your time, Bishop," Marietta chimed in, following her twin with a lidded pan and a container of ice cream. "We're not going anywhere."

Jeremiah prayed his response would sound believable. "Truth be told, I was hoping to catch all of you together so we could talk about some upcoming events at The Marketplace."

Regina's auburn eyebrows shot up. "How'd you know about our progressive dinner?"

"A little bird told me," he fibbed quickly.

None of the *maidels* looked totally convinced, but they stepped onto the porch and went inside. Lydianne remained at the bottom of the steps with him, appearing flushed and *ferhoodled*. "Well, Jeremiah, it's *gut* to see you even though I wasn't expecting—"

"I didn't mean to intrude," he murmured. Her blue eyes were wide, and her pink cheeks told him he'd probably overstepped, yet at that moment her parted lips looked so very kissable—

And where did that thought come from? You haven't

considered kissing anyone for—well, more than three years.

Jeremiah exhaled, hoping to clear his mind of such thoughts before he said or did anything that would make this situation even more awkward.

"—but *jah*, we're happy to have you join us for dinner," Lydianne continued in a rush. "Really, we are. I'm glad you're here, Jeremiah."

His heart thumped crazily. She was being a good sport about this unplanned encounter. He couldn't recall when she'd ever spoken to him without addressing him as the bishop, and today she'd left off his title. He found that encouraging . . . and rather intimate. "Um, maybe we should go in, so the food won't get cold."

Nodding, Lydianne preceded him into the house. He'd been to her place shortly after she'd moved to Morning Star, and for the one time she'd hosted church—because afterward the congregation had agreed that her rental house was too small to accommodate pew benches comfortably. The cozy front room, set off with colorful crocheted afghans, and the pale coral kitchen walls with their white cabinets felt homier than he recalled.

The table was set for six. A platter of chicken and bowls of vegetables were arranged in the center of it, along with the bread and casserole his *mamm* had sent along. The other *maidels* stopped chatting as he entered the kitchen behind Lydianne. Four expectant smiles greeted them.

"Have a seat, Bishop," Jo said, gesturing toward the chair at the head of the table. "We're eager to hear what you have to say about The Marketplace."

It didn't escape Jeremiah that the other young women had chosen their chairs so that Lydianne would be sitting to his left . . . where a wife would be. He set that thought aside as he sat down and bowed his head for a silent grace.

Lord, I'm on a tightrope here, and I'll be grateful for Your guidance. I'm thankful to be having such a nice meal, even if these gals have seen right through my excuse for coming this morning.

When he cleared his throat, everyone looked up and began passing the food. "It's very gracious of you to let me share this fabulous meal uninvited," he said as he helped himself to two pieces of beautifully roasted chicken.

"Oh, but it's a treat to have you here, Bishop Jeremiah," Regina teased as she playfully glanced from him to Lydianne.

He took some of the carrots, onions, celery, and potatoes that had been roasted along with the chicken. It was time to head off any further hints of romance between him and the district's new teacher—who was also the financial manager of The Marketplace.

"Is there anything I can do to help you prepare for the two upcoming family reunions that will be held at The Marketplace?" he asked in a businesslike tone. "Even with all the tables and chairs the Flauds are providing, and Jo's kitchen facilities, it'll be quite an undertaking to host the Shetler family event in the middle of September and then accommodate the Flauds a couple of weeks later."

As though relieved to have a safe topic of conversation, Lydianne spoke right up. "We've already received deposits from both families—and, in fact, they've paid the full amount rather than waiting until later to pay the balance," she added as she accepted the platter of chicken and vegetables from him. "Delores and your *mamm* have already said their families will be bringing all the food—"

"And they've agreed to provide the additional chairs and the large folding tables they'll be needing for the food, as well," Jo put in. "I've suggested they can use the coffee stand for their beverages. Your mother and Delores have assured me that the women will leave my kitchen and the central serving area even cleaner than when they arrive."

"*Jah*, they already know they're responsible for taking home any leftover food and disposing of their trash, too," Regina said with a nod. "It's all spelled out on our rental agreement form."

"And the church will receive the same ten percent commission from the proceeds that our shopkeepers kick in from their sales," Lydianne added as she placed a large helping of vegetables on her plate. "We're really glad Martha Maude suggested that we host reunions and parties because they'll make us some easy money. We'll earn enough to pay the utility bills for the next several months, as well as to set aside funds for any building maintenance we might need."

Jeremiah nodded, swallowing a mouthful of delectable roasted carrots and celery. The silence around the table as they began to eat suggested that the *maidels* were finished discussing reunions—and looking to him for further conversation. The grins they tried to hide as they chewed their food told him they weren't going to let him off the hook, either.

"Sounds like you ladies have everything under control," he said after too many moments had gone by. "Not that I doubted your ability to handle these reunions, of course."

"Of course," Jo echoed. She gazed purposefully at the corner space between him and Lydianne, as though she wondered if they were holding hands under the table.

Jeremiah quickly brought his napkin to his mouth, so his left hand was fully visible. When Lydianne also realized what her friend was looking at, she grabbed the bread basket with both hands and passed it to Marietta.

"So how are things coming at the new schoolhouse?" Regina asked sweetly. "Now that you're not staining furniture, Lydianne, I bet you'll be over there getting the classroom set up, ain't so?"

"Oh, *jah*, I've picked up all manner of posters and supplies at the bookstore—and the textbooks are already there," Lydianne replied quickly. "I'll spend most of this week figuring out where I want things to go."

Jeremiah wondered if Regina's question was intended to inform him of Lydianne's schedule, because the *maidels* had surely already heard what she planned to do in the coming week. Did this mean they might watch to see if he joined her at the schoolhouse?

He sighed to himself. Even though he'd received some worthwhile information about the family reunions, he sensed Lydianne's friends intended to grill him for as long as he stayed—and then ply her with their curious questions after he left. Although Jeremiah could've enjoyed a second plateful of the wonderful food, he excused himself when he'd finished the first one.

"*Denki* again for letting me join you," he said as he rose from his chair. "I'll let you ladies continue your celebration. It's *gut* to hear that our investment in The Marketplace building and property is paying off even better than we'd anticipated."

"Don't forget your *mamm*'s casserole dish," Jo piped up.

"And thank her for the bread, too!" Regina added with a mischievous grin. "It was *gut* to see you today, Bishop!"

As Jeremiah went outside and mounted his gelding,

he was well aware that he hadn't fooled a soul with his trumped-up story. He felt bad that Lydianne would have to endure her friends' questions—yet he was glad he'd come over. Having her seated to his left during the meal, where Priscilla had sat for so many happy years of their marriage, had given him an unexpected sense of fulfillment. He found himself hoping he'd enjoy other, more private meals in Lydianne's cozy kitchen as time went by.

Maybe Mamm's right. Maybe I need to make my interest and intentions known—before somebody else does.

"Do tell, Lydianne!" Regina teased as they cleared the food from the table. "A blind woman could see that something's perking between you and Bishop Jeremiah."

"*Jah*, the temperature in this kitchen rose twenty degrees when you two sat down next to each other," Molly put in.

Lydianne waved them off. "You girls are so full of baloney—"

"Oh, I think not!" Jo joined in, slipping her arm around Lydianne's shoulders. "But honestly, how could you possibly do any better than Jeremiah Shetler? He's tall and strong and *gut*-looking—not to mention how well he does with his farming."

"You couldn't find a kinder, gentler man, either," Marietta insisted as she put the leftover chicken and vegetables into a lidded container.

Lydianne searched desperately for the words that would set her friends straight. For years they'd all been close friends who'd agreed that they got along perfectly fine without husbands, yet now that Regina was engaged, their group dynamic had shifted. "If that's your story, let's talk about how cozy you twins and Pete seem to be—"

"*Cozy* is nothing, considering that I heard Margaret intends to move out, so you and Jeremiah can feather your nest in that big white house without her."

Lydianne felt suddenly dizzy. She looked Jo straight in the eye. "Who told you that?" she rasped.

Giving her shoulder a final squeeze, Jo set about wiping the table with a dishcloth. "Martha Maude told Mamm, and Mamm mentioned it to me the other day," she replied with a triumphant shrug. "Who am I to question those sources?"

"And we all know that Margaret wouldn't want just anybody marrying her son," Molly put in with a nod. "Remember how she fussed at Jude when he announced he was courting Leah Otto? And how she moved out of Jude's place because she wanted no part of being in that house after he married her?"

Lydianne inhaled deeply, trying to regain her emotional balance. Did everyone in the church district believe she and Jeremiah were sweet on each other?

"*Jah*, and Margaret wouldn't have sent over that casserole and bread today if she weren't trying to help her son get your attention," Regina pointed out. "No matter what you say, Lydianne, folks have noticed how twinkly you both look when you're in the same room together."

Twinkly? Lydianne made a point of picking up Marietta's pan of brownies and heading for the door. "You girls have it all wrong, and so does everyone else," she insisted. "I have no intention of marrying the bishop—or any other man, for that matter. I love this home, I love my life, and I'm going to pour my heart and soul into being the best teacher Morning Star's ever had. So let's go to Regina's place for brownies and ice cream, shall we?"

Chapter Eight

On Wednesday afternoon, Lydianne gazed around her classroom with a heady sense of excitement. She'd stashed the extra desks downstairs in the storage area, behind the pegged wall where the scholars would hang their coats. Textbooks of the appropriate grade levels sat on the desks in front of her, along with cheerful name placards she'd made for each of her scholars. Colorful posters and instructional materials were arranged on the walls and above the whiteboard. Near the windows, where the yellow curtains Martha Maude had sewn fluttered crisply in the breeze, sturdy tables provided room for the first two class projects she was planning. She'd also cleaned the restroom building, which sat behind the schoolhouse.

As she stood at her desk, Lydianne couldn't stop smiling. The new classroom was ready for her eight students, and she was eager to see their bright smiles and hear their voices filling the fresh, welcoming space. Some of her favorite memories came from her years in school, and now it was her turn to create a caring, vibrant environment for the children she would nurture each day. In a week and a half, Lydianne would be living her new dream—and secretly playing a vital part in her daughter's upbringing and education.

Thank You, Lord, for fresh starts and answered prayers. Help me to use these gifts in the way You intended.

She sat down and slipped a spelling book from the row of texts arranged on the left edge of her desk. Except for being a new copy, it was the same book she'd used as a seventh grader, so Lydianne felt she was visiting an old friend as she opened it to the first lesson. She'd learned her weekly spelling lists by copying each word on notebook paper, writing its definition, and then using it in a sentence—and that was the method she would use with her four older students.

As she jotted notes in her planning book, Lydianne savored the peacefulness that surrounded the schoolhouse. Except for Saturdays, when The Marketplace attracted hundreds of shoppers, the property was vacant—which made it the perfect place for her scholars to learn. For morning and afternoon recess, bins of new balls, bats, jump ropes, and other playground equipment awaited them downstairs. They would play outside on the new ball field, or on the swings and seesaws, or at the volleyball net.

In her mind, Lydianne could already hear the girls' sing-song chant of jump rope rhymes, and the crack of a bat followed by the boys' jubilant cries as they encouraged a batter to run the bases.

The clatter of an approaching horse-drawn wagon jarred her out of her daydreams, however.

When she looked out the window, the sight of picnic tables made her suck in her breath—but when she saw the expectant smiles on Glenn's and Billy Jay's faces, her heart sank.

You really should be grateful to God that Glenn's

*moving through the sorrow he feels for his wife—and be
thankful for the gift he's bringing, too.*

Lydianne sighed. There was no escaping Glenn's attention, because the open door and windows announced her
presence. The wagon had barely come to a halt beneath
the trees before Billy Jay hopped down and made a beeline
for the schoolhouse.

"Teacher Lydianne, is that you in there?" he called out.
"Look what we brung ya!"

Putting on a bright smile, she walked to the doorway—
and was nearly bowled over as Billy Jay threw his spindly
arms around her waist.

"And what brings you out here to the new school?" She
rubbed his shoulders and then gently eased away from his
embrace. His dark blue shirt was faded but neatly pressed.
The black pants fluttering several inches above his shoe
tops suggested that he was going through a growth spurt.
"Would you like to see the new schoolroom now that it's
all set up? Maybe find your desk?"

For a few moments, the boy gazed around the classroom with wide eyes, but then he seemed to quickly recall
his original mission. "Come and see what Dat made!" he
said, grabbing her hand. "Now we can have a picnic every
day, if we want to!"

As she stepped outside with her exuberant student, she
couldn't miss the wide smile on his father's face. Glenn's
hair was still damp from a shower, and the dark beard
framing his face appeared freshly trimmed.

"*Gut* morning, Glenn," Lydianne said as she followed
Billy Jay toward the trees. "That's an intriguing load on
your wagon."

After his gaze lingered on her for a few moments too
long, Glenn looked at his son. "Remember how I told you

that you're not to cling to Teacher Lydianne?" he said gently. "She's your teacher, not your *mamm*—and she'll have other scholars who need her attention during the school day."

As the boy obediently dropped her hand, Lydianne was pleased that Glenn had mentioned this matter even as she felt very sorry that Billy Jay was so hungry for her attention. She smiled at the boy—although she wondered if Glenn was using his son's neediness to inspire her affection for *him*.

Focusing on the picnic tables, which were cocoa colored with very smooth boards, Lydianne approached the loaded wagon. "These tables look different from most I've seen," she remarked. "They're not made from wood, are they?"

Glenn smiled as though she'd made a very astute observation. "Nope. I latched onto some composite materials a lot of English use for decks these days," he replied as he lifted one of the benches off the wagon bed. "These tables should last for years because they won't deteriorate like wood, and they won't need paint to keep them looking nice."

Lydianne noticed the ease with which Glenn continued removing the tables, which surely had to weigh more than wooden ones. "Can I help you steady—"

"Oh, no—I've got this." As he set the last table on the ground, his short-sleeved shirt strained taut against his muscular shoulders and arms. "If you could lift the other end, though, you could show me where you want—"

"I'm your helper, Dat—remember?" Billy Jay piped up as he scrambled to the other end of the table. "Where do you want this one, Teacher Lydianne? Under this shade tree?"

"That would be perfect," she replied. It wasn't at all unusual to see fathers and sons working together, yet she had the sense that Glenn and Billy Jay were orchestrating this task to impress her.

And what will they expect in return?

It was an uncharitable thought, and it made Lydianne uncomfortable. Glenn Detweiler was an industrious fellow with a pleasant disposition, and from all outward signs, he'd provided Dorcas a happy life.

But I can't encourage his attention. It would be dishonest and unkind to let him believe I'm the untainted schoolteacher everyone thinks I am.

By the time Glenn and Billy Jay had positioned three full-sized picnic tables and one that would seat about eight little children, Lydianne's thoughts were spinning in a tight spiral. "*Denki* so much for the time and money you spent on this wonderful-*gut* gift for the schoolyard," she said nervously. "I'm sorry I don't have any water or lemonade to offer you—"

Glenn had apparently been waiting for just such an opening. "I was hoping we might go into town for lunch—maybe pick up some sandwiches at the deli and take them to the park," he said with a hopeful smile.

"*Jah*, and I could play on the swings and the jungle gym!" Billy Jay exclaimed.

As the boy hopped up and down in his excitement, Lydianne felt trapped. She didn't have a legitimate excuse—but if folks in town saw the three of them sharing lunch in the park, the grapevine would be afire with the news that she and Glenn were seeing each other.

"I appreciate your offer, but—"

At the sound of an approaching horse and buggy, Lydianne turned and almost cheered. Bishop Jeremiah was driving toward the schoolhouse. As he waved at them, his expression told her he was assessing the situation between her and Glenn. He pulled his rig up to the hitching post, leaving a trail of dust in his wake.

"So these are the tables you were talking about?" the bishop called out as he slid out of his rig. "I'm glad you're here, Glenn. If you've got a minute, you and Billy Jay can help me position the four bases on the ball diamond. Works better if two people are pacing off the distance between bases and pulling the rope between them to keep the baselines straight."

If Glenn was irritated by the bishop's interruption, he did a fine job of covering it. Lydianne wondered if Jeremiah had originally intended for her to be his helper— or had he found out the Detweilers were coming to the school today? Either way, it was the opportunity she'd been praying for.

"I have to be going, so I'll leave you fellows to your work," she said, carefully avoiding the mention of her destination. "*Denki* for all your help getting the school and the yard ready for our scholars."

Before either man could detain her, Lydianne hurried into the building, gathered some texts, and shut the windows. As she closed the door behind her, she realized Glenn and Jeremiah might sense she was running from them, but she didn't let that slow her down. She waved at the trio carrying the bases toward the ball field, hitched up her horse at the pole barn, and drove toward the road without looking back.

How could she convince Glenn and the bishop that she didn't want to date either of them, without giving them the real reason why?

Chapter Nine

Monday, September second, dawned clear and bright without the heat and humidity that had made August so uncomfortable. It was perfect weather for the first day of school.

Nervous and excited, Lydianne arrived at the schoolhouse way too early because she couldn't stand to stay home another minute. She knew her classroom was in order, yet she had to check each scholar's desk and textbooks for the umpteenth time. She rearranged the paper, crayons, and markers on the worktable where her scholars could make posters of their names to decorate the wall when they weren't actively engaged with their first day's lessons. She smoothed her new teal cape dress and sat in the chair at her desk, watching the clock on the back wall as she rehearsed how she would introduce lessons—especially for her three beginning students.

At last, the clatter of wheels and the sound of laughter announced her scholars' arrival. Lydianne went to stand on the front stoop—and her heart flew into her throat. Billy Jay was driving a large cart up the lane, urging his brown Shetland pony to go so fast that Stevie Shetler, seated beside him, lost his hat. Little Ella sat behind the boys, clutching her *kapp* to her head—and laughing as though she were riding the Ferris wheel at the county fair.

Lydianne's first impulse was to cry out that Billy Jay should slow down, but when the boy spotted her, he immediately reined in the pony. The cart rolled along the final ten yards at a sedate pace, with its three riders all wearing angelic expressions that made Lydianne chuckle to herself. Teaching school was a far cry from working at the Flaud factory—and it would be anything but boring.

Not far behind Billy Jay, Lucy and Linda Miller drove their larger cart, followed by Lorena and Kate Flaud, who'd given Gracie Wagler a ride in their rig.

Suddenly, the moment Lydianne had been awaiting for weeks had arrived—and she froze. She had no idea what to say or do.

"*Gut* morning, Teacher Lydianne!" Kate called out, and the other scholars echoed her exuberant greeting.

The joy on their faces filled Lydianne's heart. How could she remain nervous and tongue-tied, surrounded by such bright smiles? "*Gut* morning, my dear scholars," she replied as she opened her arms wide. "It's going to be a wonderful-*gut* day, and our best school year ever. After you've pastured your ponies and put your lunches on your shelves downstairs, please come up and find your seats."

As the students drove to the corral, Lydianne walked around the white schoolhouse to stand at the lower-level door. When her three beginners approached with their lunch pails, she showed them inside, where wooden partitions along the walls contained pegs for hanging their wraps as well as shelf space for their lunches—and for their boots when the weather turned snowy. "Everyone has a spot with his or her name on it," she explained. "The girls are along this wall—"

"And us boys are on this side," Billy Jay put in as he steered Stevie toward their partitions. "Stick with me, Stevie, coz I can read!"

What a blessing it was to hear the clatter of shoes on the stairs and classroom floor mingling with the scholars' voices as they gazed at the wall displays in their new schoolroom. Lydianne had arranged the smaller desks in the front row, and as she guided Ella and Gracie to their seats, Billy Jay read the name placards aloud until he found his spot at the end.

"I don't get to sit by Stevie?" he asked with a hint of mischief. "Why's he sitting clear down at the other end?"

Lydianne playfully raised an eyebrow. "Because you're in second grade, and he's with the other first-graders, *jah*?" she asked, gesturing toward Ella and Gracie.

"Billy Jay has always been in a class by himself," Lorena quipped. "But we love him anyway."

"We do!" Lydianne agreed quickly. She went to her desk and pointed up to the passage she'd printed across the top of the white board. "Our Bible verse for the day is from Psalms 118, the twenty-fourth verse. Say it after me. 'This is the day which the Lord hath made; we will rejoice and be glad in it.'"

Her eight students obediently repeated the verse.

"Loud and proud now!" Lydianne encouraged them. "If we can't rejoice about being in a brand-new school, all of us together to learn, we might as well go home, ain't so?"

This time the scholars filled the room with their confident, eager voices. And from there, the day sped by with lessons in spelling, reading, English, and math—as well as time for the scholars to create their name posters with crayons and markers. At recess, the two boys took turns batting—and chasing after—the softball that Lydianne pitched for them, while the six girls played together on the swings. By the time her students were driving their carts toward the road, still singing "You Are My Sunshine" as they'd done to end the school day, Lydianne dropped into her desk chair.

She was exhausted. Exhilarated. And totally devoted to the eight young souls who would share her life for the next nine months.

Most of all, Lydianne was awash with love for Ella, who sat in the front row beaming at her with attentive blue eyes. Ella already knew her alphabet and her basic addition facts, she could print neatly, and she would soon be reading. What a joy it would be to watch the baby she and Aden had created grow into a capable, perceptive scholar.

So he wouldn't distract the kids—or alert their teacher to his presence—Jeremiah rode his Percheron around to the back side of The Marketplace when he heard Lydianne congratulating her scholars on a fine first day of classes. From what he'd heard for the past hour or so, he had to agree. The young voices drifting from the open schoolhouse windows had sounded enthusiastic and confident as they'd recited their math facts and sung the alphabet song.

Jeremiah had caught glimpses of Lydianne holding up the flash cards—and then she'd used a yardstick to quickly point to the letters displayed above the white board as everyone sang the alphabet song for the benefit of the youngest students. It was a joy to watch her engaging with her class, pouring herself into the basic education that would prepare Morning Star's Amish children to become productive, competent adults.

When the kids were headed for the road in their rigs, with Billy Jay racing his pony cart ahead of the Miller girls and the Flaud sisters, Jeremiah rode toward the schoolhouse. After he hitched Mitch at the rail, he stepped up to the doorway to speak with Lydianne—but he stopped.

The teacher sat at her desk with her head resting on her folded arms. She'd turned out the gas light fixtures to make the schoolroom darker.

He sensed Lydianne was totally played out after her first day at a job that required so much more of her than staining furniture had, and he almost slipped away rather than disturb her respite. Yet the questions that had been plaguing him all week wouldn't leave him alone.

Why was Lydianne so skittish around him? Was she becoming more interested in Detweiler—maybe falling for winsome Billy Jay, as well? Was she intimidated because Jeremiah was the district's bishop, or because he'd been married before? After seeing the way Glenn had made such an obvious play for Lydianne's attention by bringing the picnic tables to the schoolyard, Jeremiah knew he had to up his ante. He had no time to waste if he wanted a chance at winning the pretty blonde's affection for himself.

He prayed for the right words and cleared his throat. "How was your first day, Teacher Lydianne? Anybody cause you any problems?"

Lydianne sat up abruptly, blinking to focus on him. "We did well!" she replied quickly. "They were *gut* as gold, every one of them—but then, scholars are generally on their best behavior for the first day, *jah*?"

Jeremiah chuckled, slowly approaching her desk. The shade from nearby trees, along with a breeze, made the schoolroom cool and pleasant. "That's probably right, although I doubt your girls will ever make much fuss. Billy Jay, on the other hand, seems to be coming out of his shell—"

"Isn't he awfully young to be driving a pony cart to school?" Lydianne interrupted. "I didn't challenge him about it, because I figured if Stevie's and Ella's parents trusted him to transport them, they must feel confident in his skills."

Stopping at the front wall to admire the colorful name posters the scholars had made, Jeremiah shrugged. "I suspect Glenn's been coaching his boy with that pony and cart, so he won't have to bring him to school each morning— and maybe to encourage him in a skill he enjoys," he suggested. "Jude tells me that Billy Jay and Stevie have done a lot of driving around at their place, using that cart to haul feed and supplies for Leah's cattle and other livestock. Boys tend to take up the reins sooner than girls, after all."

Lydianne was nodding in agreement, looking fresh and pretty in her new dress. Despite eyes and shoulders that drooped a bit with weariness, she seemed even more enticing than usual—or perhaps that was because Jeremiah finally had her all to himself. All thoughts of little boys and pony carts left him when she focused on him.

No time like the present. Never mind that it's been years since you asked a girl for a date.

Jeremiah smiled, hoping his voice didn't hitch like a teenager's. "I, um, was wondering if you'd come to the Shetler reunion with me on Sunday the fifteenth—"

"No! I—I can't do that!"

Startled by the fierce finality of her reply, Jeremiah blurted his response before he thought about it. "Why not? Are you seeing Detweiler?"

Lydianne's eyes widened as she gripped the edge of her desk. "Absolutely not! It's not a *gut* idea to get involved with—this isn't the right time to—"

The deep disappointment on his face must've alerted her to his feelings. "I'm sorry, Jeremiah," she whispered. "Please don't ask me to explain. And please don't ask me again."

The schoolroom suddenly felt airless and claustrophobic. Jeremiah swallowed hard, fighting the urge to argue with her as she stood up behind her desk, as though using it for a shield. He felt stunned, as though a rattlesnake had bitten him out of the blue.

She's left you with nothing to say, man. Better back away now before you dig a deeper hole.

"See you at church then," he murmured as he turned to go.

He gave her plenty of time to call him back, but it didn't happen. As Jeremiah mounted Mitch and rode away, his soul reeled with the sting of Lydianne's rejection. He felt like a whipped dog slinking away with his tail between his legs. He had no idea what had caused her to throw up such a sudden, totally unexpected, emotional barrier.

And he wasn't ready to talk about it when he got home, either.

As he stomped into the kitchen, his mother looked up from the jars of pickled beets she was canning. "Did you ride over to the school to check on Lydianne, like you said—"

"Let's don't go there, Mamm," he muttered. "And I don't want to be quizzed about it, all right?"

Her eyebrows shot up, but she knew better than to challenge him. "All right, then. I'll start supper as soon as I clean up the mess from these beets."

As he passed through the house and onto the back porch to nurse his hurt feelings, it occurred to Jeremiah that, despite Lydianne's blatant refusal to go out with him, life would go on as it always had.

And that was the problem, wasn't it?

Chapter Ten

Shortly before noon on Friday, Lydianne heard the creak of buggy wheels. It was a special day, and when the scholars became aware of the arrival of horse-drawn rigs, their faces lit up.

"Picnic!" Stevie whispered.

"*Jah*, here come our *mamms*," Gracie chimed in from the desk beside his.

Lydianne smiled at her three youngest students, who'd been working diligently at printing the alphabet and their names. "You've come a long way this week," she praised them, "so now we get some time to enjoy lunch with your mothers.

"Scholars," she said as she looked around the classroom, "let's set aside whatever you're working on—but leave it on your desks for your *mamms* to look at when they come in. We want them to see that we've been as busy as bees this week!"

Moments later Julia Nissley peeked in the doorway, and Ella glowed like a September sunrise. "Mamma! Mamma, come see the words I wrote—all by myself!" she crowed.

"Welcome," Lydianne called out as Delores Flaud and

Cora Miller appeared at the door. "Take a look at our projects and then we'll be ready to join you for lunch— and *denki* for feeding us all today!"

Soon the schoolroom was abuzz with mothers looking at their children's papers from the week. Rose Wagler arrived with Leah Shetler—both of them round with babies due later this month. Leah's adopted baby, Betsy, kicked happily in her carrier as she gazed around the room. The two young mothers were eager to see the pictures Gracie and Stevie had colored, as well as their early attempts at printing the alphabet on their wide-lined tablets.

After a few more minutes passed, Lydianne went to stand beside Billy Jay, who was growing worried. "Mammi said she'd be here, but I hope she didn't get lost—or get sick again, or—"

"She'll arrive any minute now," Lydianne assured him. His grandmother was a busy lady, running the household while tending baby Levi, so all manner of things could've detained her before she left the house with her picnic basket.

When Billy Jay darted over to the window to watch the road, however, his face lit up. "It's Dat! My *dat*'s comin' instead of Mammi," he announced jubilantly. "How cool is that?"

Although Lydianne was relieved and excited for Billy Jay, she—and the mothers in the room—looked at each other in surprise. Traditionally, the scholars' *mamms* brought lunch to the school every now and again; who could've guessed that Glenn would take his deceased wife's place? All eyes were on him and all smiles got wide when he walked through the doorway.

As Glenn sought out his son, who ran joyously to jump into his embrace, Lydianne thought he looked roguish—

rather defiant—wearing large sunglasses beneath a black fedora that didn't follow the usual style for men's hats in their district. When Glenn focused on her—or at least his dark, opaque sunshades turned in her direction and lingered for several moments—the other women's faces took on speculative expressions.

"*Gut* to see you, Glenn," Delores ventured. "Is Elva not feeling well?"

His black beard shifted with his smile. "Mamm's fine, but Levi's taken a colicky turn, so she stayed home with him," he replied smoothly.

"So, it's just you and me, Dat!" Billy Jay put in happily. As though he suddenly realized that he might resemble a toddler, being in his father's arms, he climbed down and stood proudly alongside him instead. "Let's go out and dig into the picnic basket! I'm ready for some of that chicken Mammi was fryin' up this morning."

"*Jah*, let's eat," Stevie chimed in. "But first, I'll race ya around the bases, Billy Jay! Last one back's a rotten egg!"

The two boys took off like a shot, and Lydianne couldn't fault them for their excitement. As everyone headed outside to the shaded picnic tables, several of the women noticed they weren't made from conventional materials.

Glenn beamed, running his hand over the smooth surface of the nearest table. As he explained how he'd come to build the tables from maintenance-free deck materials, Lydianne helped Leah find a level spot to set Betsy's carrier. The Flaud sisters came out from the school's lower level pulling a small wagon between them, which held five-gallon coolers of lemonade and ice water. By the time the *mamms* had unpacked their food and arranged it for serving, one entire picnic table was covered with casserole pans that smelled delectable, as well as a few chilled salads and an array of desserts.

"What a feast," Lydianne remarked. "*Denki* to everyone for making our first picnic such a special—and delicious— event. How about if you youngest scholars and your *mamms* go first?"

Stevie and Billy Jay lost no time picking up plates and choosing from the fried chicken, sandwiches, fruity gelatin salad, and potato salad. As the boys snatched up brownies and cookies, Ella and Gracie got in line with their mothers, and then the Millers and the Flauds filled their plates. Was it Lydianne's imagination, or had Glenn hung back so he could stand beside her—and possibly sit with her as they ate? Once again, she noticed that Delores and Cora were glancing at them with speculative expressions on their faces.

Lord, you've got to help me set Glenn straight in a polite but no-nonsense way, she prayed, as she chose a slice of meat loaf, some chicken, and a warm dinner roll. His new look unnerved her, because even in the shade he'd left his sunglasses on, which made it impossible for her to read his eyes.

Maybe you've got it wrong. Glenn might've had a bad night with the baby and he's shielding his tired eyes from the bright sun. Maybe you're just assuming he's wearing that rakish fedora to attract your—

"How about if we sit over on that blanket I spread under the tree?" he murmured, pressing his arm against hers.

Alarms went off in her mind. When she noticed a spot on the end of a picnic table across from Julia Nissley, she replied, "*Denki*, Glenn, but I'd like to speak with Ella's *mamm* while she's here. Your tables are a big hit!" she added to soften her response.

Fortunately, when the boys saw that Glenn was finally

ready to eat, Billy Jay waved his arms above his head. "Dat, we saved ya some room at the guys' table!" he called out.

Glenn nodded subtly at Lydianne as he headed toward his son, but she had a feeling he wasn't taking her *no* for a final answer. As she approached the spot near Julia, she hoped her cheeks weren't as red as they felt. This wasn't the time or place for Glenn's flirtation—she could already see the wheels turning in some of these women's minds— but she didn't want to call him on it in front of these other parents.

"We've had a wonderful first week of school, ain't so, Ella?" Lydianne asked as she sat down across from Julia and her daughter. "It makes such a difference that you've encouraged Ella to practice her alphabet on paper, and that she knows what sounds all the letters make."

Julia flashed her little girl a pleased smile. "We like to play school," she said. "What with Ella not having brothers or sisters, she spends time with her tablet and a pencil at the kitchen table while I'm preparing our meals."

Her reply painted a fond mental picture for Lydianne. "I played school with my older sisters when I was little," she remarked as she picked up a crispy fried chicken leg.

Lydianne's food didn't quite make it to her mouth, how- ever. She swallowed hard when she—and the others— spotted a familiar, dapple-gray Percheron approaching the schoolyard.

Of all the times for the bishop to show up. Will he invite me to his family reunion again, figuring I won't refuse him in front of all these witnesses?

As Jeremiah approached the schoolyard, he caught Lydianne's gaze and held it. She seemed startled by his appearance, yet not as afraid as when he'd asked her to the Shetler reunion.

Afraid? She'd looked downright terrified when she blurted, "No, I can't!" And why was that?

Again and again over the past four days, he'd replayed her rejection in his mind, and he still had no answers. Jeremiah couldn't believe Lydianne was intimidated by his role as the bishop, because she'd known him in that capacity ever since she'd come to Morning Star. And she'd been engaged before, so she surely wasn't afraid of socializing with—or committing to—a man she loved. He'd come to the school picnic to see how she was doing while the presence of the scholars' mothers would provide her a social safety net.

Then he spotted Detweiler.

As though Glenn was hoping to avoid answering the obvious question about why he was there, he rose quickly from the table he was sharing with Billy Jay and Stevie. When he said something, gesturing toward the ball diamond, the two boys lit up with excitement and raced ahead of him. Kate Flaud, Linda Miller, and little Ella Nissley followed them.

Jeremiah returned the ladies' waves as he dismounted and hitched Mitch at the rail. Something struck him as odd—

Why's Glenn wearing a black fedora and dark shades?

He recalled images from a movie poster years ago, which had featured two English fellows dressed in suits—singers, they were—who wore the same sort of hats and sunglasses. He filed this away for later consideration as Delores hailed him with a paper plate in her hand.

"Bishop, you're just in time to join our picnic!" she called out.

"*Jah*, you're lucky!" Gracie crowed. "We didn't eat all of the chicken or meat loaf, so there's still some for you!"

Jeremiah smiled at the Wagler girl, returning the nods of the women who were welcoming him. "It was very nice of you to save me some, Gracie," he said as he surveyed the array of pans and platters on the table. "I thought I'd come out to see how school was going—and because I'd heard the *mamms* were treating you to a picnic lunch today."

"School is *gut*!" Gracie exclaimed. "We all love Teacher Lydianne coz she's teachin' us how to read!"

Jeremiah considered this a valid excuse for focusing on Lydianne, to assess her reaction to his presence. "I'm not surprised," he said as he filled his plate with meat loaf and potato salad. "When you put a fine teacher in a classroom with enthusiastic scholars, wonderful-*gut* things are sure to happen."

When he'd selected the rest of his food, Jeremiah eased into the open spot between Julia and Cora, which put him across the table from Lydianne and the older scholars. "And how about you girls? Is your final year of classes off to a promising start?"

Lucy and Lorena nodded eagerly. "We're in charge of keeping the classroom tidy and changing the wall displays," Lorena remarked happily.

"And we'll be helping the younger kids with their math facts and spelling while Teacher Lydianne is working with the other scholars," Lucy put in. "Teacher Lydianne says we'll be doing a lot of writing this year, too—"

"Because if you can write clear, well-constructed sentences and stories, it means your thought process is clear and logical, as well," Lorena finished proudly.

Jeremiah smiled. These two girls obviously idolized Lydianne and seemed much more enthusiastic about school than they'd been in the past. "Every now and again I get remarks about my sermons shooting off in lots of different directions—like squirrels in search of nuts—so maybe I should take some writing lessons alongside you girls," he remarked as he spread butter on his bread.

The women around him laughed—except for Lydianne, who appeared very self-conscious as she focused on her food. Why did she seem so nervous around him?

"I can't imagine anyone criticizing your sermons that way, Bishop," Cora put in kindly.

"Neither can I," Julia insisted. "It's a rare gift you have, to stand in front of a roomful of folks and preach about our beliefs, or about what went on in Bible times— especially without any notes or preparation. I certainly couldn't do that."

"Me neither," Rose agreed. "I've always been thankful that, as a woman, I'll never be called upon to deliver sermons."

"Amen to that," Delores chimed in.

A movement off to the side of the table caught Jeremiah's attention—and when Lydianne turned her head to see what it was, she seemed to curl further in upon herself. Glenn had come over to the large coolers to fill a glass with lemonade. He nodded briefly at Jeremiah, but he took his sweet time about holding Lydianne's gaze as he drank half a glassful of the cool liquid before topping it off with more.

Jeremiah filed this moment away for later, too. Something had apparently passed between Detweiler and Lydianne earlier—something that had put her on edge. And once again that sly green-eyed monster—envy— reared its ugly head within him.

Glenn's entering forbidden territory, wearing English getup and giving Lydianne such an obvious, shameless once-over—mere weeks after losing his wife. As his bishop, you're responsible for setting this errant member straight before he wanders too far down the path to perdition.

He made quick work of the rest of his meal and excused himself, thanking the ladies for the lunch he'd shared with them. He figured it was best to let Teacher Lydianne resume her school day as soon as possible, without two men circling her like dogs snarling over a choice bone.

And why did he feel that way? It was wrong to disparage Glenn or to compete against him for Lydianne's attention—especially when she'd stated she didn't want to date either one of them. Yet, uncomfortable emotions crowded out his usual goodwill toward a member of his flock who needed his emotional support more than ever.

That evening, as the men gathered on his front porch for their weekly singing, Jeremiah watched with interest as Glenn and his father stepped down from their rig. They were the picture of Amish propriety in their black straw hats, suspenders, and broadfall trousers worn over purple short-sleeved shirts cut from the same bolt of cloth.

Jeremiah had no intention of letting Glenn's earlier apparel go unnoticed, however. "I was surprised to see you at the school picnic today," he remarked nonchalantly as the Detweiler men ascended the porch steps.

Glenn shrugged. "Billy Jay no longer has a *mamm*, so I went in her place. Why were *you* there?"

Detweiler might as well have waved a red blanket in front of a bull, the way Jeremiah's adrenaline level rose to his challenge. Even Saul, Matthias, and the Flauds, already seated in porch chairs, were wide-eyed at Glenn's tone of voice.

"I'm a school board member," Jeremiah reminded him carefully, keeping his irritation in check. He hadn't planned to call Glenn out in front of the other men, yet it occurred to him that perhaps this conversation was best held with witnesses present. "As your bishop, I have to wonder why you were wearing that fedora and those dark, opaque sunshades, Glenn. It reminded me of that movie about the Blues Brothers—and it seemed you were setting a very *English* example in front of our scholars."

"Can't a man have a little fun?" Glenn shot back. "And *I* have to wonder why you seem to show up at the schoolhouse every time I'm there. If you're trying to discourage my relationship with Lydianne—"

"I think you're on the rebound too soon after losing your wife," Jeremiah put in firmly. "I'm concerned about your emotional well-being—"

"—it's because you want her for yourself, *jah*?" Glenn challenged in a rising voice. "Don't you dare criticize my need for a new wife, Jeremiah! When you lost Priscilla, you weren't left alone to raise two kids. *Gut*ness knows you've had plenty of time to win Lydianne since then—and meanwhile, you don't have to listen to your son crying himself to sleep every night!"

Jeremiah gripped the arms of his wicker porch chair, alarmed at the escalation of their contentious conversation. He was acting like the dog in the manger from Aesop's fable, snapping at Detweiler to prevent his access to Lydianne—even though she didn't want to be with *him*, either. It was an improper frame of mind for any man, and as a bishop he needed to rise above it.

"Gentlemen, I think we should take time out for a word of prayer," Deacon Saul suggested quietly.

"From what I've just overheard, I agree with your assessment, Saul," Preacher Ammon Slabaugh said as he approached the porch to join everyone. He studied Glenn and then focused on Jeremiah, planting his hands on his hips. "I don't need to know all the particulars to hear the strife and bitterness that's come between you and Glenn, Jeremiah. We won't be fully able to sing our praises to the Lord while this disagreement hangs over us like a storm cloud."

Jeremiah exhaled sharply. He knew Ammon was right—but he didn't like it much. "*Jah*, let's pray for wisdom and guidance," he agreed, focusing on Detweiler. "If we lose track of our intention to put God first, our priorities get out of kilter and our relationships with Him and each other suffer. *Denki* for pointing this out, Saul and Ammon."

He bowed his head, yet even as silence enveloped him, Jeremiah's thoughts were far from prayerful. Did Glenn truly feel he had to raise Billy Jay and baby Levi alone, even though his parents had moved in with him so they could help him every single day? And did Billy Jay really cry for his mother at night? If anything, Jeremiah sensed that since the beginning of school, the seven-year-old had rediscovered his sense of excitement—his joy—and that he was recovering pretty well from the loss of his mother.

But it's not my place to guess what's happening with Glenn or to judge him for it, Lord, Jeremiah reminded himself. *Help me to mind my words and thoughts.*

A few moments later, Preacher Ammon murmured "amen." The men on the porch awaited Gabe's direction, noting that he wasn't handing out songbooks as he normally did.

"What with the Shetler reunion only two weeks away," Gabe began eagerly, "I think we should choose the tunes we want to perform, and practice singing them without the music. We're ready to do that if we put our minds to it!"

Jeremiah admired Gabe's spirit—his ability to move

beyond the conflicting egos that had gotten their rehearsal off to a rocky start. As he pulled out a pen and paper to write the song titles the men suggested, Gabe glowed with goodwill and positive energy.

You would glow, too, if you were engaged to a pretty young woman.

Jeremiah's eyes widened at this thought, which had struck him from out of nowhere. Gabe and Regina Miller were so delightedly in love with each other that it was almost painful for him to watch their long gazes and listen to them gush about each other during their premarital counseling sessions. Unfortunately, Lydianne had made her feelings very clear—and Jeremiah had no appetite for any more of her rejection.

He supposed he should feel better, knowing she wasn't interested in seeing Detweiler, either. Maybe he'd be doing Glenn a favor if he revealed that Lydianne didn't intend to encourage his attentions—or fall for his rakish fedora and shades.

Nah. He won't believe that, coming from me. It's better if he gets burned just like I did.

This line of thought wasn't very charitable, but it raised Jeremiah's spirits. As the men around him began a rousing rendition of "Bringing in the Sheaves," he joined in with a renewed sense of enthusiasm. He was still baffled by Lydianne's apparent fear of dating, but she wasn't playing favorites. One of these days she'd put Glenn in his place, too.

And God would see that all things worked together for the common good.

Chapter Eleven

On Saturday morning, Lydianne was happy to be working inside The Marketplace with Jo, who was baking pies
and cakes to freeze for the Shetler reunion the following
weekend. As she carefully pulled two sheet cakes from the
oven, Lydianne inhaled the rich aromas of chocolate and
butterscotch. She was grateful that Glenn and Bishop Jeremiah were busy outside with the produce auction, which
had drawn another huge crowd. She had no idea how to
deal with either man's attentions, so after a restless night,
she preferred to remain out of sight in Jo's bakery kitchen.

"So, is it true, about Glenn showing up for the school
picnic looking like a gangster?" Jo asked breezily.

Lydianne was so startled she burned her forearm on the
hot cake pan when she dropped it onto the stainless-steel
countertop. "Where'd you hear about that?" she asked with
a gasp.

Jo hurried to the drawer to pull out the first aid kit.
"Delores was buzzing like a bee about it when Mamm and
I saw her in the bulk store that afternoon," she replied.
"Here—let's put some ointment on your arm. Sorry I caught
you off guard—"

"Silly me, hoping the grapevine wouldn't carry that tale," Lydianne put in with a tired sigh. "I guess I shouldn't have been surprised by Glenn's coming—especially because Elva keeps so busy with baby Levi. But his dark sunglasses and English hat might as well have been neon signs that announced 'I'm flirting with you, Lydianne' in bright shiny letters."

Jo's smile was catlike. "Is that such a bad thing?"

"*Jah*, it is!" Lydianne blurted more vehemently than she intended. "Glenn can't possibly be interested in me, for myself. He's still in shock from losing Dorcas, acting as crazy and clueless as a schoolboy wearing such a getup."

Jo gently pressed an adhesive bandage over the ointment. "To hear Martha Maude talk about it this morning, apparently Bishop Jeremiah was none too impressed with Glenn's outfit, either. I guess he and Glenn had quite a go-round at the men's singing session last night."

"Jeremiah has no room to talk, arriving unannounced and then sitting right across from me at the picnic," Lydianne said with a shake of her head. "And what did Delores have to say about *that*?"

"Oh, she thinks Margaret surely must be overjoyed that her son's finally interested in taking another wife," Jo replied.

"*Jah*, Molly and I are envious." Marietta's teasing voice came through the slatted wall of the adjoining noodle shop. "Now that you're Teacher Lydianne, the eligible men want to be in school again."

"Sounds like you'll have to beat them all off with a stick!" Molly said from Jo's doorway. She grinned at Lydianne. "Who're you going to pick?"

"Neither of them!" Lydianne shot back. "I don't have time for a social life right now. When I go home from here,

I'll spend my evening grading papers and planning out lessons for next week. I can't do that tomorrow, after all."

Jo chuckled. "No, it wouldn't look so *gut* if you were marking papers during the sermons. I guess I hadn't thought about the work you have to do after hours now—and you're new at teaching, so you'll have to figure out how to present all those different subjects every day."

"And I present them to kids who're learning at five different levels," Lydianne pointed out. "My two oldest girls study the same thing, and so do my first-graders, Stevie and Gracie. Kate's at her own level, as well. Billy Jay is my only second grader and Linda's the only seventh grader—and Ella's so far ahead of the other first graders, I have to figure out ways to keep her challenged."

Lydianne paused, hoping she didn't sound as though she was whining. "I really love working with these kids, but I hadn't anticipated how much time and effort it takes to be a one-room schoolteacher."

Jo considered this as she sliced apples into a bowl to make more pie filling. "I never thought about that," she remarked. "When you're a kid, you assume the teacher just shows up to teach—like the preachers come to church and present sermons without any preparation."

"*Jah*, the job looks different from the other side of the desk." Lydianne felt relieved when Molly returned to the noodle shop and three English ladies came into the bakery looking for cinnamon rolls. At least her friends would give her social situation a rest for a while.

As Jo went to the front counter to assist her customers, Regina slipped into the shop and joined Lydianne back in the kitchen. When the timer beeped, she handed Lydianne the quilted mitts and opened the oven door for her.

Lydianne smiled. Regina's presence always brightened

a room, and these days her freckled face was even more radiant than usual. "*Denki*, Regina," she said as she grasped the edges of another sheet cake pan. "How's business at the other end of the building this morning?"

"Most of the folks who'd be shopping at the Wengerds' nursery store are outside at the produce auction. There was a lull in traffic at Glenn's wood shop, so I thought I'd stop by," the redhead replied. She stepped closer to Lydianne at the back counter.

"After overhearing some of what Jo and the twins just said—and listening to Gabe's account of last night's singing session with the men—I have an offer for you, Lydianne," she said in a lower voice. "What if I manage the Shetler reunion next weekend? Sounds like you could use the time for your schoolwork."

Lydianne's eyes widened as she set the fragrant lemon cake on the countertop. "But you could surely use that time to get ready for your wedding—"

Regina waved her off. "Gabe's *mamm* and Aunt Cora already have the details under control. All I have to do is show up for the ceremony," she teased. She glanced behind them, to where Jo was bagging her customers' purchases. "It sounds like you'd have a lot of Shetlers watching your every move at the reunion. I know you'll have everything in perfect order for the Flaud gathering here later this month—and you're my favorite side-sitter—so working in your place next Saturday is the least I can do."

Lydianne threw her arms around Regina's shoulders and hugged her tight. "That would make my life so much easier," she murmured gratefully. She felt honored and very excited about standing up with Regina at her wedding— especially because Gabe had long ago asked one of his out-of-town cousins to serve as his side-sitter.

No romantic entanglements. Just the way I like it.

After a few moments, Regina eased away from Lydianne's embrace. Her expression suggested that she had something else important on her mind. "Once Gabe and I are married, I won't be coming here to The Marketplace on Saturdays anymore. I'll be doing my new embroidery work at home and selling it in the Flaud Furniture shop," she said, nodding in that direction. "Gabe's *dat* has insisted that I'm to follow the rules, once I hitch up with his son."

"That's as it should be, I suppose," Lydianne said, even as she felt a pang of disappointment. "But we'll really miss having you here, Regina. And, um, *denki* for not rubbing my nose in it, where Glenn and the bishop are concerned," she added softly.

Regina's face softened with a fond smile. "It's one thing to tease you about having two fine fellows vying for your attention. It's a horse of a different color when you're caught in their crossfire while you're trying to do your best at your new job."

Lydianne sighed, realizing how drained she felt after her first week in the classroom. Even without the stir Jeremiah and Glenn were causing, she hadn't anticipated the amount of mental and emotional energy teaching required. Spending the following Saturday evening at home would give her time to recharge her mental batteries, even if she was doing schoolwork.

"You're the best, Regina," she murmured.

Her friend shrugged. "What're friends for? I'll be the first to congratulate you if you start seeing Bishop Jeremiah or Glenn—but it should be on your terms, Lydianne. We *maidels* have become accustomed to living life our way.

None of us would be happy giving up all our freedom just because a husband—or the church—expected us to."

"And you're *gut* with staying at home after the wedding?" Lydianne asked quickly. "You've really enjoyed starting up our Marketplace adventure."

"I have," Regina agreed, her face taking on a special glow. "But Gabe and his family cared enough to buy my house back and then refinish the floors and paint all the rooms. I might not own that bungalow anymore, but it's still my home—and now I'll get to share it with Gabe. And bless him," she added tenderly, "he didn't expect me to move someplace else just because he's the man and wants to be in control."

Lydianne had to agree. Regina had caused quite a stir in the church when she'd revealed that she was an accomplished wildlife artist—and that she'd made up a fake identity so she could sell her work when The Marketplace opened. Gabe's confession about playing his guitar and the piano in the Methodist church had shocked his family and friends, as well. Yet, both of them had created worthwhile endeavors from their forbidden artistic talents—and meanwhile, they'd fallen in love.

"It's *gut* to see that you're so happy, Regina," Lydianne whispered.

"You'll find a *gut* man to marry, too, if it's meant to be," her closest friend assured her softly. "Take your time and listen to what God's telling you to do. He's got better plans for all of us than we can possibly make for ourselves, you know."

As applause filled the central commons inside The Marketplace, where more than a hundred Shetlers from all over the Midwest had gathered, Jeremiah gave up trying to find Lydianne. From where the men's group stood on a dais to perform, he could see the entire area in front of the shops—which was filled with tables where folks were sitting, eagerly anticipating the next song.

He'd come to the potluck supper a little early this evening to seek her out. But Lydianne was nowhere in sight. He'd purposely avoided her company over the past week, hoping the rumors would die down and give them both a break. All he could figure was that Regina was acting as manager in Lydianne's place—

Because Lydianne didn't want to see you? Or is she staying away from Mamm and the other matchmakers? A small town's a fine place to live because everyone knows you—but it's also a fishbowl.

Gabe announced that the next song would be "Go Down, Moses" before turning toward the singers again and softly blowing into his pitch pipe. The song about Moses ordering Pharaoh to release the Israelites from slavery was a longtime favorite, and Jeremiah could sing it in his sleep—

But he suddenly realized that Glenn, Saul, and Martin were stumbling over the melody and harmony, looking at him with perplexed expressions.

Jeremiah's face caught fire. He'd been so distracted by Lydianne's absence that he'd charged in too soon with the bass line, derailing the entire song.

Gabe called their singing to a halt, chuckling. "Well, even Moses had to try more than once before he got it right," he remarked.

The crowd laughed good-naturedly as Gabe turned to face the group again, gazing directly at Jeremiah with a raised eyebrow.

"Sorry," Jeremiah mumbled as the other singers shifted into readiness around him. "I'm on it now."

The song went without a hitch, and as the group continued singing for another ten minutes, Jeremiah focused on the music. Singing usually made him feel more upbeat and energized, yet his spirits lagged. Even after their finale—a quick, tricky version of "I'll Fly Away"—when his friends stood around him soaking up the extended applause they received, Jeremiah felt as if he were isolated inside a thick bubble.

It didn't help that his mother had jumped the gun, telling family members of his relationship with Lydianne.

"Where's that new teacher your *mamm*'s told me about?" his great-aunt Sylvia asked as she gazed up at him through her thick lenses.

"*Jah*, Margaret says you've found another wife!" his elderly cousin Edwin chimed in with a chortle. "Happy to hear it, Jeremiah! You deserve happiness after being alone for so long."

Jeremiah wanted to escape out the back exit and not return, except the reunion would last all the next day as well. And because it was a visiting Sunday, most of these folks would be coming to his place around noon for a barbeque and picnic.

"That's wishful thinking on Mamm's part," he said firmly. "Just because I'm on the school board and I've been helping our teacher get set up in the new schoolhouse doesn't mean there's anything going on between us."

But you wish there was, the voice in his head taunted.

As Detweiler and the other singers said their good-byes before the Shetler potluck supper began, Jeremiah was even more disappointed that Lydianne wasn't present. It was a pleasant September evening, perfect for a stroll around the property surrounding The Marketplace. Maybe if they had a chance to talk without being interrupted or watched, they could reach an understanding . . . and he could ask her why she'd been so vehement, so final, about not going out with him.

Lydianne Christner was one of the most buoyant, positive-minded people he knew. It wasn't her way to shut down an idea before she'd even considered it.

After he filled his plate at the various tables loaded with food, Jeremiah ate half-heartedly. As he sat among families with young children and watched devoted couples he'd known most of his lifetime, he realized that he was a misfit in this crowd because he'd gone too long without a mate. When word got around that his relationship with Lydianne wasn't all his mother had cracked it up to be, folks stole curious, speculative glances at him while he went from table to table greeting family members he hadn't seen since last year's reunion.

Their eyes told him they wondered why his lady friend had ducked out on him. The older folks talked softly among themselves, probably speculating about why any young woman would reject a successful farmer—a respected man whom God had chosen to be a bishop and who still had a sense of humor, a full head of hair, and all of his teeth.

As the evening wore on, Jeremiah wondered about the same things. The next day at the barbeque, he was grateful that most of his relatives had given up asking about Lydianne, but he sensed they were still speculating about him—worried that his chances for remarriage might be passing him by.

* * *

The last of the far-flung Shetlers were leaving Morning Star on Monday morning when Leah, Jude's wife, went into labor. Adah was born late that evening, and Jeremiah was delighted that his new niece arrived healthy, and that Leah came through the birth in good shape and with high spirits. He was also glad that this new grandchild gave his mother something wonderful to talk about now that her hopes for him had fallen flat.

The following Sunday at church, Jeremiah had the rare privilege of announcing that two little angels had arrived. "Most of you have heard that Jude and Leah welcomed their daughter Adah into the world this past Monday," he said as he looked out over the crowd gathered in the Hartzlers' large front room. "And on Friday, Matthias and Rose Wagler were blessed with a little girl they've named Suzanna. She arrived in time for lunch—"

"And I'm the big sister!" Gracie piped up from beside Martha Maude, her *mammi*. "She doesn't like it much when I sing 'O Suzanna' to her, but she'll come around!"

As his congregation laughed out loud, elated by the good news, Jeremiah had to hide his sorrow behind a pasted-on smile. Births were a blessed event, but they always reminded him that God hadn't granted him and Priscilla any children. The service had ended, so the women were making their way into Martha Maude's kitchen to set out the common meal.

Jeremiah glanced at Lydianne—and he couldn't help noticing that, unlike the other women, she wasn't chatting happily about the new babies or about serving the meal. As she moved into the aisle, she appeared as isolated as he'd felt lately, even though she was surrounded by her *maidel* friends, who seemed as cheerful as ever.

When her gaze fell upon Ella Nissley, however, Lydianne's face lit up—until she realized Jeremiah was watching her. Her eyes widened as she glanced at him and then quickly looked away from him. Then she hurried through the crowd and into the kitchen.

And what was that about? Is Lydianne not feeling well—or does she regret shutting me down so quickly? Or does she know things she can't tell me?

Jeremiah reminded himself not to read too much into her retreat. Lydianne was very busy with her teaching, after all. And he was about to begin harvesting his corn crop— which promised to be the best he'd had in several years— so there was no point in seeking her out to get his questions answered. If the weather remained in his favor, he'd be working alongside his hired farmer, Will Gingerich, from sunrise until darkness fell for the next few weeks.

Maybe all that physical labor would make him sleep more soundly, so he'd stop dreaming about the attractive blonde who remained beyond his reach.

Chapter Twelve

As a steady rain settled in on Wednesday morning, Lydianne greeted her scholars downstairs in the cloakroom. "Let's hang up our wet wraps and start our day with an old, old story about rain," she said cheerfully.

Billy Jay made a face as he slipped out of his raincoat. "But I hate the rain! We had to ride to school in Dawdi's old rig today—and he said we probably wouldn't be goin' outside for recess. Is that true, Teacher Lydianne?"

"You'd be soaked in thirty seconds," she pointed out.

"And then you'd be sittin' in your chair for the rest of the day with your wet clothes drippin' all over the floor," Stevie said without missing a beat. "Some of us would probably say you'd wet your pants, you big baby."

"Well, no, we wouldn't be saying that," Lydianne countered, quickly steering the boys away from a conversation about bodily functions. "But we *will* be talking about all sorts of animals, and the biggest boat you ever heard of, and the promise God made when He created the rainbow."

"Noah's ark!" Gracie exclaimed. "I know that story!"

"Me, too!" Ella chimed in, clapping her hands. "I wanna

hear about how all the animals marched onto the ark two by two—"

"And think about how much poop was on the ark!" Billy Jay blurted with renewed enthusiasm. "Noah probably had to muck out the stalls every day—"

"And throw all that poop overboard!" Stevie declared with wide-eyed wonder. "There woulda been camel poop and bear poop and . . . and dinosaur poop!"

"Ewww," thirteen-year-old Linda put in, holding her nose. "I'm glad I wasn't living on that stinky ark. That's enough about manure, boys, or I'll let you take my place at shoveling out the stable when we go home today."

Lydianne smiled to herself. She'd discovered the advantage of having older girls in the schoolroom who kept Stevie and Billy Jay from getting too far out of hand. At least the boys seemed interested in the special project she'd been saving for a rainy day, and she hoped it would keep them occupied during recess when they'd be staying indoors—without a chance to run off any steam outside.

"I brought us a special story rug to sit on," she said as she led the scholars up the stairs and into the classroom. "I like to think of it as a magic carpet, because stories take us to faraway, fascinating places. Today we'll go all the way back to Bible times in the Old Testament."

Lydianne's magic carpet was actually a colorful braided rag rug her dear, deceased mother had made—large enough that it had nearly covered the floor of the small attic room where she and her older sisters had played when they were children. Her heart thrummed with memories as she watched the Flaud sisters and the Miller girls nimbly sit on the rug, carefully tugging their cape dresses over their crossed legs before patting the places between them.

The four younger scholars situated themselves in those spots and looked eagerly at Lydianne.

Easing onto the rug, she carefully arranged her long, loose skirt so she was modestly covered. Lydianne held up a big picture book she'd recently bought for the schoolroom's library. "Long, long ago, God tried many, many times to tell humans how they should love Him and live in peace together," she began, paraphrasing the text as she focused on the colorful illustrations. "He became so disappointed in their wicked, sinful ways that He was sorry He'd ever created them."

The classroom fell silent as the kids thought about what this statement meant. Pleased that they were taking the story seriously, Lydianne turned the page.

"God so was tired of His people's violence and meanness that He figured the only way to fix it was to wipe everything away," she continued, shaking her head sadly. "He decided to destroy the world He'd created—even the animals and the birds."

"With a big ole flood," Gracie whispered solemnly.

"That's right," Lydianne said, flipping to the next page. "But whose family did God save?"

"Noah's!" Stevie cried out. "He was one of the *gut* guys!"

"And God told him how to build this big, huge ark that would float on all that water He was gonna send," Billy Jay put in.

"And Noah had to bring in every kind of animal, two by two," Ella continued the familiar story. "There was lions and tigers and g'raffs and horses and cows and goats and chickens—and thank *gut*ness there was puppies, too, or I wouldn't have Brownie to play with!"

Lydianne nodded, her heart overflowing with love for

the bright little blonde who so closely resembled her father. "God didn't give Noah and his family a lot of time to prepare for the flood. Noah and his sons began to build the ark of cedar wood, higher and higher, with a single door and just one window, near the top," she told them, pointing to the details in the pictures. "The neighbors all thought Noah was crazy to build such a boat, because they lived nowhere near the ocean. But Noah, a man of deep faith, believed what God had told him."

Turning the page, Lydianne smiled at the rapt expressions on her scholars' faces. "Then Noah called out to the animals, and they came to him, because God had spoken to them, too. It was already starting to rain when the last of the animals showed up."

Gazing at her students, she asked, "Meanwhile, what do you think Noah's wife and daughters-in-law were doing? What would you need if God said you'd be living in a boat during a flood that might last a long, long time?"

After a moment's silence, Lorena's face lit up. "Food! Noah's wife and daughters-in-law surely had to be preparing the food they'd need—"

"And think of all the feed those animals would eat," Kate said in an awed voice. "They probably didn't have baled hay for their herds—and how would they provide the leaves and grass the deer and other wild animals needed?"

"And what about acorns for the squirrels? And bird seed? And puppy chow?" Ella asked with a worried frown.

Billy Jay's eyes widened. "Do ya s'pose some of the big animals ate some of the smaller animals while they were in the ark all that time?" he whispered. "Wild animals do that."

Lydianne smiled at their astute questions. "The Bible doesn't go into those details," she replied.

"But maybe God didn't allow any of the animals on the

ark to die, because He wanted them to be alive after the flood waters receded," Lucy speculated. "God can do *anything*—and He wanted a peaceable kingdom where lions could lie down with lambs instead of having them for dinner—"

"Maybe He made it so the predatory animals didn't *want* to eat the other ones," Kate put in thoughtfully. "Otherwise, a lot of species would've become extinct."

"Excellent points," Lydianne said, smiling proudly at her older girls' insights. "Here again, the Bible doesn't spell out a lot of things that went on in the ark. We can figure that the women might've baked bread and gathered grapes and olives and other grains beforehand. We do know that Noah and his family and all those animals lived together while it rained for forty days and forty nights. The Bible says the water covered the entire earth—even the trees and the tallest mountains."

Billy Jay exhaled loudly. "That's a long time not to go outside and play, Teacher Lydianne," he murmured. "Do you s'pose all those monkeys and chickens and pigs got crazy like we do when we're cooped up?"

Lydianne chuckled along with her students. It was a real blessing that the boys were enthralled by the untold possibilities in this story, thinking beyond what the Bible presented. "What did Noah do then?" she asked. "How did he find out if it was safe to leave the ark?"

"He sent out a dove, and when it came back with an olive branch, Noah knew the water had gone down enough that the trees were uncovered," Lorena recounted.

"And how did God mark His promise with Noah—His covenant—that He would never again destroy His creation with a flood?" Lydianne asked as she closed the storybook.

"It was a rainbow! Up in the sky!" Ella crowed ecstatically.

"So every time it rains," Gracie put in confidently, "God sees the rainbow, and it reminds Him to stop the water before the whole world gets flooded again."

As Lydianne rose from the rug, her heart was filled with happiness. She hoped the retelling of this favorite Bible story would keep her scholars busy and engaged during this run of rainy weather.

"Let's start our day with a special Noah's ark spelling list. It's written up on the board," she instructed. "We also have some math problems involving the size of the ark—and what a cubit is—and we'll explore some Bible history about what people wore and the food they probably took into the ark with them. Later on, we'll have some special projects—like coloring a big poster for our wall, and molding clay animals, and maybe even building a model ark!"

As the day went on and the rain showed no sign of letting up, Lydianne unrolled the huge poster of Noah's ark surrounded by pairs of animals—with a large rainbow that stretched across the sky. To use up some of the kids' energy, she allowed them to play a relay game that raced them up and down the stairs a few times, and then they began coloring the poster. It didn't surprise her that Ella placed her chair where she could work on the wide stripes of the rainbow.

When Billy Jay and Stevie were losing interest in coloring, Lydianne gave them modeling clay and suggested they make animals to display on the table below the spot where the completed poster would hang. That afternoon she unwrapped an ark kit she'd found in the bookstore, and soon Lucy and Lorena were helping Billy Jay and Gracie fit the wooden pieces together.

By the time parents began arriving in their rigs to fetch the children, Lydianne believed that she and her scholars had shared their best day yet. As the buggies headed toward the road through the pouring rain, a blessed peacefulness settled over the classroom. She felt drained, yet elated. She wanted to rest her head on her folded arms for a bit—except the last time she'd done that, Jeremiah had come to the schoolhouse and invited her to the Shetler reunion.

Considering the steady downpour that drummed on the schoolhouse roof, Lydianne doubted he'd show up again today, but how could she know? Jeremiah certainly hadn't been harvesting his corn, as he'd mentioned at church this past Sunday, so chances were good that their busy bishop was out taking care of other business. He might stop by to ask her about why she'd turned him down—and she certainly couldn't give him a full, detailed answer.

With a weary sigh, Lydianne straightened the room, gathered her books, and started for home. Wouldn't it be wonderful if she didn't have to elude Jeremiah Shetler? He was such a compassionate, handsome man, that any woman would be blessed to have him as her husband—

But that one afternoon when I gave in to my love for Aden has made me a maidel *forever. What man could respect or trust me, if he discovered my secret? And if Bishop Jeremiah learns I bore Ella out of wedlock, I'll be shunned, and I'll lose my teaching job. How can I possibly remain in Morning Star after that?*

Lydianne swiped at a tear and quickly made her way through the rain toward the pole barn, where her buggy was parked. She might as well accept her fate and go home alone—because that was how she was destined to spend the rest of her life.

Chapter Thirteen

As Jeremiah approached the Miller home on Tuesday, October first, wearing his best black coat and pants with a new white shirt, he had mixed feelings about the wedding he was about to conduct—and that bothered him. Ordinarily, the sight of the wedding wagon—which was stocked with dinnerware, tablecloths, and extra stoves and ovens for putting on the meal that would serve hundreds of guests—lifted his spirits. His mood, however, matched the gray predawn sky, which was overshadowed by clouds.

It had been a frustrating week.

Three days of continual rain had postponed his corn harvest—and it had taken that many more days for the soil to dry enough that the draft horses and wagons could enter the fields without getting stuck in the mud.

But his farm work had to wait yet another day while he officiated at Gabe and Regina's wedding. First would come the regular church service, followed by the wedding ceremony, and then a huge meal and multi-family celebration that would last the remainder of the day. Because he was the bishop, he couldn't slip away from any of these festivities to tend his personal business—even though his livelihood depended upon working while the weather was good.

Jeremiah sighed as he drove closer to the house and the big white tents the Millers had rented to accommodate the long tables for the wedding meal. He suspected that Regina would've preferred holding the meal and reception in the commons at The Marketplace, but her uncle, Preacher Clarence, had probably insisted upon the traditional wedding arrangements because he was paying for some of them.

Again, Jeremiah reminded himself that Gabe's and Regina's families deserved his full attention—his best, most inspired wedding sermon—because the Flauds and the Millers were not only members of his congregation, they were also his dear friends. Why did he feel so restless, wishing he could drive a farm wagon for Will Gingerich rather than officiating at today's joyous occasion?

Because it'll be sheer torture to lead Regina and Gabe in their marriage vows while you stand only a few feet away from Lydianne.

All week he'd thought about her. One night he'd had a vivid dream about his beloved Priscilla—only to be shocked awake when she'd turned to take him in her arms, and it was Lydianne smiling at him. He was delighted that Gabe and Regina would be starting their new life together—and remaining in their cozy home in Morning Star—yet he was a desperate man.

Desperate for a woman's touch and sigh.

Desperate for a sign from God that he should either try again with Lydianne or move beyond his desire for her.

"This, too, shall pass," he muttered as he parked his rig alongside the pasture fence. "Get over yourself and get on with your life, man."

Jeremiah shook his head. He was so far gone, he'd been

talking to himself lately—even a couple of times when Mamm had caught him at it. He was relieved that his mother was riding to the wedding with Jude and his kids, because she'd been spending a lot of time at their place to help Leah with baby Adah, who was still too young to be out among people.

But Mamm'll be watching you, wondering why you refuse to even chat with Lydianne. She'll believe this wedding is the perfect place for you to spend time with a young woman who'd make you such a fine wife.

His mother was right about Lydianne making him a fine wife, even if he didn't want to spend time with her during the wedding festivities, where the guests could observe them. The mood was buoyant as he met with Preachers Clarence and Ammon in an upstairs room to decide who would preach the two sermons during church. His colleagues agreed that he should preach during the wedding, as usual, before leading the couple in their vows.

As the three of them and Deacon Saul entered the Millers' front room, which had been expanded by adjusting some of its movable interior walls to accommodate the huge crowd, Jeremiah anticipated a wonderful day to celebrate a fine young couple. The congregation was nearly finished singing the hymn when he and the other leaders took their places in front of the preachers' bench.

Jeremiah looked at the front pews, occupied by the wedding party. He was aware that Gabe and Regina had gone against tradition by having only one set of side-sitters instead of two—

He coughed, stifling a reprimand that would've stopped the church service cold. Instead of Gabe's cousin sitting beside him, Glenn Detweiler held the place of honor. And he was grinning as though he'd just won the lottery.

* * *

As Lydianne settled onto the front pew beside Regina, her heart felt airy and light. Because Martin Flaud, as the school board president, had called off classes so his daughters—and everyone else—could attend Gabe's wedding, she was enjoying an unexpected day off. She felt special, wearing the new dress of deep royal blue fabric that Regina had chosen to offset her bridal dress, which her Aunt Cora had sewn from an eye-catching shade of morning glory.

With her dark red hair tucked tightly under her crisp white *kapp*, Regina radiated an exuberant joy that Lydianne envied. Even though it had been her own decision—her own secret—that had determined she'd forever remain a *maidel*, she swallowed a sigh as she leaned closer to her best friend.

"I wish you all the joy and love in the world, Regina," she whispered as she clasped the bride's hands.

"And I wish you the very same, Lydianne," Regina replied softly. "Someday the right man will come along—"

Lydianne had been so focused on the bride that she hadn't looked around the room, but movement on the men's side made her glance in that direction. She froze.

Instead of Gabe's cousin sitting beside him, it was Glenn. As he flashed Lydianne a triumphant grin, she had to clench her jaw to keep from crying out in protest.

How did this happen? Where's the fellow from out of town—the cousin Gabe had invited to stand up with him right after he proposed to Regina?

Regina sucked in her breath. "Oh my," she murmured. "I wasn't expecting—"

As Bishop Jeremiah rose to begin the worship service,

he appeared displeased about Glenn's presence, as well. Lydianne tried to focus on his low, resonant voice as he opened the service with prayer—and then she forced herself to follow Preacher Ammon's first sermon, Deacon Saul's reading of the day's Scripture, and Preacher Clarence's longer second sermon.

Her efforts at worshipping and praising God were futile, however. The longer Lydianne thought about what Glenn must've done to finagle his way into the wedding party, the more upset she got. She hoped her smile didn't appear forced as she rose with Regina to stand in front of the bishop when it was time for the ceremony.

"Dearly beloved, we're gathered here on this special day to celebrate the sacrament of holy matrimony," Bishop Jeremiah began solemnly. His voice, usually rich and sonorous, sounded tight with tension—as though he, too, had been stewing about Glenn's presence.

Lydianne's heart was pounding with such distress, she barely heard the ancient words that prefaced every wedding ceremony. She tried very hard to focus on what the bishop was saying—reminding herself that such a welling-up of negative emotions was not only inappropriate at a wedding, it was unacceptable to God, as well. But her efforts at adjusting her attitude weren't working.

This surely must be a trick! And Glenn's grin says he somehow wrangled his way into standing up for Gabe. This is just wrong!

As the ceremony continued, Lydianne was enveloped in a mental haze of smoky-red resentment. She stared down at her white-knuckled hands, clasped too tightly in front of her. She refused to look at Glenn, and she didn't want to focus on Jeremiah, either, for fear he'd chastise her about her anger later—or interpret it as a sign that she'd welcome his company instead of Glenn's.

Lydianne was vaguely aware that Regina was repeating her vows in a voice that sounded strangely nervous, considering how confident she'd seemed when the two of them had entered the room. The bride got through her part without any slips, however.

"I, Gabriel, take thee, Regina, to be my lawfully wedded wife," the groom spoke out joyfully when it was his turn.

Of course, Gabe sounds happy—he knew about the switch in side-sitters, and Glenn's his best friend, so he's fine with it. Pull yourself together! Don't you dare allow this to spoil Regina's big day.

Lydianne put on her best smile as Bishop Jeremiah introduced Mr. and Mrs. Gabe Flaud to the guests in the crowded room. Most folks had no idea there was any friction between her and Glenn or between Glenn and the bishop, so they had probably attributed Regina's reticence to wedding-day jitters. As applause filled the room, Lydianne reminded herself that as mature adults—older than most side-sitters—she and Glenn could surely get through the wedding dinner and the rest of the day's festivities without any fuss.

But the trouble started immediately. When the wedding party gathered around a small table near the preachers' bench to sign the marriage certificate, Gabe and Regina signed first, writing their names on the proper lines. When Lydianne accepted the pen from her friend, however, Glenn stepped up beside her and put his arm around her.

"Stop it!" Lydianne whispered tersely.

"Stop what?" he shot back with a wounded frown. "I thought we could slip outside and talk about—"

"I don't *want* to go outside with you," Lydianne insisted

as she signed her name. "I don't want to go *out* with you, either, Glenn, so just leave me—"

"Why not? Are you seeing Shetler?" he demanded hotly.

"No! I'm—that's none of your business!"

Glenn's jaw dropped. He looked around the large, crowded room, which had suddenly gone silent as all eyes followed their escalating exchange. "Seems you've made it *everyone*'s business now, Miss Christner," he muttered as he picked up the pen she'd dropped on the table. After he hastily scribbled his name, he stalked toward the front door to avoid the crowd on the other side of the room.

Lydianne wanted the floorboards to open up and swallow her. As Regina, Gabe, and Bishop Jeremiah gathered around her, she felt lower than a worm for stirring up a ruckus—even as she told herself Glenn was as much to blame for it as she was.

"So where's your cousin Mervin?" Regina asked her new husband in a frustrated whisper.

"He's down with a nasty case of the flu," Gabe replied apologetically. "When his brother told me about it first thing this morning, what could I do but ask Glenn to fill in? I thought it would look awkward if I sat there alone and—and because I wasn't supposed to see you until church this morning, I didn't have a chance to tell you, honey-girl. I'm sorry—"

"No, *I'm* sorry," Lydianne interrupted as she blinked back tears. "I took it wrong when Glenn asked me to—I should've gone outside, as he suggested, and told him out there that I didn't want to—"

"Glenn overstepped," Jeremiah stated in a low voice. "He's still in mourning—and even if he weren't, it's improper for him to put his arm around you in public."

Lydianne was grateful that the bishop was standing

up for her, but that didn't stop the wedding guests from whispering. It didn't fully restore Regina's happiness, either, because she was clearly worried about Lydianne.

"Are you all right?" the bride whispered, grasping Lydianne's wrist. "Even though you tell me things at school are going well—"

"They are!" Lydianne insisted.

"—you haven't seemed like your usual cheerful self lately."

Lydianne sighed, wishing she could pull herself together without so many people around. It was bad enough that Glenn might have left the wedding; she couldn't abandon the wedding party, too. The bride and groom would look woefully alone if they were seated all by themselves at the special *eck* table in the corner of the main tent.

"Maybe you should've asked somebody else to be your side-sitter," she said in a halting voice. "I never intended to—"

"I did ask Jo and the twins to join you, remember?" Regina reminded her gently. "But they thought four attendants would be too many—"

"And I was at a loss to come up with four fellows to sit with me," Gabe put in. "Glenn was still married at that time, so I didn't even consider him—until this morning when I was in a pinch."

"What really matters," Bishop Jeremiah said as he slipped his arms around the bride and the groom, "is that you two have tied the knot, and that all these folks have gathered here to celebrate with you. Years from now you'll look back on your wedding as the happiest event in your life—and you'll recall this minor incident with a chuckle. What passed between Lydianne and Glenn today won't affect your love for one another one iota."

Gabe glanced behind them, at the folks who'd resumed their conversations and were slowly going outside. "*Jah*, I suppose we should be making our way into the tent and accepting everyone's congratulations," he said to Regina. His face regained its glow. "I don't want us to miss even a minute of this day, Mrs. Flaud! Our lives have worked out just the way we wanted, ain't so?"

Regina's face flushed a pretty pink beneath her freckles. "*Jah*, you're right. It's all *gut*—and I've been waiting all morning for this meal, because I was too excited to eat any breakfast."

With a squeeze of Lydianne's hand, Regina started toward the door with her new husband. As Lydianne watched them go, she was acutely aware that she and Jeremiah were the only folks left in the large room full of pew benches. She couldn't think of a single thing to say.

"Let it go, Lydianne," he said softly. "It wouldn't be a wedding if some unexpected little thing didn't happen."

When she looked gratefully into Jeremiah's deep brown eyes, she saw a flicker of intense regret—or was it sorrow?—before he glanced away. "*Denki* for seeing it that way," she murmured. "I'll try not to cause any more trouble."

As she took her seat beside Regina at the *eck* and the meal was served, Lydianne sensed folks were watching her—but they weren't watching Glenn, because he'd chosen not to rejoin the wedding party. The traditional "roast" made of chicken and stuffing, along with mashed potatoes, creamed celery, green beans, dinner rolls, and an array of fresh pies was probably delicious, but she ate without tasting much of it. It felt odd to be the only other person seated with the bride and groom, as though she were a third wheel.

I could've been kinder. Glenn hasn't recovered from the loss of his wife.

Even so, Lydianne told herself that he'd made his own moves and she couldn't have changed them. As the first sitting of guests left the tent to allow the second sitting folks to eat their meal, she made her way between the long tables. Ladies from the congregation were wiping off table-cloths and picking up dirty dishes—but as a side-sitter, she was excused from those duties.

She stepped out into the October sunshine, wondering if she should call attention to her early departure by hitch-ing up her rig—or simply slip behind the house to walk home, and come back later for her mare and the buggy. No one seemed to notice that she was standing alone, in a stew, so Lydianne turned to go. She felt horrible, leaving the fes-tivities before Gabe and Regina had even cut their cake—

"Teacher Lydianne! Teacher Lydianne!" a familiar voice called out behind her.

Lydianne closed her eyes. It would be so rude, and such a bad example, if she kept on walking and ignored the little girl who'd spotted her . . . especially because Ella was so special, and her feelings would be hurt. Putting on a smile, Lydianne turned and, as the little blonde launched herself, had no choice but to catch her in an enthusiastic hug.

"I've been lookin' all over for you! You look real pretty in your new dress, Teacher Lydianne," Ella gushed. "It must be exciting, to sit right up front with the bride!"

Why would she want to contradict the angelic little girl in her arms—her very own daughter, who was gazing at her with adoring blue eyes so like Aden's? "It's a special honor to be a side-sitter, *jah*," Lydianne agreed. "And don't you look pretty in your new dress, too? That color of pink—"

"Mamma says the side-sitter by the bride is the one

who's gonna get married next," Ella piped up. "Is that true, Teacher Lydianne? Are you gonna get married someday soon?"

A large knot formed in her throat. How deeply ironic it was that the cherub asking her this question was the very reason she could never marry—but she could *not* admit she was Ella's birth mother, nor did she want to spoil the child's sunny, innocent mood.

"Oh, I don't know about that, sweetie," she hedged when she could find her voice. "Regina asked me to be her side-sitter because we're best friends—"

"Like me and Gracie!"

Lydianne smiled, grateful for Ella's perceptive remark. "That's exactly right. And besides," she added, tweaking her daughter's upturned nose, "if I got married, I'd have to stop being your teacher."

Ella's eyes widened and her mouth became a perfect O. "We don't want that," she whispered in a worried little voice. "So . . . if you're not gettin' married, that's a *gut* thing for us kids, *jah*?"

"That's the way I see it, too," Lydianne replied gratefully. When she saw Julia Nissley in the crowd watching them, she waved and set Ella on the ground. "There's your *mamm*, sweetie. I bet she's ready to go into the tent and eat that yummy wedding dinner, because it's your turn now."

With another endearing smile, Ella raced off to rejoin her mother. Lydianne felt oddly bereft after releasing her little girl—all the more reason to escape from the crowd and deal with the emotions that had suddenly overwhelmed her.

All the way home, she kept her face turned away from the road so no one would notice she was crying as she walked. Bless her heart, Ella had stirred up a hornet's nest of raw feelings that Lydianne thought she'd reconciled long ago.

Hadn't she accepted the fact that because she and Aden had made a baby—and he'd died before they could marry—she would remain a *maidel* forever?

As her yellow house came into view, Lydianne realized just how much of a toll participating in Regina's ceremony had taken, knowing she'd never have one of her own. Constantly reminding herself that her best friend was very happy had helped her survive the ceremony—until Glenn had assumed she was delighted to be paired up with him. His suggestive remark had triggered more angst than she could have guessed—

But that's behind you now. Change into your old comfortable clothes and spend the rest of the day licking your wounds, so you can show up at school tomorrow with clear eyes, ready to teach those dear children.

Chapter Fourteen

As she and her friends stood in the shade among other wedding guests who'd finished their dinner, Jo watched Lydianne disappear behind the Miller house—and then saw her walking along the fence toward the road. She stepped closer to Molly and Marietta. "Something's not right with Lydianne today," she murmured. "I can understand why she was startled when Glenn showed up as Gabe's side-sitter, but it's not like her to let such a thing spoil her whole day."

"*Jah*, who'd ever imagine she'd leave Regina's wedding?" Molly asked as she, too, caught sight of the retreating side-sitter.

"Those two have been best friends ever since Lydianne came here," Marietta put in. "I think they share a special bond because Regina lost her parents so young, and because when Lydianne arrived, she didn't seem to have any family, either."

"Which is pretty odd, when you think about it," Molly remarked. "She moved right into her rental house—alone. I guess because she hasn't mentioned anybody but a couple older sisters who live at a distance, we've not quizzed her about her previous home or her family."

"She's been pretty private about those things, *jah*," Jo

agreed speculatively. "But still—I hate to see her heading home so early in the day. She must be very upset about something, and I don't like to think about her dealing with it all by herself."

Molly considered the issue for a moment. "Do you suppose we should go over there? We'll tell Regina we're checking on Lydianne—and not totally skipping out on her party."

Jo sighed. Because she and her mother had given the Helfing twins a ride, she foresaw a potential problem. "It's the right thing to do—and Lydianne would do that for any of us—but I hate to leave, in case Mamm wants to go home before we return."

"We'd be happy to run your mother home," a familiar male voice behind her put in.

Jo blinked. When she turned, Michael Wengerd, who'd been chatting with a couple of the other young men in attendance, flashed her a brilliant smile. "Sorry if I overheard your conversation and butted in," he continued apologetically. "Considering all the extra meals your *mamm* cooks for us—and the way she accommodated us when we came back last night for Gabe's wedding—giving her a ride's the least Dat and I can do."

For a moment, Jo got so caught up in his sparkling eyes, watching them change from blue to gray and back again, that she forgot to respond. "Uh—oh, but that would be very nice of you!" she said a little too quickly.

He nodded, suddenly seeming as shy and tongue-tied as Jo herself felt. "I'll let Mamm know—and we girls will be off. The sooner we can talk with Lydianne, the sooner we'll be back. *Denki* for your offer, Michael."

Jo noticed the knowing look that passed between the twins, but she didn't take their bait. Why should she make a big deal out of Michael's kind offer, when there couldn't possibly be any romantic interest attached to it? Molly and Marietta were seeing what they wanted to see, but Jo knew better. Even if Michael weren't so quiet and shy, he'd never be attracted to a tall, big-boned, horsey-faced girl like her. No man in his right mind would consider Joe Fussner's look-alike daughter as marriage material.

After they found Mamm in the crowd and told her she had a ride home if she needed it, Jo led the way to the long line of buggies parked alongside the pasture on the gravel lane leading from the road to the Miller house. While Jo whistled for her horse, Molly rolled the rig backward and away from the fence. A few minutes later they were driving down the road.

"It was very nice of Michael to speak up about taking your *mamm* back," Marietta began with a knowing smile.

Jo shrugged. "Michael—and his *dat*—are both very polite," she remarked, hoping to let the matter go at that.

"So, when it's time for a meal," Molly took up the thread, "does Drusilla carry their food out to the *dawdi haus*? Or do they eat in the kitchen with you two?"

Jo laughed out loud, knowing the twins were fishing. "When they first started staying over on Friday nights before working at The Marketplace on Saturdays, she wanted no part of having them in the house. But after Nelson fixed a clogged drain and replaced the glass in a window for her, she softened up a bit."

Watching for cars, Jo navigated the turn onto the county highway that ran through Morning Star. "Now they show up around six on Fridays for supper. It saves Mamm and me the effort of toting their meal over to them and fetching their dirty dishes, after all."

"Uh-huh," Marietta teased. "You can deny it till the cows

come home, Jo, but I think you and your *mamm* enjoy the Wengerds' company more than you're letting on."

"Why *wouldn't* we enjoy their company?" Jo shot back defensively. "I could make the same assumptions about you two and Pete, but I'm considerate enough to keep my speculations to myself."

Although the twins exchanged one of their silent communications—probably confirming that they were right about her and Michael—they stopped teasing her.

The buggy rolled through Morning Star slowly because of all the cars on the road, but finally Jo guided her mare toward the familiar lane leading up to Lydianne's house. It was a neatly kept home, still painted the deep yellow her English landlord had chosen. With the maple foliage in the front yard starting to turn orange and deep red, Lydianne's place was as pretty as a picture postcard.

"What do you suppose we ought to say to her?" Jo asked as she drove up Lydianne's lane.

The twins' pensive frowns and shrugs were identical, except that Marietta's face and shoulders were much thinner because of her recent cancer treatment. "I have no idea," Molly admitted. "We mostly just want to be sure nothing serious is wrong, *jah*?"

"And that it's only Glenn who's got her so upset," Marietta confirmed.

Nodding, Jo set the brake after the horse stopped at the side of the house. "We'll hope God gives us the right words. Her windows are open a crack, so she probably knows we're here."

As the three of them crossed the porch, Jo glanced between the curtains in the front window. She saw Lydianne silhouetted in the sunlight that flooded the kitchen. "Lydianne," she called out as she knocked on the screen door. "If you're having a little pity party, that's fine—but we want to come, too, all right?"

A few moments later, the door opened. Lydianne had removed her *kapp*, and she was dabbing at her red-rimmed eyes with a tissue. "So my getaway wasn't such a well-kept secret," she remarked glumly. "I didn't want to be a wet blanket on Regina's big day, so I came home."

Jo nodded as she and the twins stepped inside. "If it's any consolation, Glenn is long gone—he didn't even show up to eat," she said gently. "So why not pull yourself together and come back to the party with us? The four of us *maidels* can keep each other company, seeing's how none of us will have weddings in our immediate future—unless Pete gets smart and takes up with one of the twins," she teased.

"Puh! I'm thinking Riley's smarter than Pete will ever be," Molly countered with a laugh.

"We'll see how that goes. His rent is only paid through September—we've not seen money for October or beyond," Marietta remarked as she gazed around the front room. "You might be the smart one, Lydianne, not having a *dawdi haus* that accommodates extra guests."

Lydianne made a weak attempt at a smile. "*Denki* for checking on me, girls, but I'd hate to walk around the party with a hangdog look all afternoon—especially because my scholars are there. I've given the other guests enough to speculate about for one day, ain't so?"

Molly's eyebrows rose in a challenge. "Could be folks are talking even more because both you *and* Glenn left the party," she pointed out. "Who's to say the two of you haven't met up somewhere to be alone together?"

"Oh, *there's* a story!" Marietta teased. "Maybe you two lovebirds staged that little tiff at the signing table so folks won't think there's anything going on between you."

"But there's not!" Lydianne protested. "Except in Glenn's imagination."

Jo smiled. The twins had pulled Lydianne out of her funk, and she was sounding more like herself. "If it's your scholars you're concerned about," she began, "won't they see a fine example of grace and personal strength if you come back with us? We *maidels* understand that sometimes you just need to get away from the whole wedding thing when it depresses you, but those kids—especially your teenaged girls—will think you let Glenn's inappropriate behavior drive you away."

"You really are above that, Lydianne," Molly said, squeezing her shoulder.

"*Jah*, it's Glenn who's got the problem, not you," Marietta chimed in. "I wouldn't be surprised if Bishop Jeremiah seeks him out for some counseling sessions soon."

Lydianne sniffled loudly, considering her options. "Well, now that you put it that way . . ."

Jo smiled kindly, letting her friend decide for herself. She'd spent many an evening in her room bemoaning her singular state, wondering whom she'd have for company after Mamm passed away, so she understood the bitter sting of reaching her late twenties with no prospects for a husband. She suspected blond, blue-eyed Lydianne wasn't destined to share that fate, but she kept her opinion to herself.

"Take your time, girl. We'll wait while you splash some cold water on your face and put your *kapp* on again," she said gently. "If you've got some eye drops with redness remover in them, you'll look no worse for wear. We can enjoy some cake and spend some time with Regina—because she'll be more of a homebody now. I'll miss having her at The Marketplace on Saturdays."

Lydianne let out a long sigh. "All right, give me a

minute," she finally said. "I'll go back to visit with the bride, *jah*—but also to keep you three from spreading tales about Glenn and me when I'm not there to defend myself."

"You've got that right," Molly teased.

When Lydianne turned toward the bathroom, Jo flashed the Helfings a thumbs-up. She could recall a few times when the *maidels* had lifted Marietta's spirits when her chemo treatments were most grueling, and it was gratifying to know that the power of their friendship had rescued Lydianne, as well—even if Jo sensed the new teacher might be dealing with issues she wasn't ready to talk about.

Glenn may have taken himself out of the picture for now, but that still leaves Bishop Jeremiah with a tendency to gaze at Lydianne when he thinks nobody's looking. It's only a matter of time before he tries again.

Jeremiah's heart stilled as Jo drove her buggy up the Millers' long lane and parked it. It was a good sign that the *maidels* had only been gone from the wedding festivities for about half an hour—and he smiled when he saw Lydianne following the Helfing twins out of the rig. She had a firmness about her jaw that told him she was determined to see this day through for her best friend—that she was no quitter.

A fresh surge of longing filled his soul. Lydianne appeared weary, as though the busy Saturdays at The Marketplace and the hours she spent at home preparing for school were draining her well of inner resources faster than she could refill it.

If you were my wife, sweet lady, you wouldn't have to work at two outside jobs. You'd have a comfortable home and a man who cherished every moment he spent with you—

But this wasn't the time to approach her. Lydianne still seemed raw from her spat with Glenn, and Jeremiah still needed to come up with some compelling reasons for her to go out with him. Besides, neither of them wanted to become the object of everyone's attention this afternoon. He was guessing more than two hundred people were in attendance, eager for something else to gossip about.

Jeremiah relaxed. Sometime during the upcoming week, while he was harvesting corn, inspiration would strike. He and Lydianne could start again, slowly—and alone, rather than someplace where folks were watching them. Maybe he'd fetch her after school one day and they could share a picnic in his favorite place, on the rocks alongside the riverbank. Seated among the trees, where the leaves whispered in the breeze and the water sang a soothing tune, surely he and Lydianne could blaze a trail toward the happiness that was missing in their lonely lives.

Chapter Fifteen

On Friday, as she trudged from the pole barn up to the white schoolhouse, Lydianne felt achy all over, as though she was coming down with something. The overcast sky promised another rain shower sometime this morning— and everyone was tired of rain.

I'm probably just worn out from staying up late to work on lessons, or because the kids still haven't settled down after having the day off school on Tuesday—and because the rainy weather has kept them indoors a lot. If I could catch up on some sleep, I'd shake this heaviness in my head.

She wouldn't be sleeping late on Saturday, however, because she'd agreed to cover the Flaud Furniture store at The Marketplace for Gabe. He and Regina would be out of town, visiting family and friends who had wedding gifts for them. And Sunday there would be church, which started promptly at eight.

Lydianne entered the schoolroom with a weary sigh. She didn't foresee any break in the dreary weather, so her students—especially Stevie and Billy Jay—would proba-bly need to work off their excess energy with some relay races on the stairs again at recess. Just the thought of the kids' racket when they played indoors made Lydianne's head throb.

When she flipped the light switch, the sight of the large, colorful Noah's ark poster—and the collection of clay animals on the table beneath it—lifted her spirits. With another session or two, the model of the ark would be completed— a tribute to the patience and persistence of the older scholars working with the younger ones as they fitted its pieces together. The Miller sisters and the Flaud girls were godsends when it came to keeping two or three of the little ones focused on flash cards, vocabulary drills, and the Noah's ark class project, while Lydianne worked individually with Ella, Gracie, Stevie, or Billy Jay.

And it'll be Linda, Lucy, Kate, and Lorena who get me through today, as well.

Lydianne erased the special Noah's ark spelling words from the white board, because they would be on the test this morning. As she wrote out the morning's reading assignments for each level, the downpour she'd been expecting drummed on the schoolhouse roof.

When the children arrived, however, the sunshine broke through, dispelling the clouds and lifting her spirits further. The angle of the autumn sun was so intense, she had to shield her eyes with her hand while she returned her scholars' greetings. Her day began, falling into its comforting, familiar rhythm.

By lunchtime, the classroom had grown so stuffy from the heat, Lydianne threw open some of the windows. It was still humid, however, and there wasn't much of a breeze.

"Can we have a picnic lunch today, Teacher Lydianne?" Gracie piped up.

"*Jah*, if we eat outside, we'll be all ready to start recess, right?" Billy Jay pleaded.

Lydianne smiled at the boy's winsome expression. Some fresh air and exercise would do everyone good—and it might help her get through the afternoon's classes. "That sounds like a wonderful-*gut* idea," she replied. "We've been working hard all morning—"

"And maybe since it's Friday, we can just play for the rest of the day, ain't so?" Stevie put in with a perfectly straight face.

As the students clamored to do as Stevie had suggested, Lydianne shook her head good-naturedly. "Have you already forgotten that we took Tuesday off for the wedding? We need to finish our math units for the week, and some of you are working on book reports this afternoon. However," she added as she glanced at the clock above the door, "we can add an extra fifteen minutes to recess to make up for all the time we've had to play indoors this week. You're excused."

Stevie and Billy Jay headed downstairs in a flash to fetch their lunch boxes from the shelves in the coat room. Soon the younger girls were calling out to the older ones to grab the jump ropes and balls from the storage units behind the coat pegs. Within minutes, her scholars were seated at the picnic tables, grateful for the shade as they quickly ate their sandwiches.

Lydianne sat with them only long enough to eat her peanut butter and jelly sandwich—a meager lunch, but it was all she'd had the energy to pack early this morning. When she slipped back inside, she became aware of how unseasonably warm the day had become—and even more aware of how tired she was.

For a few moments Lydianne allowed herself to enjoy

the blessed relief of her empty classroom. She gave in to the urge to fold her arms on her desk and rest her head on them—just for a few moments, she told herself. The sing-song chant of jumping rope rhymes outside lulled her into a light doze . . .

Next thing she knew, forty-five minutes had gone by. As she rose from her desk in a state of groggy heavy-headedness, Lydianne realized that some of the afternoon lessons would have to be cut short—and that the kids would see through whatever story she made up about why she hadn't joined them outside. When she went out to use the restroom, she was once again grateful that her four older girls were so conscientious about watching the younger ones.

Maybe they're all enjoying the sunshine so much, they have no idea how long they've been out here. And maybe— just this once—it's all right to let recess run overtime.

As Lydianne emerged from the restroom building, she blew her whistle so the kids playing on the far side of the ball diamond would know it was time to come in. She preceded the students indoors and began to write some math problems on the white board, pleased that the voices downstairs indicated that the scholars had come inside promptly. Even the youngest of her students had become immersed enough in the weekly routine to realize—without being told—that after recess, they were supposed to copy the simple addition problems written on their section of the white board onto notebook paper so they could do the computation.

Everyone was so focused on the task at hand, that when Lydianne turned away from writing on the board, it took her a few moments to realize one of the smaller desks was unoccupied. "Where's Ella?" she asked. "Did any of you girls notice if she was still in the restroom when you came in?"

Seven sets of eyes widened as everyone looked up from the math problems they were working. Gracie, Ella's closest companion, gazed at the vacant desk on the other side of Stevie's as though she could make her friend appear through the sheer power of her will.

"She used the bathroom, *jah*," Lucy recalled with a frown.

"But that was when we first went outside," Linda murmured with a shake of her head. "While Kate was pitching balls for the boys, Gracie and Lorena and I were jumping rope—"

"And I knew Ella had gone into the restroom," Lorena put in, "but I wasn't keeping track of when she came out. I'll go check—I hope she's not sick."

"I'll take a look," Lydianne insisted, already thrumming with guilt for not staying outside with her students. "You kids can continue working your problems."

She hurried down the wooden stairs and into the school's storage level, checking between the rows of shelves and pegboards where her scholars kept their lunch boxes. Ella's small cooler was in its place, so she darted outside.

But a quick scan of the horizon showed no sign of anyone in the schoolyard or on the ball field. "Ella?" Lydianne called out as she rushed toward the concrete block building that housed the two restrooms.

When she entered the girls' side of the building, however, her voice echoed around the empty stalls and the sink. For safety's sake, she checked the boys' side, too, and then jogged out toward the ball diamond. "Ella!" she cried out at the top of her lungs. "Ella! It's time to come in!"

No answer. No sign of anyone near the edge of the woods, either.

As her heart raced into overdrive, Lydianne hurried toward the pole barn and the pasture where her horse grazed alongside Billy Jay's pony and the Miller and Flaud girls' mares. All she saw was grass and fence and the four horses.

Where could Ella have gone? The only place left to look was the red stable that housed The Marketplace. As Lydianne turned in that direction, she saw the other scholars coming out of the schoolhouse. They appeared as flummoxed—and as concerned—as she was.

Lydianne motioned for her students to join her as she headed toward the big stable with its window boxes full of colorful flowers. "Look all around the building," she instructed as they came within earshot. "The doors are locked, so Ella can't be inside—"

"I wish we had our cell phone here, to call the Nissley place," Kate said. "But Mamm won't allow us to bring it to school."

Lydianne knew some of the Plain teenagers in town used cell phones during their *rumspringa,* and she was wishing the school board and Pete had thought to put a phone shack by the schoolhouse for emergencies—because this situation was quickly developing into a crisis. Well-behaved little Amish girls didn't wander away during recess—

Unless the teacher's not paying attention and falls asleep, Lydianne chided herself.

How would she apologize to Julia and Tim Nissley if something happened to their daughter because of her negligence? And how would she ever live with herself if her little girl got hurt while she'd been napping at her desk?

Never mind how she would explain Ella's disappearance to members of the school board.

The kids who'd circled the red stable came back without Ella.

"I'll ring the fire bell," Lydianne said. "We'll hope folks will be able to hear it from clear out here."

Lydianne jogged toward the large old cast iron bell, which had been transferred from the previous schoolhouse. It was mounted on a pole a few yards from the school's front steps. In earlier times, teachers had rung the bell each morning as a reminder for scholars to be on time for classes, but because her eight students hadn't shown any inclination to run late, she'd never bothered with it. Otherwise, when the bell rang out, any of the nearby men who heard it would know there was a crisis at the schoolhouse.

Would the bell's toll carry over the noise of traffic on the county highway? Would Amish farmers hear it clanging despite the big English harvest equipment that was running in nearby fields? The new schoolhouse was on the opposite side of town from most Amish homes, so as Lydianne tugged on the warm rope several times, she could only hope the bell would still be effective.

As the last peal reverberated in the air around her, Lydianne realized they shouldn't sit idly by while they waited for someone to respond. "Let's split up into pairs— an older student with a younger one," she instructed. "Lorena, how about if you and Stevie start up at the road by the fence and work your way over toward the woods and back this way? Linda, you and Billy Jay can start along the far pasture fence and circle back this way. And Kate and Lucy, you and Gracie search the area in the middle— from the far end of the ball field and into the woods a bit."

The children nodded solemnly, eager to be helpful.

"Everyone should report back in about fifteen minutes, all right?" Lydianne directed. "I'll stay here to keep track of you, and to tell the first helpers who respond to our bell what we're doing. I can't think Ella went very far— we'll surely find her. When you hear my whistle blowing, you'll know she's back, all right?"

As they took off at a trot in the directions Lydianne had indicated, her prayers went with them.

Where can Ella be, Lord? She's not the type to go running off by herself. Please keep her safe and unharmed. Please don't let this be the work of a kidnapper . . .

As the next several minutes crawled by, she tried to remain positive—and reminded herself that Ella was bright and resourceful. Maybe she'd even gone home for some reason only she knew and was safely with her *mamm.*

But she's only six. If she went into the woods, she could easily become confused about where she was. If she saw a stranger beckoning her, she'd know better than to go over—or she'd be too intimidated. Wouldn't she?

Lydianne heard the students calling for Ella as she watched the road for help to arrive, though she had no idea how she would explain this unthinkable situation. As the sun sank lower in the sky, it occurred to her that the kids' parents would be expecting them to arrive home soon.

What will you say to Julia and Tim if we don't find their daughter? How do you explain—to the other parents and the school board—that you were napping instead of supervising at recess?

As a familiar dapple-gray Percheron turned off the road and approached at a brisk canter, followed by two rigs racing to keep up with him, Lydianne's heart rose into her throat. Along with the bishop, she saw Tim Nissley and Saul Hartzler in the faster rig, coming from the carriage company. Gabe Flaud was driving his *dat* in the other one, so they'd heard the bell at the furniture factory.

"What's going on, Lydianne?" Bishop Jeremiah asked as he dismounted. "I'm happy to see there's no fire—"

"We came as fast as we could hitch up the horse!" Martin called out as Gabe pulled up beside the Nissley buggy. "It's been so long since I've heard that bell, it took me a minute to realize what it meant."

Tim scrambled down from his buggy, looking around with a concerned frown. "Where are the kids? Have you kept them inside for a reason?"

"They—they're out looking for Ella," Lydianne replied with a hitch in her voice. "I'm so sorry—it's all my fault that—that she didn't come in from recess. We got so absorbed in our math lesson—we—we didn't notice she was gone until—"

"Take it easy, Lydianne. One sentence at a time," Jeremiah murmured as he stepped up beside her.

Tim's eyebrows rose. "I don't know what's gotten into Ella," he said with an exasperated shake of his head. "Twice this week we've had to go looking for her when it was time to come in from doing the chores."

Lydianne couldn't allow Tim's admission to keep her from confessing her lapse. "But if I'd been paying attention—if I hadn't been—"

"Here come some of the kids now," Saul interrupted, pointing toward the road.

"And the rest of them are heading this way, too," Gabe said as he gazed in the other direction.

But Ella wasn't with them.

As the scholars arrived, every one of them insisted that if he or she had been paying attention, they would've seen Ella leaving the schoolyard. Their large eyes and frightened voices cut Lydianne to the core, because the blame fell squarely on her shoulders. The teacher was ultimately responsible for the welfare of her students, after all.

Bishop Jeremiah raised his hands to stop the kids' outpouring. "You've all done your best to find her, like the *gut* friends you are," he assured them gently. "At this point in the afternoon, let's get you scholars home to your *mamms*. We'll round up your *dats* and some other fellows to expand the search."

"I can't think such a wee girl would get far," Martin put in. "If we fellows divide up into the woods and head farther down beyond the pasture, I bet we'll find her before the others even get here. Gabe, drive us all the way down to the pasture property line. We'll get started looking in that direction."

As the Flaud buggy took off, Deacon Saul looked at Tim. "How about if you drop me off at the carriage factory? I'll shut down the line and have our men search along the county highway and into the woods from there," Saul suggested. "If we consider the schoolhouse the gathering point, anybody who finds her can report back here."

"All right—and then I'll stop by home to be sure Ella's not there," Tim replied. "Wouldn't surprise me that she's figured out you can get to our place by cutting across the lot behind The Marketplace and zigzagging through town.

"And Teacher Lydianne," he added with a strained smile, "don't think for a minute that we'll let you take the blame for this. We've tried to teach Ella that she needs to *tell* folks she's going for a walk instead of just taking off. Obviously that lesson hasn't taken hold yet."

"*Jah*, we all learn the hard way sometimes," Saul remarked. "I bet Ella won't wander off again after she sees how many folks have been tracking her down."

By the time the bishop had instructed Billy Jay to take Stevie home, and both boys to alert their *dats* to the search, the Miller girls were heading across town to tell Preacher Clarence and other men along the way. Only Jeremiah remained with Lydianne, and he was kind enough not to quiz her about how she'd lost track of a student. Her pulse had almost returned to normal, but she had to face up to the underlying cause of this whole ordeal.

"None of this would've happened if I'd stayed outside with the kids for recess," she blurted miserably. "I gave them an extra fifteen minutes—figured the older girls would keep watch—and made the huge mistake of resting my head on my desk. I didn't wake up for forty-five minutes!" she added with a hitch in her voice. "I—I was so upset with myself that when the kids came in, I delved right into their afternoon math problems on the board and—and didn't even notice Ella was missing until I turned around!"

She hugged herself tightly, desperately wishing she could put her arms around her missing daughter instead. "I feel so awful, Jeremiah! How could I not know that the little girl who sits right in front of my desk wasn't there?"

To her horror, she burst into tears.

Chapter Sixteen

Jeremiah's heart went out to the young woman who wept beside him. Because no one else was around, he dared to slip his arm around her. "Shall we talk about this inside?" he asked gently. "I know you won't want the men to see you this way when they arrive."

Head hung low, Lydianne preceded him into the white schoolhouse. When he'd closed the door, however, she turned and clung to him like a frightened child. "But— but what if we don't find her?" she cried inconsolably. "Or what if she's hurt, and she can't call out to the men who're searching for her?"

He allowed himself a few moments to hold her, savoring her nearness despite the agony she was putting herself through. "We'll find her, sweetheart," he murmured. "Little girls don't just disappear into thin air. And even the best teachers slip up now and again because they're human, Lydianne."

"That's no excuse!" she protested, gazing at him through her tears.

His heart stilled. She looked so small and vulnerable, so fearful for the fate of her student—and so determined to torture herself. "You heard what the others said, Lydianne," he continued softly. "The kids—even your older girls, who are *very* watchful—didn't realize Ella had slipped off, either. It sounds like she's had some practice at leaving the scene without her parents being the wiser, too."

"But I'm the teacher, so I'm responsible—"

"*Jah*, you are, honey. You're one of the most responsible people I know," Jeremiah insisted, framing her blotchy face between his hands. "That's why you rang the bell and organized the kids into search teams instead of going into a panic. When you realized something was wrong, you did all the right things. Nobody can do any more than that, Lydianne."

Jeremiah was thankful that she was settling down, because if she'd kept on weeping, it would've undone him. This wasn't the time to discuss the stress she'd been under lately—especially the scenes Detweiler had caused at the picnic and the Flaud wedding. Nor was it a good idea to mention that her beautiful blue eyes had been underscored with dark circles lately.

If he gave Lydianne something constructive to focus on, they'd both be better off. It would *not* be wise to let the men catch him holding her.

"How about if you go splash some water on your face and pull yourself together?" he suggested gently. "Is it all right if I erase what you've written on the board? I'd like to sketch a rough map of the area so that, as the men start searching, we can keep track of the areas we've covered."

Lydianne nodded, exhaling wearily. "*Denki* for your patience. I'll be back in a few."

As she went out to the restroom, Jeremiah followed her progress through the window and noticed that the sun was nearly down. Even so, the schoolroom was still so warm he rolled up the sleeves of his shirt. He hoped the unseasonable heat would be an advantage if their search lasted into the night.

God, please guide Ella to safety, and help the searchers find her quickly. If she's indeed lost, she's terrified. The darkness and chilly evening temperatures will only make things worse for her. And while You're at it, please be with Lydianne. She's not nearly finished tormenting herself over this ordeal.

As he erased the day's math problems, which were neatly arranged and color-coded for each grade level, he marveled at Teacher Lydianne's precise handwriting. Her classroom chore chart made him smile, too. And the entire wall that was covered with a colorful poster depicting the story of Noah's ark, along with the clay animals and model of the ark beneath it, displayed an amazing amount of class cooperation and teamwork. He envied the kids who spent their days in this vibrant, exciting schoolroom with Teacher Lydianne.

Get your mind off the teacher and sketch the map, Shetler.

He drew parallel lines to represent the county highway, and then sketched the schoolhouse to the left of it. By the time Lydianne returned, Jeremiah had added The Marketplace, Saul's carriage factory, and the main fences that designated property boundaries, as well as the nearby woods.

"Should I include the farms on the other side of the highway, and the business district?" he asked softly. "I hate to think of Ella crossing all those streets, little as she is."

"So do I," Lydianne said as she checked the clock above the door. "But considering she's been gone for nearly four hours, who knows how far she could've gone? Or in which direction?"

He was pleased to hear the rational tone of her voice. The skin around her eyes was still puffy, but she had her emotions under control. "And who knows what gave her the notion to leave?" Jeremiah mused aloud. He began to sketch the streets of the business district and the farms beyond that. "A bright child's mind runs at the speed of imagination, and to a six-year-old, each new thing she sees is a springboard to adventure. We can at least be certain that Ella was *not* running away from school."

"*Jah*, she loves to learn," Lydianne said with a fragile smile. "Ella's like a sponge that soaks up every drop of knowledge—and then she can't wait to know more. She's a—a joy to teach. If I let her work ahead as fast as she's able to grasp the material, she could easily be ready to start second grade by Christmas and then catch up to Billy Jay."

Jeremiah's eyes widened. "Do you think that's a *gut* idea? Down the road, it would mean she'd graduate from school earlier—at thirteen or even twelve, if she keeps skipping ahead."

"*Jah*, it would have some definite social disadvantages," Lydianne put in with a pensive sigh. "We don't encourage our students—especially our girls—to academically outdistance the other kids their age. But I hate to hold Ella back or let her get bored. I've been praying on it."

"Always the best avenue to take, along with conferring with her parents. There," Jeremiah added as he made a few final marker strokes. "I hope we don't have to search all of this area, but we can't make any assumptions about how far Ella's walked—or where she might've sat down to wait for someone to find her."

He replaced the cap on his marker, holding Lydianne's

gaze. "Is this a *gut* time to talk about why you've looked so troubled lately? Or shall we wait until Ella's back?"

Lydianne swallowed hard. As she went to the window to see whether any of the men might be approaching the schoolhouse, Jeremiah wondered if he might've contributed to the cloud of anxiety and exhaustion that hovered around her. He could certainly vouch for a number of evenings when Lydianne had cost him a good night's sleep—but he'd brought that on himself. He couldn't blame her simply because she was alluring and had a pleasing personality and enough confidence to hold her own as a bishops's wife—

"Maybe it's time I gave up spending my Saturdays at The Marketplace," Lydianne confessed with a sigh. "Some days I meet myself coming and going. I feel I'm never getting enough done—"

"That comes with being a first-year teacher, I suspect," Jeremiah put in. "You don't have prepared lessons to fall back on. And even though we only have eight scholars right now, it's surely a challenge to stay a few steps ahead of each and every one of them. I'm impressed that you've already pegged Ella as a student who could advance so quickly."

Lydianne's tender smile made his chest flutter. Would there ever come a day when she took on such a glow when she was thinking about *him*?

"Oh, Gracie's plenty smart, too. But she's not as curious, and not as willing to apply herself to subjects that don't interest her—like learning her math facts," she added with a wry smile. "Ella's conquered basic addition and subtraction, and sometimes after she's finished the first-grade problems on the board, she also does Billy Jay's math assignment. If someone taught her about carrying and borrowing, she could tackle three- and four-column addition and subtraction."

Jeremiah's eyebrows rose. "I suspected that Julia worked with her at home, but I had no idea Ella was picking things up that fast."

"But she's still just a wee girl, and she must be frightened out of her mind if she's been wandering lost all this time." Lydianne looked ready to cry again as she gazed out the window. "Here come the Flauds. Ella's not with them."

Gabe and Martin were the first in a parade of men sent out to search an area on the map that Jeremiah assigned them. Glenn and Jude had joined the effort, and so had Preachers Ammon and Clarence, all of them carrying kerosene lanterns. Saul and Tim bore determined expressions as they, too, chose another area across the highway to continue looking. A group of Saul's employees were combing Morning Star's business district after a search of the area around the carriage factory had proven futile.

After he'd dispatched the last of the Hartzler employees and marked the areas they were searching on his map, Jeremiah gazed at Lydianne. "Will you be all right here if I go out and join the search? I feel I could be doing more to—"

"Well, so do I!" Lydianne blurted. "This waiting around—not knowing what's happened to Ella—well, it's driving me crazy. Maybe I should brew some coffee in one of the big coffeemakers at The Marketplace for the men to drink, or—"

"Great idea," Jeremiah assured her. The tone of her response told him Lydianne would probably come unraveled if he left her here by herself. "I'll go into town and get us something to eat, and pick up some snacks for the men, to go with your coffee. We *will* find Ella," he added as he squeezed her shoulder. "At least it's staying really warm. By now, she's probably found a place to rest—in someone's stable, or maybe even in a home—which will make it harder for our searchers to spot her."

Unfortunately, his last remark made Lydianne's face pucker again. She fought back her tears, however. "All right, I'm going over to make that coffee," she said in a strained voice. "You're right. Somebody has to stay here in case we get word of where Ella is, and to keep track of what areas haven't yet been searched. Leave a note on the board saying I'll be back in a few—and I'll see you later, Jeremiah. I have a feeling we're in for a long night."

The weary, frightened expression on Lydianne's pale face did nothing to quell his own concerns about how the search was going. She looked small and done in as she fished her keys from her purse and walked toward the big stable that housed The Marketplace. As he swung up onto Mitch's back and rode toward town on this moonless evening, Jeremiah sent up more prayers for Ella and for the search party.

Guide us toward Your little lost lamb, Lord. And hold Lydianne close as this difficult night plays upon her worst-case assumptions.

As the water heated and the coffee brewed, its gurgling reminded Lydianne of a hungry stomach—and how long it had been since she'd eaten her meager lunch. But she had no appetite.

What kind of mother doesn't know when her child goes missing? Ella's probably lost in the dark, frightened out of her mind—because her own mother wasn't paying attention.

What if she fell and hit her head? How will I ever live with myself if my little girl—Aden's daughter, and the Nissleys'— doesn't come out of this nightmare alive?

She hugged herself hard as she paced the area around The Marketplace's refreshment area, trying to hold body and soul together. When the coffee finished perking, she filled several thermal carafes and loaded them into a handcart along with some coffee cups. Setting up a serving area on a table in the back of the classroom gave her something to focus on, but the minutes still stretched like hours before Jude and Glenn grimly reported back for a new search assignment and left again.

She sighed as she watched the darkness swallow them. Glenn had barely made eye contact with her. Lydianne felt bad about that, yet maybe he'd finally gotten the message that she didn't want to socialize with him.

What would he say if he found out Ella was my daughter? What would any of these men say if they knew they were out searching for my secret baby?

Lydianne was pretty sure the answer to that question would lead to the loss of her job—but before she could sink deeper into her pit of mental despair, she heard a horse approaching. A few moments later, Bishop Jeremiah's hopeful smile fell a notch when he stepped inside and saw that Ella wasn't with her. He tried to keep his words upbeat.

"Brought us some sandwiches and bags of snacks from the convenience store on the highway," he said as he set a large paper bag on the table near the carafes. "Not a feast, but at this hour it was the only place open. I also stopped by the Nissley place, to see if Ella had found her way home. Julia's holding up pretty well, but she said she'd leave a note on their door and come to sit with you."

Although her heart was grateful for the bishop's kindness, Lydianne's mind balked at the idea that Jeremiah believed she needed a keeper . . . especially if that keeper was Ella's adoptive *mamm*. "I suppose it's a *gut* idea for her to keep me company so you can join the search, if you'd like to," she murmured.

"No sense in both of you gals fretting alone when you could commiserate together," he agreed with a gentle smile. "I'll go as soon as we've eaten. That way, I'll know you ate something. We can't have you falling ill on top of being worn thin from this ordeal, honey."

Lydianne's heart wanted so badly to accept Jeremiah's kindness—not to mention his affection for her. Rather than saying anything to encourage him, however, she dutifully sat down at one of the older scholars' desks and took a bite of the warm ham and cheese sandwich he'd brought her.

About halfway through their makeshift meal, she heard buggies approaching.

"Still no sign of our girl?" Preacher Ammon asked as he entered the schoolroom.

Lydianne shook her head dejectedly. She let Jeremiah chat with Ammon and Clarence about where to look next, glancing at the clock above the doorway.

Ten-twenty. Far too late for a first-grade girl to be unaccounted for. My little daughter should be snug in bed, secure in her mother's love—but I failed her. Maybe God has taken her away from me because I obviously can't take care of her.

She shook her head to free it of this thought, which cut her like barbed wire. Then Julia Nissley came through the door. Instantly, Lydianne rose from the desk to embrace the tearful mother who was raising Ella. Julia clutched her tightly.

"I am so sorry I wasn't paying attention at recess," Lydianne sobbed.

"I'm so sorry Ella's putting you through this," Julia insisted at the same time. "She should've *asked* you— we've tried to tell her—"

As the two of them looked at one another, Lydianne was again amazed by the lack of blame in Julia's gaze and words—the same acceptance and forgiveness she'd experienced when Tim had joined the search party. These young parents had to feel as worried and frightened as she did, yet they displayed no ill will toward her.

If you knew the truth about Ella—and me—you wouldn't behave so graciously.

Lydianne busied herself offering coffee as more men came in. She took comfort in the confident way Jeremiah spoke as he directed the groups of men toward areas that hadn't yet been searched.

When the searchers had left again, Jeremiah hastily finished his sandwich and wadded the sack into a tight, wrinkled ball. "I'm going out there to look for her," he said wearily. "We can't give up until we find her, and the more men we have on the lookout, the better our chances are."

"Well, if anyone has an in with God about where my little girl might be, it would be you, Bishop," Julia remarked, smiling through her tears. "Our prayers go with you. We have to keep believing she's found a safe place, or that someone will eventually find her and bring her home."

Jeremiah nodded. As he stepped out into the unfathomable darkness, Lydianne sensed—no matter what the bishop and Ella's *mamm* said—that they were all facing the longest night of their lifetimes.

Chapter Seventeen

As the next hours passed, Jeremiah's arms grew leaden from holding up the lantern. His legs felt as heavy as concrete columns with the effort of combing the wooded areas behind the schoolyard. The thick trees followed the narrow, winding fork of the river well beyond the city limits of Morning Star, and more than once he stumbled over roots and debris he couldn't distinguish because the lantern's glare fooled his tired eyes. He'd started out walking west, covering areas other men had searched earlier—figuring that Ella would've kept moving, perhaps in circles, as she became confused in such unfamiliar territory. He'd left Mitch in the pole barn at the school because riding the tall Percheron among the dense trees would've been hazardous to both of them.

At least he hadn't spotted a small, lifeless body floating in the river, or caught on the rugged rocks along the shoreline.

"Ella? Ella, are you here?" he called out every now and again.

To stay awake—to keep from sitting on a stump too long and falling asleep—he prayed out loud whenever he stopped to rest. "If I really do have an in with You, Lord— if it's Your will that I find Ella," he said loudly, "then please guide me in the direction I'm supposed to go. I don't believe You'll allow Your little lamb to come to harm."

Jeremiah firmly believed what he said. But as he doubled back to the schoolhouse—twice—and read the deepening despair on the two young women's faces, he began to wonder. The best he could hope for was that a family in Morning Star had spotted Ella and taken her in for a warm meal.

But wouldn't they take her home as soon as they found her? Wouldn't Ella tell them her parents' names and where she lived? Are we missing something, Lord? Looking in all the wrong places?

As the hours plodded by, occasionally punctuated by the calls of other searchers in the distance, Jeremiah had no idea what time it was. Time ceased to matter to him, except that every passing minute represented the potential for Ella to fall and hurt herself, or to meet up with other forms of danger he didn't want to ponder.

Jeremiah reached a point where he needed to regroup, mentally and physically. His lantern was getting low on kerosene again. After checking in with Lydianne and Julia, he mounted Mitch and rode carefully toward the road, grateful for the streetlights as he passed through town. Spending ten minutes at home to drink a glass of water and grab a quick snack would give him a chance to warm up before he began searching again.

He started up the lane and then stopped Mitch halfway to the house. Pink ribbons of dawn were visible on the horizon, and the air around him took on a serene stillness. The countryside vibrated with a silence only heard along winding, unpaved roads, away from the noise of town—a silence that reverberated within Jeremiah's soul.

His heart told him to visit his favorite spot on the riverbank, where he so often meditated and received inspiration. Exhausted as he was, he felt an urgent need to sit on his large, flat rock for a few moments to listen to the whisperings of the river and watch the sunrise.

When he'd ridden to the edge of the woods just beyond his stubbly, harvested cornfields, Jeremiah dismounted and left his horse to wait for him. The dawn illuminated the leaves on the maple trees, which were taking on their autumn colors. As he approached his special rock, he sucked in his breath.

There, aglow with the first light of day, a little girl lay curled up asleep.

"Ella!" Jeremiah cried out hoarsely. "Ella, honey, are you all right?"

By the time he'd reached her, she was stirring—and she bolted upright as though she had no idea where she was or how she'd gotten there. She blinked at Jeremiah with sleepy eyes akin to a newborn kitten's. Her *kapp* was gone and her blond hair had loosened from its little bun, framing her dirt-smudged face with tendrils of gold that caught the first rays of the sun breaking through the trees.

Scooping her into his arms, Jeremiah hugged her fiercely. "Ella, you're safe! Thanks be to God," he said in a voice gone raspy with emotion.

"I got tired, so I took a nap," she murmured matter-of-factly. "This rock, it was nice and warm from bein' in the sun all day."

His eyes widened. "You've been here all night? Since yesterday afternoon?" His feet were carrying him toward his horse, even as he focused on the wee angel in his arms.

"I was gettin' lost, so I stayed right here in one spot where somebody would find me," she replied with a decisive nod. "And here you are, Somebody."

"And here *you* are, Ella," he said with a relieved chuckle. "We're going to take you back to your *mamm* and Teacher Lydianne. They'll be really glad to see you, sweetie."

His exhaustion forgotten, Jeremiah carefully positioned Ella against his shoulder and mounted Mitch for the ride into town. He wanted to laugh and cry and sing and pray all at once—but he focused on the road to be sure he delivered his precious armload safely to the schoolhouse. As his Percheron clip-clopped along the shoulder of the county highway, staying safely away from the cars, Ella watched their surroundings pass by from over his shoulder.

Jeremiah allowed himself the sheer joy of feeling a child in his arms. She was probably snuggling against him to stay warm in the chill of the dawn, but for a few moments he pretended Ella was his own dear child—because she did resemble his Priscilla. As he turned into the lane leading to the schoolhouse, the autumn sun broke away from the horizon to rise in the sky like a golden beacon behind the simple white building.

"Lydianne! Julia!" he called out as he approached. "Look who's here!"

When the two women burst through the doorway, little Ella sprang to life. Before he could even stop his horse, she was extending her little arms.

"Mamma! Teacher Lydianne!" she sang out as Jeremiah carefully handed her down to her mother.

Julia rocked her daughter gratefully in her arms for several long seconds, murmuring endearments—until Ella reached for Lydianne. As the girl wrapped her arms around her teacher's neck, Lydianne burst into tears and clutched her close.

"I—we—were so scared when we couldn't find you, Ella!" she rasped. "It's so *gut* to have you back safe and sound."

Jeremiah's heart turned a happy, lopsided somersault and his whole body felt shimmery. Years from now, he knew he'd recall this deeply touching scene as the moment he fell in head-over-heels, no-going-back love with Lydianne Christner.

Then he blinked. Lydianne's exhausted outpouring was understandable, yet as she continued to embrace Ella, her emotional investment in this child's welfare struck him as far more than the usual teacher-student relationship.

He sucked in air when he saw Lydianne and Ella nose-to-nose. He told himself his eyes and mind were tired after searching all night, yet he couldn't miss the startling resemblance . . . the jawlines, the rosy complexions, the tilt of two noses that were identical except for their size.

"Ella, whatever possessed you to take off during recess?" Julia's crossed arms and no-nonsense tone broke through Jeremiah's musings. "We've talked about this, *jah*?"

Ella had the presence of mind to compose her answer rather than just blurting it out. "We went outside for recess after it stopped rainin'," she recalled, "and there was a big, beautiful rainbow in the sky—just like in our story about Noah's ark!"

Lydianne nipped her lip, nodding as she waited for the rest of Ella's explanation.

The little girl looked up at the sunlit sky, a sense of wonder lighting her face. "I thought if I followed the rainbow to wherever it touched down, I'd find the ark! Or maybe even *see God*!" she added in a reverent whisper. "So, I kept on goin'."

Jeremiah's breath caught. How could anyone be upset with a little angel who'd embarked upon her journey with such sincere, childlike faith?

"Oh, Ella," Lydianne murmured, pressing her forehead against the little girl's. "You do love that story, don't you? We've talked about it so many times, it's become real to you, *jah*?"

"But it *is* real," Ella insisted solemnly. "God really did make it rain forty days and forty nights, and He really did make the rainbow for Noah when it was safe to come out of the ark with all the animals. The Bible says so."

"You're absolutely right," Jeremiah said as he stroked the little girl's loose hair back from her face. "I bet your *mamm*'s ready to take you home now, because it's been a long night. But before you go . . . did you see God, Ella?"

Her face lit up. "I sorta did! He told me if I got up on that rock, I wouldn't be lost anymore, coz somebody would come and find me. When I turned around to look for Him, though, He was gone."

"Oh, He stayed right there with you, child," Julia reaffirmed as she held out her hand. When Lydianne set Ella down and the girl had clasped her mother's fingers, Julia gazed purposefully at Jeremiah. "Didn't I tell you about that *in* you had with God, Bishop? *Denki* so much for listening to my suggestion, and for following as the Lord led you to my little girl."

As Jeremiah watched the two Nissleys get into their buggy, he was filled with awe. It was one thing to study the Scriptures and preach what God put into his head on a Sunday morning, but it was another blessing entirely when one of his flock put God's promises into everyday action—and then thanked him for it.

"I'd better let our searchers know our lost lamb is back in the fold," he said as Julia drove toward the road.

Lydianne nodded. "I'll gather up the carafes and cups so I can drop them back at The Marketplace on my way out. And I'll leave Jo a note about why I won't be working today—even though we're hosting a special Mums and Pumpkins Auction."

Jeremiah nodded. He observed the relief in Lydianne's expression, the return of the spring in her step as she entered the schoolhouse.

Tugging on the rope and hearing the loud, clamorous clanging of the cast iron bell in the schoolyard relieved the tension he'd been holding in his shoulders, but the racket didn't drown out the questions that were buzzing like bees in his mind. It probably wasn't the right time to bring it up, but he wouldn't sleep until he'd put his suspicion to rest.

When he entered the schoolroom, Lydianne was stacking mugs on a tray, tidying her back table. Even in her exhaustion she was beautiful, reminiscent of a Madonna in one of those ancient religious paintings he'd seen in magazines.

But appearances could be deceiving. And the right question could reveal quite a lot about why Lydianne Christner remained so emotionally distant, insisting that she couldn't get involved with a man.

Jeremiah placed his hand on her shoulder, waiting until she looked at him. "This is probably way out of line—and if it is, please forgive me," he began in a voice tight with concern. There was nothing else to do but ask the question that seemed so obvious as he gazed at the face that was the spitting image of Ella Nissley's. "Lydianne, are—are you Ella's mother? Is she the reason you came to Morning Star—the reason you keep your heart locked away?"

Lydianne's mouth dropped open. The color rushed from her face as she exhaled so forcefully that Jeremiah grabbed her shoulders in case she fell over. When she tried to talk, nothing came out—

And that was all the answer he needed, wasn't it?

The sound of male voices outside brought Jeremiah back to the present moment. "I'll go tell the men Ella's back," he murmured. "Let's you and I go home and rest, as well. And then, as your bishop, I hope you'll talk to me about this matter, Lydianne. Is it all right if I stop by this evening?"

She looked ready to shake her head and bolt away from him. Then, however, her shoulders sagged. She nodded, her eyes closed against the tears that were dribbling down her cheeks. "I—I guess that's the way it needs to be," she whispered.

Chapter Eighteen

When Lydianne got home that morning, she collapsed on her bed and stared up at the ceiling. Exhausted as she was after her all-night vigil, she knew she'd get no rest as she awaited Jeremiah's visit—and his condemnation. Her body felt like a shoelace that was knotted so tightly no one could ever untie it.

Her secret was out. She'd never felt so frightened in her life.

Even after Aden had died and she'd learned she was carrying his child, Lydianne had felt a sense of hope buried deep within her soul. She'd had to run away from her judgmental family and everything she'd held dear in her former life to escape the shame of bearing a child out of wedlock, yet she'd believed she could create a new future for herself. And she had, here in Morning Star.

Now, however, fear filled her soul. She saw only humiliation in her future. She would surely be shunned and lose her job. Then she would have to give up her home, as well, because she couldn't afford the payments. Why would anyone in the Morning Star church district—especially Bishop Jeremiah and the preachers—ever trust her with their children again? And it was a sure bet that Martin Flaud wouldn't rehire her at the furniture factory when he learned about the lies she'd told—or at least about the truth she hadn't revealed when she'd interviewed for the teaching position.

She could already imagine the scornful reproach Deacon Saul would deliver . . . the disdain on Martha Maude's face when she learned of Lydianne's sin . . . the harsh Old Testament judgment Preachers Clarence and Ammon would bring down upon her as she confessed before a shocked congregation. Just weeks ago, her best friend, Regina, had been shunned. Lydianne recalled the way folks had turned their heads and refused to accept anything directly from Regina's hand, because that was standard—if harsh—procedure for an Old Order shunning.

Her integrity was shot. Not even her *maidel* friends would forgive her.

Glenn will probably be relieved that I shut him down before he got too involved with me. And Jeremiah will feel so . . .

Lydianne began to cry again when she thought about facing the kind, gentle bishop who'd given her every benefit of the doubt. Jeremiah's disappointment would slice her like a knife. He surely felt betrayed now that he'd figured out why she'd discouraged his affection—a relationship she would've welcomed, had she been the honorable, virtuous young woman he'd believed her to be.

But my life here is ruined. Why in God's name did I ever think I could come to Morning Star—much less take the teaching position—without my love for Ella giving me away?

With a sob, Lydianne sat bolt upright. Hers was not the only life that would never be the same.

How can I face Julia and Tim? This revelation—my confession—will surely shatter their happy family. They, more than anyone else, won't allow me to return to the schoolroom.

Scared and anxious, Lydianne rose from her bed and walked from room to room in the home that might not be hers for much longer. Where could she go? How could she start over, when she had a house to sell and so many other loose ends to tie up? Depending upon how insistent the preachers were about getting her out of their schoolhouse and out of their town, she might have to leave Morning Star on very short notice—and then she'd face the daunting task of relocating as winter closed in. She would have to start over yet again, in a place where no one knew her.

And she would have to leave Ella behind forever.

As the walls threatened to close in on her, Lydianne stepped outside to take a long, mind-clearing walk—

But Bishop Jeremiah was driving up her lane. She couldn't escape her terrifying thoughts, nor could she pretend she hadn't seen him. Lydianne clung to a porch post, feeling so lost and guilty, she couldn't look at him as he got out of his rig and approached her.

"Came earlier than I'd figured," he said with an apologetic sigh. "I suspected you weren't any more able to sleep than I was. Shall we talk this through, Lydianne?"

She nipped her lip. His empathy was so much harder to take than the stern reprimand she'd been expecting—and deserved. This discussion would be a lot easier if he was older, a father figure rather than a potential husband. Nodding forlornly, Lydianne turned and preceded him to the door.

Basic manners demanded that she offer him coffee and

cookies, but this was hardly a social call. Lydianne chose to sit in the armchair, thinking to keep a safe distance between them because he would sit on the couch—but Jeremiah pulled the rocking chair over and positioned himself right in front of her. He studied her with his deep brown eyes for a few moments before he spoke.

"Do you want to tell me about this situation, Lydianne? Or shall I ask you questions?"

She closed her eyes. "I don't know what to say—where to begin."

Jeremiah cleared his throat, seeming nearly as nervous as she was. "Was I right, that you're Ella's birth mother?"

Lydianne nodded. Her love for her misbegotten daughter was so intense that an acute panic grabbed hold of her heart, rendering her speechless. The bishop would surely pounce on her now, bringing his condemnation down upon her—and rightfully so.

Instead, he gently raised her chin with his finger. "Look at me, Lydianne," he whispered. "I can't stand to see you caught up in so much pain."

When her eyes flew open, she realized that Jeremiah had showered and changed into clean clothes. His face was a deep, healthy tan from working outside, and freshly shaven above his trimmed beard. He smelled like a man she wanted to cling to forever, but there would never come a time when she could bury her face in his chest as he held her close.

Startled by such thoughts, Lydianne became instantly aware that her hair was mussed beneath her *kapp*, which had become skewed while she'd been lying down—and she was still wearing the clothes she'd put on before school on Friday morning, more than twenty-four hours ago. Her face was damp from her most recent crying fit, and her eyes felt sore from worry and staying awake for too many endless hours.

"Was Ella the reason you came to Morning Star?" Jeremiah continued softly. "Until recently, it didn't occur to me that I knew next to nothing about your family, except that you've lost your parents and your siblings are scattered—and the man you were betrothed to drowned the day before you were to marry him. It's no wonder you wanted to be near your child, Lydianne. She's all you have."

A sob escaped her, and she buried her face in her hands. How could the bishop be so gentle, so understanding, after he'd pieced together her incriminating story from the few details she'd given at her interview?

"Tell me about the man you loved, Lydianne. Take your time."

As he pressed a clean, blue bandanna into her hand, she became even more flummoxed. This talk—this confession of her deepest sin—wasn't going at all as she'd imagined it. Jeremiah was being so compassionate. The least she could do was answer his questions. He, more than anyone else, deserved the story she'd held back from even her closest friends.

"Aden was everything I'd always wanted," she began, and the floodgates of her heart opened before she could take control of them. The years slipped away, and as Lydianne recalled everything about that fateful day, her heart-wrenching memories spoke for themselves.

"We were so in love, ready to begin our life together," she whispered as she blotted her face. "We thought a few weeks wouldn't make any difference. I suspected I was carrying his child when we slipped away for an early picnic by the pond in the park the day before our wedding, but I never got a chance to tell him. Aden was feeling so happy about getting married, he jumped in to swim across the pond and back.

"But he didn't make it," Lydianne continued in a faltering voice. "From the look on his face as he went under, he must've gotten a bad cramp. When he didn't come back up, I ran for help. But it was too late."

"Oh my," Jeremiah breathed. "What an awful way to— I'm so sorry, Lydianne."

She stared at him in disbelief. *I might as well get the whole story out before I lose my nerve. Sooner or later, Jeremiah's going to pronounce me guilty and sinful, and I'll be confessing all over again at a Members Meeting after church tomorrow.*

Lydianne exhaled with a shudder. "As time went on, it became obvious that I was expecting. My older sister and brother-in-law confronted me," Lydianne continued dolefully. "They—and Aden's parents—were so upset because I'd shamed them. Before they could set me out—or send me to live with a different sister—I left."

Jeremiah's brow furrowed. "That seems awfully harsh, even in a conservative church district," he murmured. "It's not as though other young couples haven't jumped the gun before their wedding day—"

"But my sister's husband was the deacon in their district. He didn't want to be responsible for a young woman who was obviously loose and immoral," Lydianne put in bitterly. "Aden's *dat* insisted that I'd led his son into temptation, instead of waiting until we were married. So, I did us all a favor and took off."

Jeremiah sat back in his chair and rocked for a few

moments, troubled by what he'd heard. When he was sitting still again, he held her gaze. "Where did you go? How did you get by?"

Lydianne considered her answer carefully. The bishop was showing her such understanding, that she didn't want to offend him. "I'd read about Higher Ground in *The Budget*—about how the bishop who'd founded that settlement had been a renegade with a questionable reputation before he died," she began tentatively. "An article from the scribe in Willow Ridge mentioned that they hadn't even held a drawing of the lot for a new leader in Higher Ground, so I figured I could slip in under the radar there. I needed to find a job in a place where nobody would ask questions or try to send me back to my family."

Jeremiah scowled, shaking his head. "That's exactly why I didn't like my nephew Pete having his apartment there. Any town that claims to be Plain without following the most basic rules for establishing church leadership is on the path to perdition and is *not* Amish," he said tersely.

Lydianne nodded. "*Jah*, I knew that, but it was a place to land when I had nowhere else to go," she explained. "I took a job at the pet food factory and rented a small apartment. The only thing that kept me going was the knowledge that a part of Aden had survived inside me, but I knew I couldn't possibly support a child."

The difficulty of those days came back to Lydianne in a rush, and she had to breathe deeply to settle her emotions. "I—I arranged early on to give my baby up for adoption as soon as he or she was born at the birthing center," she murmured. "The midwife I'd been working with— Carla—was very kind. She told me a wonderful couple from a nearby town was going to take my baby home as soon as it was born."

She paused, recalling every grueling moment of her labor and delivery—not details she cared to share with a man.

"The birthing process was . . . difficult for me. From across the room I—I watched Carla clean the baby up after she was born, telling me she was healthy and perfectly formed. But Carla thought it'd be best if I didn't hold her," she added miserably. "She might as well have cut my heart out with a dull knife when she walked out of that birthing room with my little girl."

Jeremiah sucked in his breath and looked away, as though her words had caused him great pain. "And how did you find your precious child, Lydianne?" he whispered a few moments later.

She blinked, still amazed at the way the bishop was following her story without showing any sign of condemnation. "The aides at the birthing clinic encouraged me to get up and walk around as soon as possible after the delivery. As luck, or a careless employee—or maybe God Himself—would have it, I caught sight of the adoption papers on the front counter," she replied softly. "I saw the couple's name and their Morning Star address—"

"And information like that burns itself into your brain," Jeremiah remarked with a sympathetic smile.

Lydianne nodded, blotting her eyes with his blue bandanna. "After I was able to return to my job, I *knew* that passing through Morning Star and just *happening* to locate the Nissleys' place was a really bad idea," she said with a rueful chuckle.

"But you couldn't stay away."

"I convinced myself that it was no coincidence when I spotted a help-wanted notice on the bulk store's corkboard, for a finishing job at Martin Flaud's furniture factory," she continued. "And when I found this house that was renting for an affordable amount, it was all the more reason to believe that God was leading me to live here, near my child."

Lydianne watched Bishop Jeremiah's face to gauge his reaction to her tale—especially the part about believing God had led her to Morning Star despite the trouble it had gotten her into—the very reason she was confessing to him now. His dark eyes and handsome face registered no sign that he thought she'd been listening to her own wayward inner voice rather than to God, so she continued.

"It was even more of a bonus when I met Regina and Jo and the Helfing twins at church the first Sunday I attended," she recalled with a smile. "I knew it was all right to be a *maidel* in this district. And I fit right in from the very first."

"*Jah*, you gals have been fine friends from the get-go," Jeremiah agreed. "And look what you've accomplished together, starting up The Marketplace. I think your friends were as surprised as I was when you blurted out that you wanted to apply for the teaching position—but no one can deny that God was at work amongst us that day, and that you've been a blessing to our kids ever since, Lydianne."

His statement, although spoken with utmost sincerity, made it difficult for Lydianne to swallow the painful lump forming in her throat. Their calm conversation had lulled her into a momentary sense of security, but there was no getting around it. She was about to forfeit the wonderful life she'd made for herself in this town and this church district.

"I suppose I have to do a kneeling confession at church tomorrow, now that my sin has come out," she whispered hoarsely. "I've deceived everyone, Bishop. Surely the parents here won't want an unwed mother teaching their children anymore—especially because it was my negligence that allowed Ella to slip away unnoticed."

Jeremiah stood up and walked to the window. The longer he gazed outside, silent, the more Lydianne's fears jangled her nerves. She couldn't move. The house got absolutely quiet, except for the steady ticking of the battery wall clock that surely measured out her shameful fate with each endless passing minute. She sat there like a shamed scholar who'd been scolded by the teacher, staring at the pale, clasped hands in her lap without seeing them.

"I need to pray on this," the bishop finally said. "And I need to sleep on it, so I'll have a clear idea about how to proceed. I'll see you at church tomorrow, Lydianne."

Before she could demand that Jeremiah clarify his thoughts about whether she'd be confessing before the congregation the next morning, he was gone.

Chapter Nineteen

As a busy Saturday morning at The Marketplace got underway, Jo kept baking so she'd have enough goodies in her glass cases when the special Mums and Pumpkins Auction was over. Most of the men around town—even Michael and Nelson Wengerd—had responded to the tolling of the emergency bell the previous evening, so Jo and her *mamm* had heard about Ella Nissley's escapade over breakfast. Because they'd advertised this special auction in several places around the county, they were expecting a large crowd for it. Jude Shetler, Glenn, the Wengerds, and the other men involved were running the sale on coffee and adrenaline after a nightlong search that hadn't ended until nearly seven this morning.

Jo had arrived to find the coffee carafes and cups Lydianne had returned, along with her note apologizing for leaving them dirty—and saying she wouldn't be coming in to work. Cleaning up after the search was a small task, however, compared to the ordeal the men and Lydianne had endured. Jo and her helpers, Alice and Adeline, made quick work of washing the dirty cups as they brewed extra coffee to keep the auction workers alert.

She'd also baked an additional pan of cinnamon rolls as her gift to them, for when the sale was over.

As she was spreading the white frosting over the hot rolls, Michael came into the bakery.

"Put my name on one or two of those rolls—unless you've baked them for a customer," he said as he reached into his back pocket.

"Put your wallet away," Jo insisted as she smiled to herself. Even though Michael appeared exhausted, he was still the nicest, cutest young man she knew. "Take what you'd like, and then go spread the word with Jude and the other fellows that they have refreshments waiting for them when they're finished with the auction."

"You're very thoughtful, Jo," he murmured.

She shrugged, not wanting to let on about how wonderful Michael's compliment made her feel. "How's the sale progressing? If you think it's a *gut* time, I could send Alicia and Adeline out with coffee for those men."

"They'd probably rather wait. The auction's going pretty fast—and Dat and I have sold a *lot* of those big jack-o'-lantern pumpkins, as well as all of the mums and tied-up clusters of Indian corn we brought in," Michael replied enthusiastically. "It would've taken us weeks to move that many if we'd only sold them around Queen City. Glad we planted an extra field this year."

As he peeled away the outer layer of the roll she'd placed on a plate for him, Jo watched his long, agile fingers. Everything about Michael Wengerd was thin and elongated. He wasn't muscular in the usual way, yet his wiry frame was extremely strong—she'd reached this conclusion after secretly watching him every chance she got, ever since he and his *dat* had been renting the *dawdi haus* for the weekends. She envied the way he could pack away meals and sweets without gaining any weight.

"Mmmm," he moaned as he chewed his first bite. "These rolls are even better than my *mamm's* were—but don't tell Dat I said that," he added quickly.

Michael's kind words stunned her nearly as much as his blue-gray eyes did when he focused on her.

"*Jah*, it—it's usually best not to correct the way our parents remember their wives or husbands," she stammered. "My father was a fine man, but now that he's gone, my *mamm* has forgotten how she scolded him for tracking mud on her floors or for being late to meals most of the time. These days, she considers him a saint."

Michael's smile, bracketed by dimples, lit up his tired face. "That's the way it goes, *jah*. And, um, what else have you baked today, Jo? Something smells like pumpkin and spices." Once again, he turned shy on her, focusing on her display shelves after she'd dared to hold his gaze for a moment.

"Your nose is right on target," she replied. "With the changing of the season, it seems like a *gut* time to make pumpkin bars and bread, as well as cinnamon bars and ginger snaps. It's my favorite time of the year."

"Mine, too." Michael made quick work of his roll and flashed her a lopsided smile. "Better get back out to the auction, or Dat'll think I'm lollygagging. *Denki* for the roll, Jo. Now that I've had my sugar fix, I'll be able to handle the rest of the sale."

When he'd left the store, Jo returned to her baking with a big smile on her face. She knew better than to dream that her friendship with Michael would ever turn into anything more, but that was all right. He and his father always paid ahead for the Friday nights they stayed in the *dawdi haus*, they helped around the farm with maintenance chores that were difficult for Jo and her *mamm*, and they were so appreciative of the meals she and her mother cooked. Mamm would never admit it, but she was sorry to see them leave on Saturdays after The Marketplace had closed for the day.

"That's an interesting grin on your face, Josephine Fussner."

Jo looked up, her eyes widening when Lydianne entered the bakery. "I wasn't expecting you today. You must be exhausted after the scary night you had while Ella was gone for so long."

"She gave us all a fright, *jah*. Who could've guessed she'd get all the way over to Jeremiah's farm, and that he'd find her sleeping on a big rock by the river?" Lydianne mused aloud.

As Lydianne sank into the nearest chair behind the counter, Jo noticed she hadn't addressed the bishop by his title—and she suspected there were other things her friend wasn't saying, as well. "What was Ella's explanation when he brought her back?"

Lydianne's blue eyes sparkled despite their pink rims and the dark circles beneath them. "Ella saw a rainbow during recess on Friday. She thought if she followed it to the end, she might find Noah's ark—or even see God," she whispered in awe. "I was nearly struck dumb when I heard that. And when Jeremiah asked her if she did see God, Ella said she sort of had, and that He'd told her to wait on that big rock until somebody found her. It—it was an amazing moment, even if we'd all been worried sick about her."

Jo nodded, thinking the thrum of Lydianne's voice still sounded awfully intense several hours after Ella had been found. "You really should go home and get some rest," she suggested gently. "You'll be snoring all through church tomorrow."

"Oh, I doubt *that*."

Emotions Jo couldn't name flickered across Lydianne's face before she spoke again.

"I thought I'd stay until the auction's over, to gather up the receipts so I can do the accounting," she said. "If I work at home, maybe that bookkeeping will lull me to sleep, because otherwise I'll be keyed up for a while. I— I feel so horrible that Ella slipped away while I wasn't paying attention."

Was she hearing more than Lydianne was willing to say? Jo didn't feel right pressing for an explanation when her friend appeared exhausted enough to lay her head on the worktable for a nap. She put a frosted cinnamon roll on a small plate and slid it across the table. "Here. Sugar and cinnamon make everything better, ain't so?"

Lydianne smiled gratefully before snatching up her treat. "You've got that right, Jo. What would I do without friends like you?"

As Jeremiah climbed the stairs with the two preachers and Deacon Saul before the Sunday service at the Wagler home, exhaustion and anxiety nipped at him like aggressive, circling dogs. He'd prayed through the night, because every time he stopped, Lydianne's story—her plaintive voice—filled his mind. He'd considered courses of action appropriate to the Old Order faith, yet none of them stood out as *right*. He wanted to know God's opinion and hear His direction before he discussed Lydianne's situation with the preachers and Saul, but it seemed the Lord wasn't going to whisper in his ear or show Jeremiah the sign he so desperately needed.

"Jeremiah, are you with us?"

"*Jah*—Earth calling Jeremiah!"

He blinked. Clarence, Ammon, and Saul were all focused on him as though one of them had asked a question and he'd been too deep into his woolgathering about Lydianne to realize it. "Sorry. Long night."

Ammon's eyebrows rose. "Surely you slept better last night, knowing Ella was home safe and sound," he remarked. His statement sounded like an unspoken question, an invitation to talk about whatever was bothering him before they went downstairs to worship in the Waglers' front room.

Voices drifted up through the heat grate in the floor. The congregation was singing the morning's first hymn, slowly and methodically, as though nothing unusual had transpired. Jeremiah, however, felt as though the world was tipping on its axis like a seesaw—first in one direction, and then in another. Each disciplinary option he'd been considering seemed favorable at first, and then it felt totally wrong to him. He couldn't bring himself to mention Lydianne's revelation as the four of them discussed the Scripture passages listed in the lectionary.

"It was indeed a blessing to spot Ella on that rock by the river," he remarked as they all rose from their chairs to go downstairs. "We have a great deal to be thankful for."

"So, I'll preach first, and Ammon will take the main sermon?" Clarence clarified.

"*Jah*, that's what we decided," Jeremiah replied, although he didn't actually recall their making that decision—and that startled him. He prayed again that God would guide him during the church service, and that by the time he pronounced the benediction, he would know what to do. Lydianne deserved a clear answer, and she hadn't backed away from making the confession the *Ordnung* called for.

When he'd opened the service and taken his seat on the preachers' bench for the first sermon, however, Lydianne's pale, downcast face tore at his heart. A row ahead of her on the women's side, Julia sat with her arm around little Ella, who leaned against her quietly with a faceless doll in her lap. Mother and daughter were the picture of a tranquility that transcended blood ties and had been crafted by the Creator Himself. On the men's side, Tim sat peering between the heads in front of him, gazing at his wife and child.

Jeremiah clasped his hands hard, trying to get a grip on the situation. Did he have the right to rip apart the Nissley family's deep, sweet relationship with their six-year-old adopted daughter? That's what would happen if Lydianne made her confession. If he asked her to kneel before the congregation and spill out the tale of her sin, her story would overturn the well-being of the entire church district—not to mention the way it would disrupt the education of the eight scholars who adored their teacher.

As the bishop, it was his duty to see that souls in need of confession spoke out—cleared their hearts of secret burdens that came between them and a full, honest devotion to God.

But wasn't it also his calling to ensure the emotional security of the souls and families God had entrusted to him?

The horns of his dilemma prodded him all through the three-hour service. Jeremiah was aware that they'd been singing hymns and that the longer, second sermon had been delivered. He'd led the congregation in prayer, but he wasn't sure what he'd said—and he hoped his words had been appropriate and coherent. When he stood up to pronounce the benediction, he still had no clear notion of what God wanted him to do about Lydianne's situation.

When he observed the heaviness of her tormented expression as she sat with her head bowed, however, he couldn't bring himself to throw her to the wolves. He saw no point in announcing Ella's safe return, because everyone had heard her story. The women had been expressing their relief to Julia in Rose Wagler's kitchen before the service had started.

So, Jeremiah came to the end of his usual benediction and stopped, putting a smile on his face despite his inner upheaval. As folks rose from the benches, ready to set out the meal, he knew he'd left Lydianne hanging. She felt no more relief than he did, because she was still emotionally pregnant with the confession she hadn't delivered.

But it was the best he could do. He needed to speak with her again, but not while they were surrounded by their entire congregation.

"Lydianne, are you all right?" Jo murmured as they shuffled between the pew benches toward the center aisle.

"*Jah*, I thought you'd be ecstatic that the bishop found little Ella," Marietta put in gently, "but you look like you haven't slept a wink all weekend."

Lydianne tried to compose her expression, because her observant *maidel* friends wouldn't leave her alone until they'd pried the truth from her. But if the bishop hadn't called a Members Meeting so she could make her confession, he must've had a very good reason—and she wanted to hear it before she revealed her situation with a slip of her tongue.

"I haven't slept," she confirmed wearily. "It still bothers me that Ella wandered away from the schoolyard while I was taking a nap. I should've been out on the playground, paying attention."

Regina slipped her arm around Lydianne's shoulders. "In your place, I'd feel bad about that, too," she murmured. "But it all turned out fine, so you need to let go of that guilt, sweetie. From what I saw when Julia was talking to you before church, she feels no ill will—"

"*Jah*, she's been telling everyone that Ella has taken to running off at home, too," Molly remarked, "so I'd accept the fact that everybody gets caught napping once in a while, so to speak. You're human like the rest of us, Lydianne."

Jah, that's wise advice, but if you had an inkling of the truth about my connection to Ella, you'd be appalled.

To further compound Lydianne's guilt, she was worried about letting her friends down if she stopped working at The Marketplace on Saturdays. Because she wasn't running a shop, she was the perfect person to keep the accounts or to fill in for shopkeepers who couldn't come in on any given day—and Regina's absence was already making a difference in the workload the four of them shared to keep The Marketplace running smoothly. With Jo baking and maintaining the refreshment area, and the Helfings being much better at noodle making than numbers, Lydianne believed the bookkeeping would suffer if she left.

And that would attract the attention of Deacon Saul. The *maidels* were delighted about creating and managing such a profitable enterprise, so it would be a shame for Saul to take over the finances.

Lydianne quickly put on a tired smile when she realized she hadn't responded to Molly's statement. "I am human," she mumbled. "And you're right—even teachers make mistakes, and they need to move on. Ella's home, and that's what counts."

Could that belief sustain her while she and Bishop Jeremiah discussed her options? She suspected she wouldn't be home from church for very long that afternoon before he paid her another visit.

Chapter Twenty

Early that evening, Jeremiah stepped onto Lydianne's front porch, determined to settle the matter of her sin and her confession of it. Before he could knock, she opened the door and gestured for him to come in. As always, her punctuality and prettiness charmed him—and she had coffee and cookies waiting for him on the kitchen table, as though she'd been expecting him, watching for him. It would be so easy to make Lydianne a permanent part of his life—she always seemed to do the right things at the right time.

But this is not the right time to consider anything resembling a lifelong relationship.

Jeremiah seated himself on one side of her small, rectangular table rather than assuming the position a husband would occupy. When she sat down across from him, however, he realized it would be even harder to hold their discussion face to face, because he couldn't avoid looking into her big blue eyes.

Those eyes held a lot of questions as Lydianne folded her hands on the table in an attitude of prayer and submission. "What have you decided?" she asked before he could begin their conversation. "I was ready to confess after church—"

"And I admire your willingness to follow the *Ordnung*, Lydianne," Jeremiah put in quickly. "Most folks have to be convinced to admit their wrongdoing, and some almost have to be dragged kicking and screaming into the ritual of confession. But every time I looked at Julia sitting there with Ella today, while Tim gazed at them from across the room, I realized how badly their world would be shattered if I asked you to break your news in a public setting."

Lydianne sighed. "*Jah*, there's that."

"Not to mention the disruption to the education of those eight scholars who believe you hung the moon, and who love to learn because you're their teacher," he added. "As I've pondered our options, I see three."

Her expressive eyebrows rose. "Bishop, I'm grateful for your open-minded attitude," she said in a low voice. "In the district I came from, there would've only been one option—baring my soul on my knees and accepting my punishment, no matter the consequences for anyone else."

Lydianne glanced away with a pensive sigh. "I'm guessing the first option is the standard confession I just mentioned? Most likely followed by a six-week *bann*— and then a lifetime of knowing I'd caused a great deal of strife for the Nissley family."

Jeremiah nodded. "The second idea is a bit more complicated. I could find a replacement teacher and remove you from your teaching duties without making your situation public—because you have confessed to me, and as the bishop, I can choose to keep your confession confidential."

Jeremiah rested his elbows on the table, leaning toward her as he watched the play of expressions on her lovely face. "If this is the route we go, you'd need to leave Morning Star as soon as I find another teacher—and I would have a *lot* of questions to answer. But I would do that for you, Lydianne. Rather than living alone again, I would strongly encourage you to reunite with the family you left behind after Aden's funeral. Have you had any contact with them?"

Lydianne's head jerked as she stared at him. "No," she replied with a vehemence that widened his eyes. "They made their condemnation very clear, and I can't think their attitude about me will have changed in the years since I went away. Even if my sisters might be curious about my whereabouts, they'd go along with their husbands' insistence that I shamed them by leading Aden into temptation."

Jeremiah frowned. "Where's the forgiveness in that?"

"If you'd like to ask them that question, go right ahead," Lydianne blurted without missing a beat. "But even after all this time has passed, I don't believe my brothers-in-law—especially Deacon Ralph—will feel inclined to welcome me back. Most likely, they were grateful that I ran off without telling them where I went."

The small kitchen felt charged with negative energy. Clearly, Lydianne would rather subject herself to the punishment of the Morning Star church district than return to a place where she'd never felt particularly welcome after her parents had passed. Being a *maidel* and a wage earner and a homeowner suited her better than living under a judgmental brother-in-law's roof. Even though her previous district's attitude went against the Old Order's tenets about supporting unmarried female family members, nothing he could say would make Lydianne's family take her back on better emotional terms.

"So now that I've refused to go along with your second

option, Jeremiah—at least if my family's involved—what's the third one?"

He blinked. Her question brought Jeremiah out of his musings. "What if you and I get married, Lydianne?" he blurted. "Your secret would be safe with me, and the Nissleys would never have to know—"

"Get *married*?"

Jeremiah searched her sweet face, heartened by a momentary softening of her beautiful blue eyes even as her tone expressed dismay.

"That's the worst reason I've ever heard of—" With an exasperated sigh, Lydianne rose from her chair. "You've put me between a rock and a hard place, Jeremiah. If I don't marry you, will you force me to go back to my family to preserve the Nissleys' happy life? If I do become your wife, you'll be holding my secret over my head every day—"

"I would never do that!" Jeremiah sprang from his seat, distressed by the direction their talk had taken. "I didn't phrase my idea properly, and I didn't intend to put you in such a spot, Lydianne. I'm sorry!" he insisted. "I can't stop thinking about you, and I believe you and I could make a fine life together. Even before you admitted you were Ella's mother, I had feelings for you. I—I love you so much more than I ever thought possible after I lost Priscilla."

He sensed he was only digging himself into a deeper pit, but he couldn't give up. As Jeremiah reached across the table to grasp Lydianne's hands, he prayed for the words that would make her see him for the man he yearned to be in her eyes.

"Your past is behind you, sweetheart, and I wouldn't dream of holding it against you," he said in a hoarse whisper. "*Please* give me a chance to win your heart—to prove I'm not the sort of man who'd try to manipulate you because you had a child out of wedlock. That doesn't matter to me."

"But it matters to me, Jeremiah," she stated, easing her hands out of his. "It feels *wrong* to marry you as a cover-up. I can't do that."

Once again, her outright rejection made his heart shrivel, made his eyes burn—even if she'd made a valid point. It had been one thing to refuse his invitation to the family reunion, but Lydianne had just slammed a much bigger, more important door in his face. He knew better than to keep begging, however.

"Well then, we'll have to keep talking until we've reached a satisfactory solution," Jeremiah somehow managed to say. He felt as though Mitch had kicked him square in the chest, knocking the breath and the fortitude out of him.

There was no point in lingering, so he took his leave.

As a man, he needed to lick his wounds and recover his dignity. But as a bishop, he had to resolve this conflict in a way that upheld the Old Order and allowed all the involved parties to become right with God again.

It was a tall order. And for the first time since the bishop's lot had fallen to him several years ago, Jeremiah doubted that he was the right man with the right words to do the right thing.

As Lydianne watched Jeremiah's rig roll down her lane toward the road, she regretted the way she'd shut him down. How many times had she dreamed of marrying the handsome bishop, sorry that her secret sin would prevent such a relationship?

But he knows about Ella and he still wants to marry me!

He said he couldn't stop thinking about me—and that he loves me! It would be the answer to all my problems—if my pride didn't get in the way.

She'd dismissed Jeremiah's proposal without a moment's thought, however. She'd been so upset about his suggestion that she reunite with her family, she'd blurted *no* before his marriage suggestion had even reached her heart.

Worse than that, I hurt his feelings. Sure, Jeremiah didn't make the romantic, perfectly worded proposal I've dreamed of, but he was sincere and genuine. I know what a wonderful, loving husband he would be, yet I slapped him down even after he'd forgiven the sin I've been hiding since before I came here.

Lydianne sighed sadly. They were no closer to a solution about how to handle her confession, either. Now it was Jeremiah who was between a rock and a hard place, because she'd so thoughtlessly put him there.

The next day at school she had to behave as though everything was normal—because as far as her eight scholars were concerned, Ella was back at her desk and all was well. Lydianne, however, had never felt so unprepared. She'd spent her weekend whirling in an emotional tornado rather than planning lessons, so she moved ahead in each of her student's textbooks, introducing the new spelling lists and vocabulary words for the week. She was grateful for a sunny October day, because recess could be outside, which would give her students the chance to work off steam between their study sessions.

All during the day, whenever the scholars worked quietly at their desks, Lydianne gazed at Ella over the top of the textbooks she was pretending to study. Her little daughter glowed with the radiance of discovery as she turned the pages of a new library book. Ella spoke out confidently when they reviewed addition and subtraction facts. After she chose crayons for a coloring sheet that featured an autumn arrangement of pumpkins, gourds, and mums, her smile reflected the joy she felt as she neatly completed her picture.

And how will Ella feel if she learns I'm her mother? Think of how confusing that will be for a six-year-old— and think of the wedge it might drive between her and Julia. If Ella became so obsessed over a rainbow in a Bible story, what might she fixate on as she tries to figure out the implications of being born to a mamm *who has no husband to be her* dat—*a woman who gave her up?*

At long last, the school day ended. Lydianne stood on the front stoop of the schoolhouse, waving as Billy Jay drove Stevie and Ella home in his pony cart. She smiled as the Flauds and Gracie left, followed closely by the Miller sisters. Relief washed over her as she sank onto her desk chair for a few moments of quiet contemplation. She wasn't surprised when Jeremiah stepped through the schoolhouse door about ten minutes later.

"How was your day?" he asked as he carried a chair from the back and placed it beside her desk. As he removed his black straw hat, he looked as unsettled as she felt.

"We made it through. The kids are fine," Lydianne replied with a wan smile. "I was so busy flying by the seat of my pants to keep their lessons going, I didn't have much chance to worry about our dilemma. But I've come to some conclusions."

"Like what?" Jeremiah settled himself on the wooden chair, focused on her.

Lydianne shook her head. "I never should've taken this

teaching position," she replied ruefully. "It's not a *gut* idea for a parent to teach her child in the classroom, and now I've created a very difficult situation for everyone— all because I selfishly thought I could keep my secret. I've put you in a tough spot, as well, Jeremiah, and I'm sorry for the way I spoke to you yesterday."

His dark eyes widened. "Care to clarify that? We, um, talked about a lot of big issues."

Lydianne closed her eyes, praying she wouldn't torment this generous, forgiving man more than she already had. "You were offering me options, and I threw them all back in your face because I still feel bitter about the way my sisters and their husbands treated me," she murmured. "I need to forgive them every bit as much as they should for- give me—not that I gave them that chance when I took off."

The bishop's smile looked tired, but at least he was nod- ding. "I'm glad you can see that angle now, Lydianne."

"And today, as I watched the joy Ella felt in her school- work, I knew how confused—how upset—she'd probably be if she found out that Teacher Lydianne is her mother, especially because I gave her up," she continued with a sigh. "If I'd just had the sense to keep my job at the furni- ture factory—"

"The parents of our district don't see it that way," he interrupted firmly. "If they learned the truth, and you went through the proper steps of confession to gain their forgiveness, I believe they'd still be pleased with the way you're educating their kids."

"But it's Ella I'm worried about! She's my child, but I forfeited the right to—"

"You came here to watch her grow up," Jeremiah put in earnestly. He reached for her hands, gently clasping them as he leaned closer. "That's what convinced me you were the woman I wanted to spend my life with, Lydianne. When I saw you holding her close and crying, after I found her on—"

A noise made them look toward the doorway, and Lydianne's mouth dropped open. Ella was standing just inside the schoolroom. She was wide-eyed, holding a colorful bouquet of zinnias as she gaped at them.

How long had she been there? How much of their conversation had she overheard? Lydianne had been so engrossed in talking to Jeremiah, that she'd lost all track of what might be going on around them.

"Ella! What a nice surprise," Lydianne said as she hurried toward the little blonde. "Does your mother know you've come back to school?"

"*Jah*, she helped me pick these flowers in our yard. She's waitin' out in the buggy," Ella replied quickly. "They're a present for *you*, Teacher Lydianne. I'm sorry I left the playground the other day—"

"I know you are, sweetie," Lydianne replied earnestly. It was a blessing to watch her young daughter own up to a mistake and apologize for it. "These are *beautiful*! *Denki* so much for thinking of me, Ella. I'll put them in a vase on my desk right now."

Casting a curious glance at Jeremiah, the little blonde thrust the flowers at Lydianne and darted out the door. Lydianne stepped outside to wave at Julia, who sat in her rig a short distance from the building. "These are lovely! *Denki*, Julia!" she called out.

Julia waved before helping Ella into the rig. Then they were off.

Lydianne was relieved that Julia had shown no inclination to visit. As she found a glass canning jar in the cupboard by the sink, however, her thoughts took off much faster than the Nissleys' horse had. "Do you suppose Ella heard what we were talking about?" she asked over her shoulder.

"I don't know," Jeremiah replied. "If she did, I'm guessing word will get out pretty fast. If we're lucky, Ella will be more interested in the fact that I was here talking to you, holding your hands, than about the circumstances of her birth."

As she ran water into the jar and placed the pretty zinnias in it, Lydianne wondered if Jeremiah intended to further pursue the topic she'd purposely been avoiding before Ella had interrupted them. The little girl's untimely appearance had apparently jarred all thoughts of his proposal from his mind, however.

"We'll see where this leads, Lydianne." Jeremiah stood up and put on his hat. "If Ella was listening for very long, there's no telling what spin she'll put on this story."

Chapter Twenty-One

On the very next day, Jeremiah ran into Julia and Tim Nissley in front of the Dutch bulk store. As they wheeled their shopping cart toward their rig at the hitching rail, Tim gestured for the bishop to follow them. Jeremiah sighed inwardly as they recounted Ella's latest tale, shaking their heads.

"Where on earth would she get the idea that Teacher Lydianne is her mother?" Julia asked him softly. "That's all she could talk about when she came from the school-house yesterday afternoon."

"We've not yet told Ella she's adopted, because we believe she's too young to handle that information," Tim put in earnestly. "Most of all, we need to squelch this rumor before the grapevine gets wind of it and folks start to quiz Lydianne, or doubt her reputation."

Jeremiah racked his brain for a response—a way to handle the hot-potato situation that had just landed in his lap. Only about an hour remained of the school day, and it seemed prudent to take the direct approach. "Can you folks possibly meet me at the schoolhouse when classes let out for the day?" he asked. "It would be best if Ella could go somewhere else—maybe to Gracie's house—while we talk about this matter."

The Nissley's exchanged a puzzled glance.

"*Jah*, she loves to go to Gracie's," Julia remarked, "so we could arrange for Matthias to pick her up from school, or—"

"Are you saying there's some truth to Ella's story?" Tim interrupted in a whisper. "She's at that age where children pretend, and I'm not sure she always knows the difference between what's real and what she wishes would happen."

"*Jah*, we certainly saw her imagination in high gear when she followed that rainbow, hoping to find the ark," Julia pointed out. Her face, usually bright and cheerful, had taken on a few worry lines as she processed the bishop's response.

Jeremiah exhaled slowly, praying he'd do the right thing. "Like you said before, we don't want to confuse Ella before she's old enough to handle the fact that she's adopted. It's also best that we speak with Lydianne, so you'll know the facts firsthand."

His words caused the young couple a moment's hesitation, but they both nodded. "I think we should straighten this out right away," Tim agreed.

"We'll meet you at the school," Julia said with a nod. "Ella will think it's a real treat to go home with Gracie—and we'll go to the Waglers' right now to be sure that'll work for Rose."

"If it won't, we'll ask if Ella can spend some time with Stevie at your brother's place," Tim said.

"That'll be fine. See you there."

Jeremiah entered the bulk store to buy the items on his *mamm*'s shopping list, hoping he'd have a few moments to warn Lydianne that the Nissleys were coming in for a very important talk. As he drove through the white plank gate near The Marketplace, however, he spotted the Nissleys' rig parked at the side of the schoolhouse. Julia stood outside having an animated conversation with her daughter, and when Ella and Gracie's blond heads bobbed excitedly, he knew the girls would be spending time together at the Wagler home. After he waved at Billy Jay, who slowed his pony cart to a more sedate speed when he realized the bishop was watching him, Jeremiah wasted no time pulling up beside the Nissleys' rig.

He felt a pang of regret when he entered the schoolroom. Comprehension dawned on Lydianne's pretty face the moment she saw that the Nissleys were with him. "Do you have time to chat with us?" Jeremiah asked as the three of them approached her desk. "It seems Ella overheard quite a bit yesterday. She's told her parents that you're her mother, and they're understandably . . . curious."

The schoolroom got so quiet that he could hear Lydianne suck in a fortifying breath. "*Jah*, we'd best get to the bottom of this," she murmured, gesturing toward the table where the clay animals and the model of Noah's ark were displayed. "Let's sit in those chairs. *Denki* for coming to help us with this, Bishop."

Jeremiah sensed a deep need for guidance, not just because little Ella's well-being was at stake, but because the woman he'd come to love—an esteemed teacher—had arrived at a very difficult intersection on her life's journey. As they sat down together, he said, "Before we begin, shall we pray about this?"

When they bowed their heads, he carefully composed his thoughts. They were on the brink of an important, life-altering discussion. Jeremiah yearned to use this potentially heartbreaking situation as a conduit for a positive, loving outcome they could all live with—the conclusion that he and Lydianne hadn't reached about her confession.

"Guide us, Lord, as we help Tim and Julia understand the complexities of Lydianne's situation," he prayed in the steadiest voice he could manage. "Help us make decisions that will be best for all of us—far better than if we humans try to muddle through this without You. Amen."

With her eyes squeezed shut, Lydianne listened to Jeremiah's prayer and allowed the deep timbre of his voice to soothe her. They'd come to the moment she'd antici- pated with fear and dread, because so many lives would be changed by the outcome of their discussion. When she looked up, Tim and Julia were watching her closely—and why wouldn't they be curious? Their little girl had come home from school with a story they didn't know how to deal with—the story Lydianne had carefully kept hidden in the innermost sanctum of her vulnerable heart.

Jeremiah's bottomless brown eyes were fixed on her, too, encouraging her and promising his support. She saw no reason to stall or to elaborate on matters that didn't di- rectly affect the Nissleys.

"Ella has it right," she said softly. "I am her birth mother—"

"And this only came out because when Lydianne was holding Ella after we found her on Saturday morning, I noticed the way their facial features matched up," Jeremiah explained earnestly. "When I asked her point-blank about it, Lydianne admitted the details of Ella's birth. She im- mediately offered to make her confession in church—"

"But I never intended for this information to interfere with your family life—your relationship with Ella," Lydianne insisted quickly. Despite her need to remain calm and in control of her emotions, a tear dribbled down each of her cheeks. "Maybe it's best if you ask your questions instead of listening to me babble about details that probably won't matter to you."

Julia's mouth had dropped open, but she seemed unable to voice her thoughts. Tim swallowed repeatedly, making his Adam's apple bulge.

"My word," Ella's adoptive *dat* finally whispered. "Until this minute, I never noticed the resemblance. Ella *does* look like you, Lydianne."

Lydianne let out a nervous laugh. "Funny, but when I look at Ella, I see her father," she murmured wistfully. "He drowned the day before we were to be married and—and that's why I gave her up for adoption. I wanted her to have a *mamm* and a *dat*. I knew I couldn't support her after my family—well, they thought a baby conceived in sin was the ultimate humiliation. So, I left home, and created a new life for myself before Ella was born."

Julia's eyes widened as she leaned closer to clasp Lydianne's wrist. "I—I had no idea!" she rasped. "The social worker who arranged the adoption didn't give us any details except that the baby was to be born nearby, so we'd be able to pick her up as soon as the clinic determined that she was healthy. It was the happiest day of my life—well, almost," she added fondly as she grasped her husband's hand.

Swiping at her eyes, Lydianne silently thanked God that neither parent facing her seemed overly upset about the details they were hearing. They were startled, of course, but she saw no sign of resentment or anger.

"I wasn't supposed to know where my baby went—or who was adopting her—except I caught sight of the adoption papers on the clinic counter," she admitted with a hesitant smile. "When I saw that you lived in Morning Star, opportunities just seemed to open up for me here—like the job at Martin Flaud's factory, and the house I found to rent."

She let out a long, apologetic sigh. "I *knew* better than to tempt myself by coming here, but I just had to watch my little girl grow up. I never intended to interfere—or even reveal who I was. I'm so sorry that this story has caught you by surprise."

"But what a story it is!" Julia said as tears flowed down her cheeks.

"What do we *do* about this situation?" Jeremiah asked. He gazed at each of the Nissleys in turn, allowing them time to consider the consequences of whatever they might decide. "If Lydianne confesses to her unwed pregnancy in church and is then shunned, as the *Ordnung* says she should be, everyone will know she's Ella's mother. I didn't call her to her knees this past Sunday because Lydianne and I both want to do what's best for Ella—and for your family."

Lydianne couldn't miss the way Jeremiah had spoken as though the two of them were on the same page—involved in this situation *together*. But it was no time for romantic fantasies. A young family's future was at stake.

After a few moments' consideration, Tim cleared his throat. "Ella will be devastated if Teacher Lydianne is shunned and suddenly has to stop teaching," he said. "And as a school board member, I can't think of any immediate replacement our district's parents would respect and trust the way they do Lydianne."

Lydianne blinked. Tim's support was more than she'd hoped for, considering the way he'd learned of her situation. Before she could comment, however, he continued in a voice that rose with conviction.

"Glenn's told me repeatedly that Billy Jay is so much happier because Lydianne pays him the attention he needs," Tim stated. "The Waglers—and Julia and I—are delighted that Gracie and Ella are already reading. Even Clarence Miller, who's a hard man to please, says his two teenage daughters want to become teachers because Lydianne has inspired them."

Lydianne's mouth dropped open, even as Jeremiah shot her a look that said *I told you so.*

"And Ella will be so upset if folks aren't supposed to accept things directly from your hand or include you in activities for weeks while you're under the *bann*," Julia put in with a shake of her head. "She won't understand why everyone's being mean to you, shutting you out."

Lydianne nodded, catching the agreement in Jeremiah's eyes.

"She can't wait to come to school each day, to see what you'll teach her next—because she loves you dearly, Lydianne," Julia continued eloquently. "If she couldn't hug you or talk with you—because a *bann* would mean you couldn't be in this classroom interacting with students— Ella might just refuse to come to school! And we can't have that."

Lydianne nodded. She'd thought about those very matters, and the way they might affect a bright, eager six-year-old. Truth be told, it would tear her heart in two if she didn't get to see Ella each day. How would she get through six weeks without hearing her daughter's voice or basking in the sunshine of her dear smile?

"I'm so sorry this has happened, all because I selfishly wanted to be near my child," Lydianne whispered. "I shouldn't have moved to Morning Star, thinking I wouldn't be found out—and I certainly shouldn't have accepted the teaching position—"

"Oh, don't go saying that," Tim interrupted firmly. "Nobody I know would accept that sentiment, and they'd be sorry to see you leave. But, well—I don't see any way around dismissing you, at least for the length of your *bann*."

Lydianne nodded sadly. She had no idea how she'd support herself for six weeks while she awaited the decision of the church district about whether to allow her back in the classroom, either.

Julia glanced away, blinking back tears as she considered another angle to this situation. "I'm delighted that Ella loves you so much as a teacher, Lydianne," she murmured. "But she'll understand this whole adoption situation more completely when she's older. Maybe someday I'll be stronger, too—better able to share her with you because you've given us such a blessing, Lydianne. But right now . . ."

"You're her *mamm*," Lydianne put in softly. "It's a bond that goes beyond blood, and I don't want to confuse Ella, or make her think she has to choose between us—and I don't want her comparing the two of us, either. Having two mothers is too much for a six-year-old to handle, I think."

"I totally agree," Tim put in with a decisive nod. He focused on Jeremiah as he chose his next words. "Under the circumstances, won't God understand if we keep this matter amongst ourselves, Bishop? After all, Lydianne has confessed—and we have nothing to forgive her for. She gave us our little Ella, after all."

Lydianne's heartbeat stilled. Tim's compassionate suggestion made her wipe away more tears. The Nissleys were accepting this situation so much better than she'd anticipated—and it made her even more grateful that God had led the social worker to place her newborn baby in their loving home.

"I'm certainly open to that—because you suggested it yourselves," Jeremiah replied with a nod. "Lydianne has also confessed to me, and she's told me of her concerns— her insistence that this information doesn't become a wedge between you and Ella. But what do we do now that the cat's out of the bag?" he asked. "Ella heard what she heard, and she's already repeating it."

"*Jah*, she's a chatterbox, and she'll be telling everyone that Teacher Lydianne's her *mamm*," Julia confirmed with a sigh. "It won't be long before the other preachers demand answers, and they'll be a lot more likely to insist upon shunning Lydianne—no matter what *we* want."

"We'll start by correcting Ella's story the minute we pick her up from the Waglers' place," Tim said, taking his wife's hand between his.

"And we'll point out that she shouldn't have been eavesdropping on Lydianne and the Bishop's conversation in the first place!" Julia interjected.

"—and that she must stop telling it," Tim continued firmly. "Whenever any of us hears someone suggest that Lydianne is Ella's mother, we need to set them straight right away. We have to have our words ready, so that whoever's speculating about this situation will believe it's just the mistaken story of a six-year-old with a big, wishful imagination."

Jeremiah was nodding. "The fact that you folks, as Ella's parents, are correcting her story will have a much bigger impact than if Lydianne—or I—insisted Ella heard us wrong."

When the bishop focused on Lydianne, she couldn't miss the love that shone in his eyes. "Are you all right with this solution? We all might have to cover these tracks a lot of times—"

"But I think correcting the story—even if it means we're not telling folks the whole truth—is the best thing for Ella right now," Lydianne remarked. "It means I'll have to have my words ready, as you've said. But if all four of us insist that Ella's imagination has run away with her—"

"Again," Julia put in emphatically.

"—I think the questions will eventually stop," Lydianne finished. "Then, one of these days when you're ready, you can talk to Ella about being adopted, and you can choose whether to tell her about me. I promise I'll stay out of it until you want me involved. And I'll understand if you don't."

As the Nissleys nodded in agreement, a wave of relief washed over Lydianne. They didn't want her to be shunned. They didn't want her to stop teaching, or to leave Morning Star. They had praised her ability to teach the scholars, and they believed everyone else in the community felt she was doing a good job, too. Their reaction to her situation was better than she could have hoped or prayed for—better than she deserved.

"*Denki* so much for your understanding," Lydianne murmured as she gazed at Ella's *mamm* and *dat*. "It's a privilege to teach your daughter—and I promise to start thinking of her as *your* daughter. It means so much to be near Ella and to be a part of her life, even if she'll never know who I really am."

Julia nodded, too moved to speak. Tim reached out to shake Jeremiah's hand, and then Lydianne's.

"I'm glad we've reached a conclusion that preserves all we—and Ella—hold dear," he said. "*Denki* for opening your soul to us, Lydianne. We'll fetch Ella now, and immediately correct what she overheard—"

"And we'll insist that she stop telling the story," Julia reiterated. She smiled at Jeremiah. "I feel God's been here amongst us, and that He'll lead us where we need to go over the coming years, Bishop. We're fortunate to have you—and Lydianne—as leaders in our community."

Lydianne rose from her chair to accompany the Nissleys to the door, waving as they drove off in their rig. Jeremiah was standing behind her, close enough that she felt the warmth of his tall, strong body. She felt protected and cherished.

"That went so much better than it might have," she remarked with a short laugh.

"But it's not over," he reminded her gently. "When other folks hear Ella's story and start looking closely, comparing her face to yours, they'll reach the same conclusion I did. Tim sees the resemblance, after all."

"*Jah*, but we should also point out that Ella looks very much like the fair-haired Nissleys, too—to reinforce the belief that they are her parents," Lydianne said. "Because as far as Ella knows, they *are* her birth parents."

When she turned and Jeremiah cupped her jaw in his large, warm hand, Lydianne's heart fluttered.

"You did a brave and loving thing, coming here to be with your child," he whispered. "It's only one of the reasons I love you, Lydianne."

She held her breath, unable to look away from his gaze. For the first time, her heart was willing to accept that such an upstanding, honorable man could find her desirable— and worthy of his love. She no longer feared that he might hold her past over her head to keep her where he wanted her. "*Denki* for standing by me," she murmured shyly.

His handsome face softened as he leaned toward her. "I hope to be standing by you for a long, long time, Sunshine." He brushed her lips with his. "Think about that, will you?"

Chapter Twenty-Two

As Jeremiah walked toward his rig, he kicked himself for kissing Lydianne, probably making her feel pressured after an emotionally draining conversation with the Nissleys. If he wasn't careful—if he didn't show more control—he might also fire up the grapevine. Gossip could force Teacher Lydianne to have to answer even more questions than they anticipated about the story Ella was spreading. The impressionable little girl had caught them alone together, after all.

But Lydianne looked so receptive. She looked grateful for my support. She looked so beautiful even though she's exhausted and—hey, it wasn't nearly the kind of kiss I really wanted to—

"Jeremiah? Wait!"

The way Lydianne called his name made his heart prance like a frisky colt. When he turned, she was on the schoolhouse stoop, shielding her eyes from the rays of the setting sun. Her gaze didn't waver as she looked at him.

"*Jah?*" he asked, sounding painfully hopeful.

When Lydianne started toward him, Jeremiah had a heady sense that his world was about to take a huge turn for the better. Her smile appeared vulnerable and a bit shy, yet her steps didn't falter.

"I—I'd really like to invite you to supper, Jeremiah, but there's nothing much to eat and the house is messy and I—"

"Sounds like a fine night for me to get a pizza and a salad uptown," he suggested. He hoped he hadn't overstepped by inviting himself to her house—or incorrectly assumed she was as open to their relationship as he was.

Lydianne's blue eyes widened with gratitude. "That would be perfect. And maybe, for once, we'll actually get to eat a meal uninterrupted."

"Sounds a lot better than going into the pizza place, where any number of folks we know might see us," he remarked. "Of course, I would be *proud* to be seen with you—"

"Not yet. Right now, my emotions feel as fragile as a spider web. People's assumptions at seeing us together are more than I want to handle."

Suddenly, Jeremiah felt infused with the setting sun's warmth and bright splendor. This day was ending a lot better than it could have, and for that he was grateful to God—and to Lydianne, for giving him another chance. "I understand," he said with a nod. "What if I head into town and get our supper ordered, and I'll be at your place right after they box it up for me?"

Her eager nod, so childlike and happy, sent his heart into somersaults. Lydianne was such a delightful young woman, easy to please and able to move forward despite the unexpected surprises that had come at her since last Friday. Jeremiah reminded himself that if he rushed ahead in this relationship, however, she might slap him down again—maybe for good this time.

"It's such a relief that you know about me now, yet you . . . you don't hold any of my secrets against me," she explained softly. "Ever since I knew I was carrying Ella—and even after I gave her up—I believed my future as a *maidel* alone was pretty much set in concrete. What man would have me, if he ever found out about my past?"

"*I* would," Jeremiah immediately whispered. He reached out to stroke her cheek, yearning for a deep, serious kiss to commemorate this moment. But it wasn't the right time or place. "How about if we talk more about this at your place? You have school tomorrow, so I promise I won't stay very late—although I really want to."

Lydianne glanced back toward the schoolhouse. "I'll gather up my books and head home now. I'm too keyed up to write tomorrow's lesson lists on the board anyway. See you when you get there."

Jeremiah got into his rig with a fresh spring in his step. He reminded himself that they were only sharing a simple supper and some conversation—and the conversation needed to stay light. This was no time to gallop ahead and tell Lydianne that another reason he loved her was because she could give him children—

Don't lay that on her yet! After losing her fiancé and enduring her family's judgment and giving up her child to start a new life—and then having to confess that Ella is her child—Lydianne has had more than enough domestic drama. She needs to know I love her for who she is rather than for what she can give me.

As a bishop who'd dealt with other people's personal problems for years, Jeremiah knew the voice in his head—which might well be the voice of God—was right.

But as a man, he had dreams. After years of longing for a family and then losing Priscilla, he rejoiced in the chance to start afresh.

He had to bide his time, however. Patience was a virtue

that could help him avoid more false starts with Lydianne. And once the folks in their church district realized he was courting her, a whole new set of expectations would come into play. He and Lydianne would be living in a fishbowl, with everyone wondering how soon they would marry—and, consequently, how soon their children would need to adjust to a new teacher.

But you're putting the cart before the horse again. Just get that pizza and enjoy a quiet—short—evening with the wonderful woman who finally wants to be with you.

About an hour later, Jeremiah urged his buggy horse into a canter, headed toward Lydianne's house just outside Morning Star's main business district. The aromas of sausage, cheese, and spices drifted from the box on the seat beside him, and he was suddenly famished—but for more than mere pizza.

How long had it been since he'd enjoyed the company of a woman who would require his best behavior? Being a married man had allowed him to slip into a comfortable routine with a wife who'd known his habits, preferences, and foibles—and had loved him anyway. And living with his mother had spoiled him in other ways, because he'd never needed to impress Mamm or tell her his preferences.

With Lydianne, he'd have to rethink his assumptions. He'd need to make room in his heart and home for a woman with tastes that would differ from Priscilla's.

Will she want to use her own dishes and kitchen equipment? Will she want to make changes in my house so it will feel like home to her? What if she wants to remain in her own home, the way Regina did?

Jeremiah laughed at himself, shaking his head to clear it of questions that didn't yet require answers. Tired as he was from Ella's disappearance and Lydianne's recent revelations, he felt like a new man as he guided Mitch up the lane toward the yellow house nestled among trees adorned in autumn's glorious colors. After he hitched his horse at the side of her home and bounded up onto her porch, Lydianne's voice came through the screen door.

"Come on in, Jeremiah!"

He was so ready to hear that. He stepped into the front room with their dinner and looked around. There wasn't a sign of a stray newspaper or any books strewn on the floor or coffee table, as was often the case at his place. A crocheted afghan was perfectly centered on the sofa. A battery lamp glowed in welcome on an end table. "For a house that's supposedly so messy, your place looks very neat and tidy to me, Lydianne," he called out.

When she appeared in the kitchen doorway, drying her hands on a white flour sack towel, her smile was catlike. "Don't open any closets," she warned with a lifted eyebrow. "All the clutter I just crammed into them will fall out and knock you flat."

Jeremiah laughed loudly. When Lydianne's laughter mingled with his, it filled his soul with a mirth he'd forgotten how to feel—so he kept laughing as he approached her. When he slipped his arm around her shoulders, still chuckling, she stepped into his embrace as though it were a longtime habit instead of something new and exhilarating.

When Lydianne gazed up at him, he forgot everything else. When he kissed her, softly at first, her willing lips moved with his in such a perfect fit that Jeremiah deepened the kiss and poured all his hopes and dreams into it. Moments later, he heard the pizza bag hit the floor, but he didn't care.

Lydianne was in his arms. She was clinging to him, returning his affection in a way that sent his body into a state of eager need. It would be so simple, so natural to remove her *kapp*, to pluck the pins that held her long, blond hair—

Her gasp brought Jeremiah back to his senses.

"Oh, but we can't go down this road right now," she rasped as she reluctantly stepped away from him. "The last time I did, I had Ella, after all."

Jeremiah inhaled sharply. "I'm sorry. I should've known better than to—"

"Don't be sorry. We've both needed that kiss for a long time," she whispered. She smoothed her apron, as if to set her emotions to rights along with her clothing. "How about if we pick our dinner up off the floor and go sit with a kitchen table between us. That sounds a lot safer, *jah*?"

He chuckled. As the older, more experienced person in the room—not to mention as the bishop—he hadn't expected Lydianne to set the boundaries for their behavior when they were alone together.

But thank God she did. It would've been so easy to forget all about food . . .

"You're a wise woman, Miss Christner," he murmured as he stooped to grasp the bag's handles. "Maybe that's why you're the teacher and I'm suddenly feeling like a smitten schoolboy again, *jah*?"

As they entered her kitchen, Jeremiah noted that it was much smaller than the ones in most Amish homes—but then, why would a woman living alone need as many cabinets or a table that expanded to seat ten or twelve family members? He waited for Lydianne to choose one of the chairs that had a plate in front of it, then sat down across from her. Jeremiah felt her gaze as he took the pizza box and the container of salad from the bag.

"I'm feeling as tossed as that salad," Lydianne admitted with a little laugh. "At least the lid stayed closed."

"We have a lot to be thankful for," Jeremiah agreed as he opened the cardboard box in the center of the table. "The pizza stayed intact, too. Pretty much, anyway," he added as he straightened the slices that had flipped on top of others.

When he bowed his head, he reached across the table for her hand—just as he'd done with Priscilla for so many years. It felt exactly right to have Lydianne's fingers curled around his while they shared a silent prayer before their meal. Her gentle grasp centered him, helping him focus on the moment despite the way the aromas of warm sausage and cheese made his stomach rumble.

Lord, this is Your doing, and I'm so grateful for this chance to laugh and love again. Help me not to mess it up.

When he opened his eyes, Lydianne was gazing at him with such a gentle smile, Jeremiah knew he would feel at home no matter where he was, as long as she was with him. As they ate, he purposely kept the conversation light, mostly centered on the upcoming activities she was planning for the scholars as the holidays approached. They were each picking up a third piece of pizza when loud banging on the front door startled them.

Wide-eyed, Lydianne rose to answer the knock while Jeremiah got up to peer out the kitchen window. He let out a sigh when he recognized the rig parked alongside Mitch—and heard familiar voices in the front room.

Deacon Saul said, "Lydianne, I regret our need to barge in and bother you—"

"But we've heard a very *interesting* story," Martha

Maude interrupted in a strident tone. "We came here right away to hear what you have to say about it."

Jeremiah closed his eyes wearily, regretting this intrusion even though he wasn't particularly surprised about it. Before the Hartzlers could trap Lydianne in a conversational corner, he went out to greet them. They'd seen Mitch, so they already knew he was here.

"Good evening, folks," he said as nonchalantly as he could. "We were just having some pizza after a rather unsettling day. Care to join us?"

Two sets of curious eyes gazed first at Lydianne and then at him, as the deacon and his outspoken mother drew their silent conclusions about his presence in Lydianne's kitchen.

"Would your unsettling day have anything to do with the *exciting news* Ella was telling us about?" Martha Maude asked. "I was helping Rose with baby Suzanna when Ella burst into the kitchen with Gracie after school. The first words out of her mouth were about you being her *mother*, Lydianne. She sounded absolutely certain about this—said she'd heard you talking about it—"

"And meanwhile, at the schoolhouse, Tim and Julia were telling us the very same story," Jeremiah put in matter-of-factly. Lydianne's face had paled, and she seemed at a loss for words, so he hoped his explanation would nip the Hartzlers' curiosity in the bud. As two of the most influential members of their church, they might well determine how convincing—and how successful—he and the Nissleys would be at extinguishing this blazing-hot news about Teacher Lydianne.

Jeremiah gestured toward the kitchen. "Come sit down. I'm sure you have questions."

"Oh, *jah*—questions. That doesn't begin to cover it," Saul said as he studied Lydianne's facial features.

Jeremiah was grateful that Martha Maude was heading toward the table, so her son would follow her. He prayed fervently that God would give him words to convince the Hartzlers to stop this story in its tracks . . . even if he had to lie a little to protect Lydianne and the Nissley family. "Let me start by saying that Lydianne and I were talking at her desk after school on Monday, about a lot of different things—"

"And we didn't realize that Ella had come in," Lydianne added in a voice that shook with emotion.

"Our best guess is that she overheard just enough of our conversation to piece things together as only an imaginative six-year-old can," Jeremiah continued valiantly. "Like a lot of first-year scholars, Ella has become so attached to Teacher Lydianne—the first woman after her *mamm* to be her teacher—that she's gotten it in her head that Lydianne could be her mother because she *wants* her to be."

He watched the reactions play over their guests' faces as they took the other two seats at the table. Martha Maude's hawk-sharp mind could cut unerringly through fibs and smoke screens, and she never hesitated to state her opinions. Saul tended to reserve judgment—to keep track of loopholes and discrepancies on his mental tally sheet—until he'd heard enough to say that the particulars of a story didn't add up.

"Don't you recall that kind of attachment, Saul?" Jeremiah continued earnestly. "I was so in love with my teacher, I was telling everyone I intended to marry her—and I was quite a bit older than Ella when I was spreading this tale."

The deacon's lips lifted. "*Jah*, I recall having such a crush, but everybody knew the story wasn't true—chalked it up to little-boy talk," he countered. "In this case, Lydianne is certainly old enough to have had a child—back before she came to Morning Star. And the resemblance is impossible to miss, once you start looking."

Resisting the urge to grasp Lydianne's hand, Jeremiah persisted with his argument. "But—even though we adults know that the Nissleys adopted Ella as a newborn—she could certainly be Tim and Julia's biological child if you compare her features and complexion to theirs," he said earnestly. "My *mamm* has always said I'm the spitting image of my *dat*, yet other people tell me they see her features all over my face."

Martha Maude had been following the conversation closely, her forehead furrowed with thought. "*Jah*, beauty's in the eye of the beholder," she quipped. "Saul would've been better off if he'd inherited more of my features, don't you think?"

As her son scowled at her off-hand remark, she sat back in her chair. "I'll never forget the day—I was a first-year scholar just like Ella—when I slipped up and called my teacher *Mamm*, right in front of my mother. As you've said, Jeremiah, first-year scholars form a close attachment to their teachers because they spend all day with them instead of with their *mamms*, drinking in every word they say."

Jeremiah let her statement stand, hoping Saul would follow her logic.

"I also recall knowing a few kids who were adopted, as well as daydreaming that I might've had different parents, too," Martha Maude continued softly. "It's a phase a lot of kids go through, I think. I didn't quiz Ella too closely about her story, because I don't believe she knows that Tim and Julia adopted her as a newborn."

"That's right—they haven't told her," Jeremiah chimed

in, grateful for the opening Martha Maude had given him.
"They want to discuss Ella's adoption with her when she's
older and better able to understand. Even as we speak,
they're instructing Ella not to repeat what she overheard
because she might've gotten it wrong—and because eavesdropping on adults' conversations isn't proper behavior."

Saul's eyes narrowed as he considered this. "But if
Lydianne really is Ella's mother—"

"This matter is not up for discussion." Jeremiah leaned
toward the deacon, holding his gaze. "As the bishop, I have
chosen to honor the Nissleys' request to keep this matter
confidential—to preserve the privacy of all involved. God
already knows the details, after all."

Saul scowled. "But if Lydianne really is—you can't just
sweep her situation under the rug as though—"

"*Jah*, he can—and for *gut* reason," Martha Maude
interrupted as she, too, held Saul's gaze. "Think of the
unfortunate consequences for Tim and Julia and *Ella*—
and for the other scholars and their parents—if we were to
pursue this matter the way you're thinking we should, son.
You don't always have to be right."

Saul's eyes widened. When he opened his mouth to
argue, his mother kept talking so he wouldn't have the
chance.

"God chose Jeremiah as our bishop," Martha Maude
said firmly. "We should accept his decisions about family
matters and allow this situation to play out in its own *gut*
time, the way the Nissleys have requested. I have all faith
that Jeremiah has crossed the t's and dotted the i's, as far
as Old Order beliefs about confession are concerned."

Saul shook his head vehemently. "But we need to at
least inform the preachers—"

"*My* lips are sealed," his mother shot back, making a

zipper motion with her fingers across her mouth. "I intend to tell anyone who repeats Ella's story that she's a little girl and she got it wrong. If other folks whip this situation into a frenzy, demanding a Members Meeting and Lydianne's confession, we'll know who told them to do that, won't we, Saul?"

The kitchen rang with silence. Only when the deacon's shoulders fell as a sign of his resigned acceptance did Jeremiah allow himself to breathe again. "*Denki* for your vote of confidence and your compassionate understanding, Martha Maude," he murmured.

"*Jah*, I—and the Nissleys—appreciate it more than you know," Lydianne whispered hoarsely.

Martha Maude reached over to grasp Lydianne's shoulder. "Every one of us has a secret or two we've tucked into our hearts, because some things really are best kept between us and our Lord," she said gently. "Bless you for all the *gut* work you've done with our scholars, Lydianne. We'll go now and leave you to finish your dinner."

Saul didn't appear entirely satisfied with the outcome of their conversation, but he knew it was over because his mother had declared that it was. With a nod at Jeremiah, he followed Martha Maude out of the kitchen.

Jeremiah and Lydianne escorted them to the front door with a minimum of small talk. Only when the Hartzler buggy was on the road did the bishop slip his arm around her shoulders. "That conversation certainly could've ended differently."

Lydianne let out a strained laugh. "I had no idea Martha Maude would take our side—or that she'd stand up to her son," she said. "In most districts, the deacon's opinion would've overruled anyone else's—except the bishop's."

Jeremiah gently turned her toward the kitchen again.

"Martha Maude calls a spade a spade, no matter who's holding it," he remarked, "but I was grateful that she realized the consequences of bringing this matter to a Members Meeting. I wish I'd done a better job of keeping your identity as Ella's mother out of it, but I didn't want to tell Saul an outright lie."

"I would never expect you to lie for me, Jeremiah," Lydianne murmured as she sank wearily into her chair at the table. "As it was, I was too nervous to give you much help. If you hadn't stood up for me and the Nissleys, my reputation would be toast. I'd have to start packing."

"We don't know that. The congregation might accept you back into the fold after your shunning—"

"But the damage would've been done, and Ella would know that Julia and Tim aren't her birth parents," Lydianne insisted. "Thank *gut*ness Martha Maude believes the Nissleys should handle that information as they see fit, instead of making it a matter for public discussion."

As Jeremiah glanced at the remainder of their cold pizza and the salad that had gotten soggy, he didn't have much appetite for it. "I suspect you need time to process what's happened today, and to prepare for your classes tomorrow, so I'll be on my way," he said softly. Then he chuckled. "I also suspect that Mamm wonders why I've not come home for the supper she's fixed. At least she'll be pleased that I was with *you*, even though I won't reveal what we've been dealing with."

"Margaret will get some ideas about our supper, *jah*— and I won't be surprised if the Hartzlers mention to folks that they found us together, as well." Lydianne's eyebrows arched. "Some news is just too *interesting* to keep quiet about, ain't so?"

Jeremiah was pleased to see hints of happiness in her

expression, considering the times she'd turned him away. "When you're the bishop, you live in a fishbowl, Sunshine. I hope you won't mind it that folks in the congregation will be paying very close attention to our comings and goings now."

She shrugged. "If they're talking about us and our potential future, they're leaving other topics alone, right? At least I hope they will," she added with a sigh. "A lot of the more conservative church members would believe I'm not fit company for you if they knew I had Ella out of wedlock."

"Phooey on that." He clasped her small, sturdy hand between his. "We're adults. We'll decide what's best for us regardless of what other folks might say. Are you with me on that, Lydianne?"

When she held his gaze and nodded, Jeremiah felt something wonderfully satisfying lock into place, as though his heart was a jigsaw puzzle and he'd finally found the missing piece he'd been searching for.

Chapter Twenty-Three

As Jo watched the Wengerds' horse-drawn wagon pull off the road to come down the lane, excitement tickled her all over. After four and a half months of having Michael and Nelson stay in their *dawdi haus* each Friday night and then spend Saturdays working at The Marketplace, her life had fallen into a pleasant, predictable rhythm—and had taken a turn for the better. Although she knew nothing serious or permanent could come of her friendship with Michael, she enjoyed his company immensely. Even Mamm seemed happier these days because—though she didn't admit it—she looked forward to sharing Friday night's supper with Nelson and his son.

"The Wengerds must be coming," her mother remarked from the stove, where she was stirring a big pot of venison stew. "If you were a dog, your tail would be wagging a mile a minute, twitchy as you are."

Twitchy? Jo turned from the window to finish setting the table with four places. "You enjoy them, too, Mamm," she challenged. "Back in June when they first began coming, I *never* would've guessed you'd invite them to join us for supper each week."

"Puh! It's the only polite thing to do, considering they arrive around five o'clock," Mamm countered. "And it seems only right to feed them, as a return for all the odd jobs and maintenance they do around this place without my asking them."

Jo was removing a pan of fresh dinner rolls from the oven when one of their guests knocked on the door. "Come on in!" she called out as she hurried through the front room to greet them.

When the door opened, she saw a huge pot of bright yellow mums that appeared to have sprouted two legs in broadfall trousers. "Special delivery for Miss Josephine Fussner," Michael teased before peaking around his armful of flowers. "Dat has another plant for your mother. Where would you like us to put them?"

"What a nice surprise—and so pretty!" Jo exclaimed. "Is there room for a pot on either side of the porch steps? They'll get some nice sunshine there."

"That would be my choice of locations, *jah*," Nelson replied from the doorway. His handsome face creased with a smile. "After selling out of our mums at the auctions, it's a *gut* thing we saved these two back for you ladies. It's our way of thanking you for your hospitality—and a way to celebrate how profitable it's been for us to sell our flowers and vegetables in Morning Star."

"I—I'm glad it's worked out so well for you, considering the drive you make each week to get here," Jo remarked. "All of our businesses do better because customers come to The Marketplace for your produce, pumpkins, and mums."

She watched the two men position the big pots in their new spots, pleased with the pop of color the mums added to the shrubbery growing there. When the Wengerds returned to their wagon, Nelson carried their duffel bags to the *dawdi haus* while Michael returned to the front door carrying a large sack of apples and a plastic jug.

"For this weekend, we brought some baskets of apples and some pressed cider from a neighbor who has an orchard," Michael explained as he rejoined Jo. "Folks out in the countryside don't get the amount of customer traffic at their roadside stands that we see here at The Marketplace, so we offered to sell some of his crop tomorrow. For you!" he added, offering her the sack and the jug.

"Oh, these apples look so shiny and fresh—and it's been an age since we had cider," Jo remarked happily. "Come on in—the stew's ready."

"Happy to bring you ladies a little something," Nelson put in as he came up the steps and into the front room. "It's the least we can do, considering that your hospitality goes above and beyond what we'd originally agreed upon."

"Come get your supper!" Mamm said. She'd been waiting for them in the kitchen doorway, more eager to see the Wengerds than she would ever let on. "Then you can tell me whether you'll keep coming here all winter, or whether you're staying in Queen City to put your feet up until spring."

Michael and Nelson's laughter filled the kitchen. "Funny you should ask that question, Drusilla," Nelson teased. "If you could visit the new greenhouses we built over the summer, and see what's growing in them—"

"You'd know we're not going to take a lot of time off," Michael chimed in. "At least not until after Christmas."

As the men washed their hands at the sink, Jo set the cider and apples on the side counter. She filled a basket with warm rolls and put it on the table as Michael and Nelson took their usual seats at the table.

"You've hinted that you might be expanding, or trying something new, but you've kept us guessing about what you're doing," Jo said. She noticed the curiosity that lit Mamm's eyes as she carried a steaming bowl of stew to the table.

"Poinsettias!" Michael blurted with a boyish smile.

"*Thousands* of poinsettias," Nelson clarified. "We've always done well supplying the grocery stores, florists, and other outlets around Queen City and Kirksville each Christmas season, but when we realized how much business we were doing here with our other products, we decided to go all in. We used to raise around five thousand potted poinsettias in a season, but we now have eight thousand of them—"

"And we're hoping you gals who manage The Marketplace will agree to advertise an open house or some other special event to help us sell them all!" Michael looked from Jo to her mother, and then his gaze lingered on Jo. "Of course, we figured on supplying some of those plants as decorations for the shops and the refreshment area, come December—"

"But that still leaves you with a *lot* of flowers to sell before Christmas," Jo put in with a laugh. "Eight thousand poinsettias! I can't imagine how colorful your greenhouses will look when they're all in bloom!"

Michael and his *dat* shared a furtive glance. "Maybe you ladies should come and see for yourselves sometime in early December. We—we could show you around our gardens and greenhouses, and—"

"You could stay at our place," Nelson added matter-of-factly. "So, it would be a nice little outing that wouldn't cost you anything but a day or two of your—"

"Why would we want to do that?" Mamm demanded. Her earlier happiness dissipated like the steam from the stew bowl. "That's a long trip. And we wouldn't have the foggiest notion of how to get there, or—"

"That's why we figured you could ride back to Queen City with us some Saturday night after The Marketplace closes," Nelson said smoothly. "And Michael could drive you home whenever you're ready."

"Oh, but that would be fun!" Jo murmured wistfully.

"No, it wouldn't!" Mamm shot back at her. "You know how cranky and sore I get when I have to sit in a rig more than ten or fifteen minutes."

Sighing, Jo glanced apologetically at Michael. After all the time he and his *dat* had spent here, they knew Mamm could get cranky about the least little suggestion that might vary her routine—even if it didn't involve a buggy ride.

Michael winked at Jo. "Well, it was only an idea."

"Just something to think about," Nelson agreed cordially. "Let's bow our heads before this *gut*-smelling stew gets cold, shall we?"

Jo closed her eyes, but her thoughts were far from prayerful. *Lord, why can't my mother ever be happy? Michael and his* dat *are being so nice, inviting us to see their greenhouses, and—well, if there's any way at all You can bring us a positive outcome, please bless us with Your assistance.*

After the grace, as they were passing the food, Nelson looked at Mamm. "Drusilla, is it inconvenient—or a disruption to your rental business—if Michael and I continue to stay in your *dawdi haus* through the holidays?" he asked. "If it is, we'll find other Friday night lodging—"

"Don't even think about it!" Jo blurted. "You've been a steady source of income for us all summer, and we've still taken in other guests on weeknights. And besides that," she added when Mamm appeared ready to object, "we don't get nearly as many reservations during the winter months. We'd be delighted to have you."

Michael's smile told Jo he understood that she was steering the conversation in a better direction. "We're happy to hear that. After our week's work in the greenhouses and our Queen City shop, it's always a nice break to drive through the countryside with a wagonload of our flowers and produce."

"*Jah*, this fall has been exceptionally colorful, with all the maple and sweet gum trees blazing in bright reds and oranges when the sunlight hits them," Nelson remarked. He closed his eyes to bite into his dinner roll, which he'd dipped into the stew sauce on his plate. "And you have no idea how much we look forward to the Friday night suppers you cook for us, Drusilla and Jo. You've been very gracious to invite us to join you. I haven't tasted venison stew in years, and this is delicious."

Mamm remained focused on her meal, pretending Nelson's compliment hadn't made her glow a little.

Jo smiled at Nelson, nodding subtly. "We enjoy your company—and hearing about your nursery business, too. With the weather getting colder, how will you keep all those poinsettias at their best? Don't they require a lot of warmth and attention?"

"The most important thing is not to let the temperature dip below fifty-eight degrees," Michael replied. "Our bishop has allowed us to install an alarm system that goes off when it gets that cool—"

"And then we burn wood chips from some nearby sawmills to run the greenhouse heaters," Nelson explained further. "Between now and the end of the year, we'll probably go through a trailer truckload of chips each week to keep our poinsettias warm enough."

"But then, as the end of November comes around and the blooms turn red," Michael chimed in eagerly, "each greenhouse is a sea of color from one end to the other! It's a sight I never tire of."

Jo could imagine how spectacular all those blooming flowers must look—and how fresh the air must smell in the greenhouses. Now that the Wengerds had invited her to share that experience, she yearned to go.

"We also raise white poinsettias and a few other varieties in shades of pink," Nelson said, "but the red ones are by far the most popular."

"When we bring the flowers to The Marketplace, we could arrange some in the shape of a tall Christmas tree—maybe right in the center of the commons area, where folks would see it when they walked in," Michael suggested. "You'd lose some of your refreshment seating that way—"

"Oh, but wouldn't that be a fabulous sight?" Jo interrupted excitedly. "But I hope you'll still be able to sell those plants—maybe tag them as folks speak for them, and they could claim them that weekend before Christmas? We don't want you losing money on them, because once the holidays are past, nobody will want them, right?"

When the Wengerds smiled at her, their faces were nearly identical except that Michael's didn't have the laugh lines that bracketed his *dat*'s mouth and eyes—nor did he have Nelson's salt-and-pepper hair.

"That sort of forward thinking is the reason The Marketplace is doing so well," Nelson remarked with an approving nod. "You and the other gals who organize things and keep track of the money understand that, as small business owners, we have to turn a profit on everything we bring—even if it's a display."

"We've made poinsettia trees a few other places, so

we'll take care of the ordering details," Michael put in as he reached for another roll. His blue eyes twinkled with anticipation. "*Denki* for allotting us some space for them. It's only the middle of October, but I think we're already on the way to a very merry, profitable Christmas season."

Though her mother had dropped out of the conversation, Jo found the Wengerds' enthusiasm contagious. The upcoming holidays—not to mention Michael and Nelson's continued company on Friday nights—gave her a lot to look forward to. And for that, she was grateful.

Chapter Twenty-Four

Lydianne entered the schoolroom early on Monday morning, determined to start the week on a positive note. She felt rested after a quiet weekend. She'd prepared detailed lessons for her scholars, so she wouldn't feel she was flying by the seat of her flapping skirt anymore. Because the previous day hadn't been a church Sunday, she'd spent some enjoyable time with her *maidel* friends in the afternoon—and they hadn't heard Ella's story, so they didn't quiz her about it.

Best of all, the Hartzlers hadn't returned. Lydianne had imagined scenes in which Saul interrogated her about the circumstances of Ella's birth when Jeremiah wasn't around to support her.

As she turned the calendar beside the white board to a fresh page, Lydianne dared to believe her secret was safely tucked away again—known to only a few forgiving souls who wouldn't publicly reveal the truth.

When the front door opened far too early for her students to be arriving, however, Lydianne's fragile hopes shattered. Preacher Clarence Miller stepped inside the schoolroom and closed the door behind him, gazing steadily at her for several moments. It was only polite to greet him, so Lydianne spoke first. She sensed he intended to remain silent and judgmental rather than striking up a conversation.

"*Gut* morning, Preacher Clarence," she said with a cheerfulness she didn't feel. "What brings you here so early on a Monday morning? I hope it's not because Lucy or Linda is ill."

"The girls are fine," he replied in a clipped voice. "I, however, am deeply upset by a story I heard concerning your being *related* to Ella Nissley. When I spoke to the bishop about it, I felt he was downplaying the details— whitewashing the facts—to protect your reputation. That sort of tactic doesn't fly with me."

Lydianne glanced at the clock above Clarence's head. Even if she could talk the preacher out of his stern, disapproving mood before the scholars arrived within the hour, she wouldn't begin the school day with the upbeat sense of joy she'd hoped to share with them.

But there was no sending Clarence away. As a member of the school board and the father of two of her students, the preacher had every right to challenge her spiritual and ethical qualifications for being the district's teacher.

"Come sit down," she suggested as she fetched a straight-backed chair from the nearby worktable. "Tell me about this story you heard."

"Oh, I think you *know* the story, Miss Christner," Clarence accused as he approached her desk. "I overheard it on Saturday when I was at Books on Bates with the bishop, selecting a new Bible for when Emma joins the church. Julia Nissley was there with Ella, who was bubbling over about a wooden placard she wanted to give you because you're her *mother*," he put in with added emphasis.

Clarence's hawklike features sharpened as he sat down.

He was a stick figure of a man, without an ounce of fat on his bony frame, and his steely-gray hair and bushy beard had always made Lydianne think of a fiercely judgmental Old Testament prophet. "As Julia shushed her, I could tell she was trying to keep the girl quiet," Clarence continued. "But you know what they say. 'Out of the mouths of babes . . .'"

Lydianne swallowed hard. She sensed Preacher Clarence wasn't nearly finished with her as he studied her facial features.

"When I heard Ella's story and her *mamm*'s reaction to it, I quizzed Bishop Jeremiah as soon as we left the bookstore, to see what he knew about the situation," the preacher blustered. "*He* began sidestepping the issue, as well, so I felt it was my duty to come straight to the source.

"*Are* you Ella's mother, Lydianne?" he demanded. "Is that why she looks just like you? Is that why we know so little about your past, and why you chose to come to Morning Star, where you have no family?"

There was no evading Preacher Clarence as he awaited her response. Every second of silence ticking by on the battery clock in the suddenly airless classroom made her guilt more apparent. Lydianne prayed for strength and the right words.

"In the interest of protecting the Nissleys' privacy as Ella's adoptive parents," she began in the firmest voice she could muster, "we have agreed not to—"

"What's this *we* business?" he blurted out. "I'm asking you for a simple yes or no, but you insist upon dodging—"

When the door opened to admit Jeremiah, Lydianne felt a surge of relief. Even though she saw no way around

Preacher Clarence's questions, she at least had the church district's highest authority on her side.

"I figured I might find you here first thing this morning, Clarence," the bishop said as he strode toward them. With a resigned glance at Lydianne, he sat on the edge of her desk. "In the bookstore parking lot, when you questioned me about what Ella Nissley had said," he began, crossing his arms tightly, "you had the air of a dog latching onto a fresh bone, determined not to release it until you'd picked away every juicy morsel."

The preacher's bushy eyebrows rose as he considered the bishop's uncomplimentary remark. "And *you* were covering up the truth about a young woman with an incriminating secret," he countered in a coiled voice. "This situation casts Teacher Lydianne in a very questionable light. It's my duty to get to the truth about—"

"The truth," Jeremiah interrupted brusquely, "is that Tim and Julia Nissley have requested that Ella's story remain confidential until she's old enough for them to explain that she's adopted. You need to trust that I, as the bishop of this district, have already handled this matter properly for all the parties directly concerned—including Teacher Lydianne."

He paused, wrapping his hands tightly around the edge of the desk in his frustration. "If you insist upon publicly pursuing this matter, you'll not only betray a confidence, you'll open a can of worms with consequences that far outweigh your right to interrogate Miss Christner. End of discussion."

Preacher Clarence's face had gone tight with his effort to control his temper. "That's no answer, and you know it!" he spouted off. He glared at Lydianne. "Why is it that you,

Miss Christner, haven't given me any straight answers? And why, if you were carrying your fiancé's baby before he died, did you not mention this at your interview?"

"Why do you think? Would you have hired her if you'd known?" Jeremiah shot back—and then something made him go to the window. "Here comes Glenn's boy driving Stevie and Gracie, as well as the Flaud sisters with Ella, and close behind them, your daughters, Clarence. Do you really want this discussion to be what they walk in on as they start their school day?"

Scowling, the preacher stood up and grabbed the back of his chair. "Fine—I'll be quiet because I've heard all I need to. But I'm not leaving."

Lydianne's stomach knotted around the cereal she'd eaten for breakfast, and she wondered if she was going to be sick as her students entered the room. Before Jeremiah turned toward the door, however, his smile settled her nerves. As he passed the preacher, who'd planted himself beside the worktable at the back of the room, she prayed fervently that this confrontation would come to a solution that left Ella—and her—unscathed.

Could Jeremiah once again rescue her from Old Order tongues that wanted to wag and demand her public confession?

Jeremiah drew a deep breath as he stood on the school's front stoop, allowing the crisp October air to clear his head. He was no stranger to Clarence Miller's narrow, stifling sense of religious duty. A few months earlier he'd freed the preacher's niece, Regina, from the tiny prison of a room Clarence had forced her to live in. Regina had confessed to assuming a fake male name to mask her identity as a successful artist when The Marketplace had opened, and Clarence had been determined to make her pay penance for her wayward artistic inclinations.

Jeremiah would *not* allow Miller's self-righteousness to shred the blanket of love and trust the young Nissleys were wrapping around little Ella. Nor did he want Lydianne's past to be needlessly exposed, just to satisfy the preacher's overzealous inclinations. As he watched the scholars approach the schoolhouse, he prayed for guidance in yet another tough situation. Would there ever come a time when he and Lydianne could explore a romantic relationship without folks prying into her personal business?

As Billy Jay skillfully steered his pony cart toward the pole barn—and he and Gracie and Stevie waved, flashing their eager smiles at him—Jeremiah's spirits lightened. Kate and Lorena Flaud also seemed happy to see him, and as Ella called out to him, he couldn't miss her excitement about being at school for another day of learning. Clarence's girls waved, as well, probably unaware that their unhappy *dat* was sitting in the back of the classroom.

Jeremiah simply had to trust that these young souls, so full of youthful exuberance, would rally to Teacher Lydianne's cause and roll with whatever happened as their school day began.

A few minutes after the buggies and the cart were parked and the horses had been pastured, the thunder of footsteps on the wooden interior stairs told him the kids had deposited their wraps and lunch pails in the lower-level cloakroom. Jeremiah entered the classroom just in time to see Gracie Wagler racing toward Lydianne without a passing glance at him or the stern man seated near the door.

"Teacher Lydianne!" she cried out, opening her little arms wide. "If you can be Ella's *mamm*, I want you to be my *mamm*, too, coz Mamma is too busy with the new baby nowadays. And she's always tellin' me to be *quiet*!"

Jeremiah's heart lurched at Gracie's remark, figuring it would only fuel Clarence's cause. But when he glanced toward the preacher's face, another set of rapid-fire footsteps claimed his attention instead.

Billy Jay had seen that Gracie's outburst had earned her a big hug, so he was rushing forward, as well. "I need a new *mamm* at my house, too—so Dat can be happy again, like me!" he exclaimed.

Stevie, always eager to keep up with his buddy, exclaimed, "*Jah*, Baby Adah takes all of my *mamm*'s time, too, so I want you to be *my* new *mamm*, Teacher Lydianne!"

Determined not to be outdone or ignored, little Ella scrambled up onto Lydianne's chair and into her startled teacher's arms. "Mamm says that God brought me to our family—not you, Teacher Lydianne—but I love you anyway. You can be my *other* mother, okay?"

Kate laughed as she and her sister stepped to either side of Lydianne. "You can be my other mother any day!"

"*Jah*, I could use another mother, too!" Lorena chimed in as they slipped their arms around their wide-eyed teacher.

Lucy Miller laughed as she joined the growing, giggling huddle in the front of the classroom. "We all love you to pieces, Teacher Lydianne!"

Linda was approaching the big group hug when she caught sight of her father at the back table. She blinked, but then she went around behind Lydianne and wrapped both her arms around the teacher's shoulders. "There's no such thing as too much love," she declared. "It's *gut* to be here in school with you, Teacher Lydianne, because you love us as we are, and you help us be the people God created us to be."

Jeremiah was stunned. As Lydianne gratefully embraced each of her students, his heart overflowed with deep emotion. The first light of morning was streaming through the windows, and as it bathed Lydianne in its radiance, she glowed with an all-over halo as she shared her scholars' genuine affection.

Jeremiah sighed wistfully. He could easily imagine Lydianne embracing the children he longed to have with her. It was a holy moment for him, magnified by the power of the love he hoped to share with her for the rest of his life.

A movement caught his eye. Before Jeremiah could say anything else to Clarence, the preacher took his leave. His parting glance expressed his dissatisfaction, yet Jeremiah sensed the preacher knew better than to disrupt the important relationships being formed in this schoolroom.

Denki, Lord, for pulling us through this one, and for putting so much love in these scholars' hearts, Jeremiah prayed silently.

When he looked toward the front of the classroom again, the children were quietly taking their seats, getting ready for another day of learning—unaware of the unpleasantness they'd dispelled with the simple gift of their love.

The grateful gaze Lydianne gave him made Jeremiah's whole being thrum with the rightness of their deepening feelings for each other. Sure that none of her students were watching, he blew her a kiss and turned to go.

But already, he couldn't wait to be with Lydianne again.

Chapter Twenty-Five

As his friends gathered Friday evening for their weekly singing session, Jeremiah welcomed them into the front room because it was too chilly to sit out on the porch. Inspired by the cider he'd purchased from the Wengerds at The Marketplace, Mamm had prepared a special treat: fresh pumpkin doughnuts stacked on a platter alongside a punchbowl of warm, spiced cider. Even though most of the fellows had just come from their supper, they flocked to the goodies as if they hadn't eaten for weeks.

Jeremiah noted the scruff of beard adorning Gabe's face, denoting his status as a newly married man. His brother, Jude, and Matthias Wagler had dark circles beneath their eyes, bearing out what Stevie and Gracie had said about new babies demanding a lot of attention and keeping their parents up during the night.

But it's a wonderful reason to be exhausted.

Jeremiah asked Matthias and Jude how things were going at their homes. He sympathized as they described their wives' feedings in the wee hours, as well as cleaning up their newborn daughters' vomit and changing their diapers.

I would welcome the chance to change a diaper or rock

a baby, even if I was walking the floors with a little soul who was screaming for relief I didn't know how to provide.

An image of Lydianne tenderly caring for his infant children filled Jeremiah's soul with such overwhelming love, he had to take some deep breaths—and another doughnut—to bring himself back into the present moment with his friends.

Gabe snagged one last doughnut and took his seat in the armchair. "Not to rush the season," he said as he passed some song sheets to the men who were filling in the circle of chairs, "but in a couple of months it'll be Christmas! Let's spend some time tonight refreshing our memories about how the harmony goes on these carols. You never know—we might be invited to sing at some holiday functions, so we should be ready!"

"What if we held a big party at The Marketplace on Second Christmas, for anyone who cared to come—and they could even bring their visiting families?" Martin asked excitedly. "That would be a great place for us to sing. And we'd have room for a couple hundred people there."

Beside Martin, Preacher Ammon raised his eyebrows. "I get tired just thinking about all the extra activities we try to cram into the Christmas—"

"Sounds like a great way to visit with folks without having them at your house all evening," Matthias put in. "That way, babies could nap in peace and the folks who wanted to party could enjoy their time together as late as they cared to stay up."

Jeremiah was listening closely to these ideas. "We can speak to Jo about that and reserve the space," he suggested. "It would be a *gut* chance for us to sing together as well as an opportunity for folks to mingle with other families' guests."

"Because sometimes spending all that time with your own relatives gets tiresome," Gabe teased.

The room rang with merriment that Jeremiah was pleased to share. None of these fellows seemed eager to quiz him about Lydianne's situation—if they even knew about it. After the week he'd spent defending her to two demanding church leaders, he was happy to think ahead to brighter times—occasions when he and Lydianne could be together as a couple.

Gabe was about to blow into his pitch pipe for "The First Noel" when voices in the kitchen caught everyone's attention. Jeremiah heard his mother offering to look after baby Levi and share a doughnut and cider with Billy Jay, which meant Elva Detweiler probably needed a break from her childcare routine.

When Glenn entered the front room just ahead of his *dat*, he nodded at everyone. "Sorry we're late," he said as he and Reuben slipped into the last two chairs. "Mamm's worn thin tonight, so we brought the boys with us."

"Glad you could make it," Jeremiah said. He couldn't begin to imagine how tired Elva must get looking after an energetic seven-year-old and a newborn, not to mention her grieving son and her aging husband. At seventy-two she was a prime example of a woman who'd stepped in to do what needed to be done after tragedy had struck her family. Jeremiah had always admired her, even if her hearing loss meant she spoke very loudly and he had to repeat whatever he said to her.

"I'm going to have a couple of these doughnuts for my supper," Reuben remarked, gazing at the three that remained on the platter. "Elva didn't fix enough to amount to anything this evening. I keep telling her she needs to get checked for her diabetes and that heart problem the doctor warned her about years ago, but she won't listen to me. Says she's got no time to be sick or go to the doctor."

"No, Dat, it was *last* night that Mamm's meal ran a little short," Glenn reminded him gently. "She was out of almost everything until we went shopping this morning, remember? And you ate two big bowls of her beef and beans for supper."

With an apologetic glance at Jeremiah and Gabe, Glenn said, "You fellows go ahead and start the singing. We'll catch up to you when we've had a doughnut and some cider."

As Gabe led them into "The First Noel" again, Jeremiah assessed what he'd just heard. Reuben had apparently forgotten the meal he'd eaten an hour ago, and Glenn's tone made it sound as though he'd steered his *dat*'s wandering mind back on track more than once recently. Despite Reuben and Elva's boasts about how healthy they'd remained without seeing a doctor, Jeremiah told himself it was time to talk with them about going in for medical checkups.

Jeremiah also realized that Glenn could use some friendly attention, and that it was time for him to let go of the hostility he'd felt because his younger, recently widowed friend had been keen for Lydianne's affection.

As the group began singing "It Came Upon the Midnight Clear," the poignant words and melody seemed to be coming from God Himself. The verse about bending low beneath life's load and toiling with painful slowness was a perfect description of life at the Detweiler place, wasn't it? Jeremiah reminded himself that it was time for him to behave like a bishop instead of a rival boyfriend. If anyone needed a chance to rest beside the weary road while the angels sang, it was Glenn.

You've given me fresh hope and a chance at a new beginning, Lord, he prayed as he watched Reuben and Glenn lick the powdered sugar from their fingers. *Help me be the blessing Glenn and his family so badly need.*

As Lydianne arrived at The Marketplace on Saturday, she felt brighter and more lighthearted than she had in weeks. Maybe it was the baskets of shiny red apples arranged in front of the Wengerd Nursery storefront, or the aromas of the fresh-brewed coffee, cinnamon rolls, and warm cider Jo was selling that filled her heart with the joyful glory of autumn.

No, silly, you're excited about the phone message Jeremiah left you, asking you to join him after you get off work this evening.

Lydianne reminded herself that if she went around with a lovesick grin on her face, her *maidel* friends would soon be quizzing her about it. When she saw the Helfing twins arriving with big boxloads of bagged noodles, she rushed over to help them. "Do you have more boxes to carry in?" she asked. "My word, it seems you bring more and more noodles as the weeks go by."

Molly laughed out loud. "Well, that was our original plan, ain't so—to increase our sales?" she pointed out. "But I think we've reached our maximum capacity now."

"*Jah*," Marietta chimed in from behind the box she was carrying. "We worked every possible hour we had this week. It's *gut* that folks like our varieties of noodles, but it makes for a tiring life, you know?"

"We've got one more box. If you want to bring it in,

bless your heart, Lydianne," Molly said over her shoulder. She deftly balanced her lightweight but bulky box against her hip to unlatch the gate to their store. "I suspect several of the noodles in that last box are broken, seeing's how Riley knocked it out of my hands when he got so excited to see me. Dumb dog. I keep threatening to send him off to the home for wayward dogs, but he's not a bit afraid that I'll really do that."

"If there *was* such a place," Marietta clarified with a chuckle. "Luckily, that's a box of flat egg noodles, and if they're broken, it's not the end of the world. They're still fine for the casseroles and soups most folks use them for."

Lydianne laughed. Molly's tone of voice was so affectionate any time she talked about Pete's golden retriever that it was doubtful she'd get rid of Riley. After some of the tales the twins had told after church recently, it was more likely they'd send Pete packing than his dog.

When she'd gently deposited the final box of noodles on the floor of the twins' shop, the sisters thanked her. "Do you suppose we should sell them at a discount?" Marietta asked as she peered through the clear bags to see if their contents were damaged.

"Just my opinion," Lydianne said, "but when I've bought any sort of pasta at the grocery store, some of it's been broken—even if it's packed in a box instead of a bag."

Marietta's grateful smile was a fine sight. She was still underweight after enduring her long, difficult chemo treatment, but her spirits were strong and she was regaining her physical strength, as well. "That's *gut* to know. We wouldn't have any idea about—"

"When you grow up with a *mamm* who runs a noodle company," Molly put in, "you never ever buy pasta from the store!"

Lydianne laughed, and after she wished them a good day of sales, she followed her nose to the adjoining shop. Jo was pulling two large pans of cinnamon rolls from her oven, setting them on her butcher-block worktable beside the big bowl of frosting she'd made for them.

"All right, missy, confess," Lydianne teased as she glanced at the clock above the sink. "It's only seven-thirty and you've already made the dough for these, rolled them out and spread them with filling, and let them rise—twice? What time do you get here on Saturdays, anyway?"

Jo waggled her eyebrows. "I have a secret," she teased in a furtive voice. "I make up a double batch of dough at home on Friday nights and keep it in the fridge. Saves me time on Saturday mornings, and I'm always sure to have fresh rolls ready when the doors open at nine."

"And the entire Marketplace already smells like cinnamon and sugar when the customers arrive," Lydianne remarked.

"I consider that free advertisement. It entices our guests beyond their ability to resist my treats," Jo said with a chuckle. "But of course, my *mamm* says I've become too focused on my business to be any help to *her* at home."

Lydianne wasn't surprised about Drusilla Fussner's attitude, yet it made her curious. "What does she say about the extra income you've been earning? Surely that counts for something—and so does the rent you get from the Wengerds, *jah*?"

Jo flashed her a long-suffering smile. "We spend some of the rent money for household expenses and bank the rest," she replied. "But when I tell her I've also been depositing my profits from the shop—for a time when we might not be able to run our roadside stand—she waves me off. Apparently, she doesn't figure on living beyond her ability to pay the bills."

"That's impressive," Lydianne murmured. "Most *maidels* and widows eventually become dependent upon a male in their family, even when they'd hoped not to."

"You know *mamm*. Never satisfied." Jo began spreading the white frosting over the tops of the hot rolls. "Not long ago, Nelson and Michael told us they plan to sell hundreds of poinsettias here during the holidays, and they even invited us to see their greenhouses in Queen City," she said wistfully. "But of course, Mamm shut them down by saying how such a long trip in a rig would be hard on her. And why would they want to look at her sourpuss expression or listen to her complaints for nearly three hours in each direction?"

It struck Lydianne like lightning—Jo was seriously sweet on Michael, and she'd give anything to see the Wengerd nurseries, to spend the time with him. In all the years she'd known Jo, this was the first time Lydianne had gotten any hint that her tall, stocky, long-limbed friend aspired to romance.

But why wouldn't she? Didn't every girl grow up dreaming of the day she'd marry and have a family?

"Couldn't you go without your *mamm*?" she asked softly. "It's not as though you have to do everything together—"

"And spend a couple of days with two men, unchaperoned?" Jo shot back. "Mamm would say I was on the road to hell in a handbasket if I did that!"

"Ah. I forgot about Michael's *mamm* not being there. Which means that Nelson would make a wonderful-*gut* companion for Drusilla—"

"Don't waste your breath!" Jo exclaimed with a shake of her head. "Nelson's a kind, considerate fellow, even when Mamm's behaving like—well, her usual self. But she would never in a million years pair up with him, or any other fellow.

"And what man would have her?" Jo continued sadly. "That's a terrible thing to say about your own mother, but it's true. She drives everyone away with her complaining."

Squeezing her friend's shoulder, Lydianne considered a more cheerful topic of conversation. "What do I need to do today? Will anyone want extra help in their shop, or shall I go upstairs and update the bookkeeping?"

Jo glanced at the clock. "You could do an hour's worth of accounting before we'll know if anyone's short-handed," she pointed out, returning to her usual practical frame of mind. "And take this with you."

She pulled a small plate from her open cabinet and placed a warm cinnamon roll on it. "*Denki* for being a friend and listening to my bellyaching, Lydianne," she murmured. "If I'm not careful, I'll end up being just like Mamm, ain't so?"

Lydianne blinked. She had no trouble envisioning Jo spending the rest of her life on the Fussner home place, taking care of her mother—yet she wanted to believe that so much more was in store for the competent, caring woman who stood beside her.

"I don't see that happening, Jo," she replied firmly. "You never know what God's got up His sleeve, just waiting for the right time to reveal it to you."

Jo glanced away, yet when she focused on Lydianne again, her lips were twitching with a grin. "You're right, of course. After all, He's brought you and the bishop together. And who could've foreseen that?"

"Don't put the cart before the horse," Lydianne insisted

as she accepted the huge cinnamon roll. But she didn't dispute what Jo had said—because what good would that do? Jo, the Helfings, and Regina had been around too many times when Jeremiah had shown up unexpectedly for her to deny the relationship that was budding between them. "God brought Regina and Gabe together, too, so we'll see what happens next for *all* of us, won't we?"

"We will," Jo agreed with a nod. "With God, *anything* is possible."

When Lydianne got to the upstairs office, she found a few receipts and notes on the worktable alongside the ledger. Her *maidel* friends very efficiently kept track of buying such items as toilet paper and paper towels for the restroom, as well as cleaning supplies—but it was the income column that made her smile as she scanned the notations of recent sales totals and the shopkeepers' monthly rent payments.

The Marketplace was also taking in some nice fees from a few local groups that were already booking holiday parties in the big reception area. Lydianne recorded the dates on their business calendar, and she was making notes about when she or Regina needed to work at those parties when a movement in the doorway made her look up.

Jeremiah's grin made her suck in her breath. Placing a finger on his lips to signal that she should be quiet, he closed the door behind him and carefully crossed the floor to slip into the chair beside hers.

"How much can folks underneath us hear when you move around up here?" he whispered.

As his breath tickled her ear, Lydianne's pulse raced. "I don't know," she replied softly. "What brings you up here to—"

"So we'll sit very still, and we won't talk." Jeremiah was a man keen on his purpose, if his bottomless brown eyes were any indication. Before she could ask him anything more, he kissed her gently, cradling her face in his broad, warm hand. As he deepened the kiss, Lydianne melted against him and got hopelessly, helplessly lost in the sweetness of his insistent lips. Questions about every-day matters ceased to exist as his thorough mouth let her know exactly how much he wanted her.

With a sigh, he finally broke away. "I couldn't wait until this afternoon to see you," he whispered, "so I slipped in the back way and came straight up the stairs, hoping you'd be here. With only a few minutes until the shops open, I'm figuring none of your friends will venture upstairs and find us."

His words were sweet and welcome, for her ears alone, after he'd had to defend her to other church members during the past week. "I told Jo I'd work on the books for a while and then check to see if anyone needed my help—"

"Oh, help *me* again, sweetheart," Jeremiah murmured before closing his eyes and meeting her lips once again.

Lydianne poured herself into the kiss, feeling wonder-fully liberated even as she sensed it wouldn't be long before Jeremiah claimed her as much more than his sweet-heart. As he pulled her closer, his love—his need for her—swept her into a state of awareness of his freshly showered scent and the smoothness of his shaved cheeks above the soft beard that brushed her chin. It would be so easy to succumb to the way he was awakening needs that had lain dormant for so long.

"Better stop right now, while I can." Jeremiah held her gaze, his eyes mere inches from hers as he inhaled deeply to settle himself. "It's been way too long since—well, we'd best not talk about that. Let's just say I'm hoping we can keep kissing this way, and that we'll come to a day when we don't have to stop there, Lydianne. Thinking about that possibility kept me awake most of the night."

Lydianne swallowed hard. "I hope I won't disappoint you, seeing's how you've had a lot more experience with—"

"You can't possibly disappoint me, Sunshine. I'm too far gone—too much in love with you to be concerned about anything except how happy you make me feel. So—" Jeremiah's smile brightened the entire office as he backed away from her. He glanced at her ledger and calendar, and then spotted the cinnamon roll. "We can't let this get stale, now, can we? Talk to me, Lydianne. Steer my mind back toward safer thoughts before I have to go downstairs."

She laughed softly, opening her mouth as he held a chunk of the cinnamon roll in front of her. As he helped himself to a bite, she savored the pastry's spicy sweetness. "When you came in, I was making notes on the reservations we've already gotten for holiday parties," she remarked, gesturing toward the calendar.

Jeremiah's eyebrows rose. "Which reminds me that Martin suggested we plan an evening of food and music on Second Christmas," he said. "I hope the twenty-sixth of December's still open?"

Lydianne pulled the calendar over to them, nodding. "That falls on a Thursday, and English folks are booking the Saturdays in December, so I'll put it down. What a fine idea!"

Jeremiah chuckled. "It all started when Gabe was refreshing our memories on some carol harmonies last night—in case we men have the occasion to sing as a group, as we did at the reunions."

"Well, if you create the occasion, everyone's sure to come, *jah*?" she asked lightly. "Who wouldn't want to hear you men sing—and then sing along? Carols sound even better when a whole roomful of people are joining in."

"We think alike, you and I," he murmured. As he unwound another few inches of the cinnamon roll, he winked at her. "I'll just help myself to another mouthful of this roll before I leave you to your work. Hopefully, no one will spot me. There'll be no end to the teasing and questions— not that I can't handle that."

His tone made her feel cherished and reminded her of all the times he'd come to her defense. "A little teasing sounds like a big improvement, considering the other issues we've dealt with recently," she said. "Do you suppose Clarence or Saul will say anything to anyone about my being Ella's mother?"

"I hope they realize the risk they run of upsetting Ella— especially since Julia and Tim have now explained that she was a gift from God to them." Jeremiah clasped her hand. "And she *is*, no matter what the circumstances of her conception."

He held her gaze for a moment, his faith and affection unwavering. "We'll have to trust that as leaders of the church, they'll respect the confidentiality of your confession as well as what's at stake for the Nissleys. Believe me, in my years as a bishop, I've heard and honored secrets much deeper and darker than yours, Sunshine. And so have they."

Lydianne blinked. His words made her curious, but she knew better than to ask what those secrets might've involved and whose they were. It was a blessing to know that her past was safe in Jeremiah's keeping, and that her relationship with Aden hadn't offended him.

"Truth be told," Jeremiah whispered as he leaned closer to her, "I'm ecstatic knowing that you'll be able to give me children, Lydianne. I couldn't possibly have loved Priscilla any more than I did—we shared a special, blessed marriage even though our nursery remained empty. But I feel so hopeful now—so ready to raise the babies we'll have together."

He cleared his throat and looked away. "But of course, I've gotten ahead of myself again, haven't I? One of these days I'll give you a chance to answer the question I haven't asked you yet."

After a moment, Jeremiah gazed at her again. "See you around five, Lydianne. I'll be parked out back, hoping we'll get away faster if we don't have folks stopping us to talk."

As he rose to go, Lydianne's emotions danced and she almost blurted out that yes, she'd marry him. But it was best to let Jeremiah follow all the steps of his courtship, wasn't it? And what was her hurry? He certainly didn't show signs of courting anyone else.

"I'll be ready," she said softly. "Have a *gut* day, Jeremiah."

He turned, with a tender smile that made her feel like the most beloved woman in the world. "It's already been the best day ever, because we've talked and kissed, Lydianne. I live for the day when we can share so much more."

When he'd disappeared into the upstairs hallway, Lydianne allowed herself to believe that her fondest dreams finally had a chance of coming true—that a man who knew of her past and loved her anyway wanted her to be his wife.

Chapter Twenty-Six

A little before five, Jeremiah went behind The Marketplace to hitch his mare to his buggy. He'd enjoyed about an hour of chatting with the Wengerds in their nursery shop, the Hartzler women in their quilt and candle shop, Martin and Gabe in the corner of the building that was filled with their beautiful furniture, and the Helfing twins as they sold the last bags of their noodles—and told a few stories on his nephew, Pete. All this visiting was only a way to bide his time, however.

What was taking Lydianne so long? When he'd last seen her, she'd been helping his redheaded nieces, Alice and Adeline, redd up the tables in the refreshment area—around four-fifteen. Didn't she know how eager he was to whisk her away? To spend time alone with her, someplace where well-meaning members of their church couldn't interrupt?

Maybe she's making me wait—playing hard to get after the way I swooped in on her this morning. Now that I've told her I love her, Lydianne knows she can say "jump" and I'll immediately ask her "how high?"

A few minutes later when she emerged, however,

Lydianne's smile made Jeremiah forget his impatient musings.

"Sorry I wasn't here sooner, but Gracie was showing me the pumpkin placemat she'd cross-stitched—as Martha Maude looked on," she explained while he helped her into his buggy. "I thought it best to give them a little of my time, seeing's how Gracie has latched onto me as her other mother, and Martha Maude's going along with that line."

Jeremiah stepped up into the rig, agreeing with Lydianne's logic. "*Jah*, I could've cheered out loud when Gracie rushed toward you and got all the kids going about how they wanted you to be their *mamm*," he replied as they backed away from the hitching rail. "But let's leave all that behind us, shall we? Seems like a nice evening for a ride and dinner at the café in Willow Ridge. Hopefully, we won't see anybody we know, like we would here in town."

Lydianne chuckled. "Everyone around here seems very aware that we're spending time together," she remarked softly. "The way their minds—and the grapevine—work, a lot of them already have us hitched up and having kids."

"Is that a *bad* thing?"

Her faraway expression teased at him as she welcomed the hand he wrapped around hers. "It's just a *sudden* thing," she clarified softly. "Every couple should take the time to know each other's sore spots and all those little habits that are easy to overlook—until that first rush of romance dies down and they grate on your nerves. Those little irritations can become stumbling blocks to a close relationship."

Jeremiah admired her mature way of making that point. "Surely you don't have any such habits!" he teased.

"Of course, I don't," she shot back. "I've lived alone for so long, I've become the perfect companion—for myself.

And you've had a wife and your mother seeing to all your needs, so you've gotten used to the way they've always done things. The minute I become Mrs. Shetler, your apple cart will get upset in a big way."

The way she'd said *Mrs. Shetler*, as though she'd tried it on for size in her mind, made Jeremiah's soul glow. "Maybe I have a few ideas for easing that transition. And Mamm's already offered to move out so we'd have our privacy," he said. "She was one of the first to see us as a *gut* match, and she reminds me of that every chance she gets."

Lydianne's eyes widened. "Where would she go? As I recall, she lived with Jude after his first wife died, helping manage his kids. But once he married Leah and her *mamm* moved in with them, she came back to your place."

"My mother's motivated to do whatever it takes to make us happy—and to bring her some more grandkids," he added with a gentle laugh. "Mamm got along fine with Priscilla, but it was her biggest disappointment when our babies didn't start arriving. She accepted our situation as best she could—like Priscilla and I had to—but our childless state hung over the household like a constant cloud."

Lydianne gazed out over the passing countryside. "*Jah*, a baby changes everything. For better or worse," she murmured.

Jeremiah squeezed her hand. "But we've got plenty of time together before we start our family," he said in a lighter tone. "After all, the school year's off to a fine start. Nobody's keen on replacing you, Lydianne—especially now that the scholars have become so attached to you."

"Not to mention the fact that you haven't proposed, and I haven't answered. Everyone seems to be overlooking that."

Jeremiah's eyes widened and he focused on the winding road. Lydianne's observation hadn't sounded judgmental or disappointed—and as they rolled along the county highway, she remained as calm as the autumn dusk that was falling around them. How many women would be able to mention a marriage proposal in such a lighthearted, matter-of-fact tone, as though it was an event that just hadn't happened yet? His first inclination was to pull onto the shoulder of the road and pop the question straightaway, yet that felt wrong.

"'To everything there's a season,'" he remarked, relying on the Bible to get him through a tricky spot.

"'And a time for every purpose under the heaven,'" Lydianne said without missing a beat. "What with writing a verse of Scripture on the board each day, I'm pretty *gut* at quoting the Bible—but being around a bishop full-time would increase my repertoire a lot, no doubt."

Jeremiah laughed out loud. "Trading verse for verse, like a contest, must surely rank as the least likely way to win a woman's heart. But it's nice to know you wouldn't back down or feel intimidated by my years of Bible study and preaching if I did challenge you."

"I don't have it in me to back down, just because you're a man and I'm not. That's one of those little habits I spoke of earlier," she said with a sweet, wide-eyed smile. "And maybe it's a *maidel* thing, too."

"You and your *maidel* friends certainly didn't back down from the challenges of running The Marketplace," Jeremiah agreed. He gestured ahead of them, feeling lighthearted as the outskirts of Willow Ridge came into view. "We're almost there, and I can already smell the meat roasting in the outdoor grills. Ever eaten at the Grill N Skillet?"

Lydianne shook her head. "I've heard it's the best place around, though. And now that I've caught a whiff of seasoned beef and pork, I could eat an entire cow by myself," she stated in all seriousness. Then she laughed. "That sounds like something Billy Jay or Stevie would say."

Chuckling, Jeremiah guided his mare along the road that ran past the Simple Gifts store, because it was faster than circling his friend Tom's dairy farm. A few minutes later, he pulled into an empty spot along the café's hitching rail.

"Always busy on Saturday nights," he murmured as he set the brake. "Guess I didn't consider that I know several folks in this town, so we may well see someone who'll find it very *interesting* that I have a pretty woman with me. Are you all right with that, Lydianne?"

Her cheeks glowed at his compliment. "If I want my dinner, I'd better take that in stride, ain't so?"

Jeremiah stepped to the ground and grasped Lydianne around the waist to help her down. He was tempted to get lost in her kiss again, right there in the parking lot, but he thought better of it. She was such a blessing—and in such a good mood this evening—he didn't want to jeopardize their first real date. He contented himself with placing his hand in the small of her back as they approached the door.

The Grill N Skillet rang with dozens of conversations as aromas of beef, chicken, cornbread, biscuits, and other down-home food on the buffet wafted around the main dining room. He quickly surveyed the sturdy wooden tables, hoping to find an empty one—

"Jeremiah Shetler!" someone called out above the noisy crowd.

"Here's two chairs with your names on them," another

fellow chimed in, just as Jeremiah spotted four arms waving in the air about halfway back.

He smiled at two longtime friends, pointing so Lydianne would know which way to go between the crowded tables. "Honest to Pete, I did *not* know these guys and their wives would be here tonight," he said. "But we'll be in *gut* company—"

"Of course, we will," she reassured him. "If they like you enough to call you over, how can I not like them, too?"

Once again, Jeremiah reminded himself that Lydianne was more than equal to the task of stepping into a bishop's life and social circle, even if she was several years younger than he was. As he shook the hands of the two longtime friends who'd called them over, he made the introductions.

"Lydianne, this is Tom Hostetler and his wife Nazareth from here in Willow Ridge, and Vernon Gingerich, who married Nazareth's sister, Jerusalem—they live in Cedar Creek," he said as she gripped the hand of each smiling person in turn. "Miss Christner's our new schoolteacher in Morning Star."

"Pleased to meet you all," Lydianne said as she took the empty chair nearest the two women.

Vernon's wife flashed her a bright smile. "Back in the day, Nazareth and I taught school for most of our lives, out East," she remarked.

"Never in a million years did we dream we'd both hitch up with bishops after we moved to Missouri," Nazareth put in with a laugh. "Just goes to show you that God's plan can take you down some totally unexpected paths."

"And His plans are always the best," Jerusalem put in. "As you can see by our plates, we've already made our first round at the buffet—"

"So your arrival is the perfect excuse for a refill," Tom

piped up with a boyish smile. "By golly, it's so *gut* to see you, Jeremiah, your meals are on me. And don't give me any guff about it!"

Just that easily, his friends had welcomed Lydianne, and minutes later they were filling plates at the buffet table. It was a joy to watch her select slices of brisket, scalloped potatoes, and spoonfuls of the various salads and side dishes as she chatted with Nazareth and Jerusalem. The Hostetlers and Gingeriches were somewhat older than he was—old enough to be Lydianne's parents—yet she was already conversing so easily with them, that Jeremiah knew she wouldn't feel left out if he talked with Tom and Vernon some of the time.

Even though Amish women had much in common from one town to the next, some gals were shy around folks they didn't know. It had taken Priscilla a long time to get beyond feeling intimidated when they'd socialized with other bishops—especially because the lot had fallen to him when he was in his thirties, and the other church leaders were so much older and sterner.

It's yet another blessing, Lord, that Lydianne can hold her own amongst my colleagues, he prayed when they bowed briefly over their plates at the table.

The meal was delicious, and the six of them moved effortlessly from one topic of conversation to the next. Every now and then he clasped Lydianne's hand under the table, and when she squeezed back, Jeremiah felt deliriously happy. When he glanced at the wall clock over his second slice of pie, he was astounded that more than two hours had passed—without a single dead spot in the conversation.

"We'll have to mosey over to Morning Star some Sunday and attend your service, Jeremiah," Vernon said with a twinkle in his blue eyes. "Just to be sure you folks're still following the proper path."

"Puh!" Jerusalem put in. "Church is all well and *gut*, but *I* want to make it over to The Marketplace some Saturday and see what all the fuss is about!"

"*Jah*, folks hereabouts are saying it's quite the place to shop, with Plain crafters and businesses all under one roof," Nazareth chimed in.

Lydianne beamed at them. "Within the next month, when we start setting out Christmas items, I suspect we'll be really busy. We've gotten off to a more profitable start than any of us figured on—"

"And with our church getting a percentage of the sales," Jeremiah remarked, "we've paid for the property and the new schoolhouse, so everybody benefits. The five *maidels* who organized it have done us all proud."

"Well, where there's a woman, there's a way!" Jerusalem crowed, and the six of them laughed so loudly that folks at other tables looked over to see what the big joke was.

After he'd thanked Tom for their dinner and they said their good-byes, Jeremiah followed Lydianne between the crowded tables to the parking lot. It had been one of the most pleasant evenings in recent memory, and he was pleased that Lydianne had enjoyed it, too.

"What lovely, funny friends you have," she remarked as he helped her into the rig.

Jeremiah laughed as he slid onto the seat and turned on the headlights and the safety flashers. "Vernon and Tom are the best," he agreed. "Their lives took a sudden turn when they met the Hooley sisters. Vernon had lost his devoted Dorothea, and Tom's wife left him for an English fellow a few years ago. It's wonderful to see them so happy again . . . and all because a couple of open-minded *maidels* took a chance on them."

As the mare clip-clopped onto the county highway, Jeremiah considered another possibility and how he should phrase it. With Lydianne sitting so close that her skirt rustled against his pant leg as the buggy moved, he didn't want to ruin their fine mood by saying something dumb or inappropriate.

"It's another plus that we've met up with Tom and Vernon," he began softly, "because one of these days—if I happen to ask a certain young lady for her hand—we'll need one of them to officiate at the wedding."

"That's a big *if*," Lydianne teased, happy to continue her flirtation concerning his proposal. Then her expression waxed more serious. "But why only one of them? No matter whom you choose, the other fellow's likely to feel bad that he didn't get picked, *jah*? After all, how often does a bishop get remarried?" she continued more fervently. "Why shouldn't your ceremony—your entire wedding day—be as extraordinary as you are, Jeremiah?"

He was so startled, he drew in his breath. He felt ten feet tall and head-over-heels for the beautiful woman beside him.

Lydianne turned her head, however. "But it's none of my beeswax, of course," she said breezily, "because I haven't been asked to participate in any way."

As his laughter rang out into the autumn night, Jeremiah slipped his arm around Lydianne and hugged her firmly. He suspected she would always be able to take him by surprise—and as long as she took him for her husband someday, he would be forever delighted.

Chapter Twenty-Seven

"Jeremiah! We need to go to the Detweiler place, right now!"

His mother's urgent voice coming up through the heating grate roused Jeremiah from his daydreams of Lydianne as he shaved early on Sunday morning. Mamm rarely interrupted his routine when he was preparing for a church service, so he quickly rinsed his face. "I'll be right there, soon as I put on my clothes," he called down to her.

All manner of possibilities, none of them good, rushed through his mind. Should he wear his Sunday suit and be ready for church, or everyday clothing more suited to a physical emergency? He opted for the shirt and pants that still lay over the back of the chair after his date with Lydianne, figuring he'd have time to change before heading to the Flaud home for the service.

The sight of Billy Jay crying in Mamm's lap at the kitchen table told him he might be in for a long morning, however. "What's happened, son?" he asked softly as he placed his hand on the boy's tousled hair.

Billy Jay sniffled loudly. "Dat sent me here to tellya that—that Mammi Elva didn't wake up this morning," he said as tears streamed down his cheeks. "I knew somethin' was wrong when I woke up and I couldn't smell no breakfast, and baby Levi was bawlin' his head off and—"

"Give me a minute to hitch up the buggy and we'll be on our way," Jeremiah said, looking at his mother.

"If you'll go out and help Jeremiah with the horse, honey-boy, I'll pack us up some breakfast to take along," Mamm suggested gently. "Won't take me but a minute."

Flashing his mother a grateful smile, Jeremiah grabbed his jacket and started toward the stable with Billy Jay close behind him. He recalled Glenn saying how run-down his *mamm* had been of late—and the remarks Reuben had made Friday evening about her diabetes and heart—but he hadn't expected her to pass on so quickly.

"Did your *mammi* fix your supper last night? Was she feeling poorly over the weekend?" he asked Billy Jay as he opened the stable's wooden plank door.

The boy shook his head. "Dat called for pizza delivery again, coz Mammi was sleepin' on the couch and couldn't even give Levi his bottle," he replied mournfully. "He almost couldn't wake her up to get her into bed last night."

Jeremiah wondered if Glenn had considered calling for an ambulance—or had thought about coming to get him last night.

But I wasn't home, the sharp voice in his head reminded him. Even though Jeremiah knew he couldn't be present every time a church member needed him, he still felt bad when couldn't help his friends.

He focused on hitching up the horse, and when Mamm came out with a picnic basket, he set it in the back of the rig. It didn't take but five minutes to drive to the Detweiler farm, but he couldn't imagine the fear and worry that must've propelled Billy Jay along the road, running at top speed to get help while Glenn managed the crisis at home along with a wailing baby and his elderly father.

When they got to the house, Mamm and Billy Jay immediately followed Levi's ear-splitting cries to find him. Jeremiah set the picnic basket on the kitchen floor and stopped to place his hand on the slumped figure at the table. He prayed that Reuben hadn't had a heart attack from the shock of waking up beside his dead wife.

"Reuben, I'm mighty sorry," he said as he pulled up a chair.

With a forlorn sigh, Reuben raised his head. "I knew the minute she went," he whispered. "I couldn't hardly sleep for worrying about her—she'd refused to go to the emergency room when Glenn asked her to—so when she shuddered all over and stopped breathing, I knew she'd gone home to the Lord."

Reuben's smile was bittersweet. "Elva never wanted to trouble anybody, you know. It was three-fifteen, and how was Glenn gonna get the undertaker at that hour?" he reasoned wearily. "So, I just stayed beside her until the baby woke up, wanting to be fed."

Jeremiah was momentarily speechless. What a great depth of love this poor elderly fellow had felt for his wife, that he was comfortable remaining beside her lifeless body in bed. "Sounds like she had a peaceful passing beside the man she loved, and now she's claimed her reward," Jeremiah murmured. "It's the best Elva could hope for, but it's tough on the rest of us. How's Glenn?"

"He's called the funeral home, but I haven't seen him since he came in." Reuben's bushy eyebrows rose as he looked toward the front room. "Well, now. Levi's quieter. *That's* a relief."

Jeremiah nodded. "I'll go check on Glenn and the baby.

Mamm brought some breakfast—she'll get you something
as soon as she can."

"No need to eat," Reuben remarked with a shrug.
"What with Elva gone, I won't be around much longer
anyway."

He'd heard many an elderly spouse express the same
sentiment after their mate passed, so he didn't try to talk
Reuben out of his depression. As he rose from the table,
his mother entered the kitchen with baby Levi hiccupping
against her shoulder and Billy Jay following her like a
shadow.

"If you'll find me the goat's milk, we'll warm a bottle,"
she was saying to the beleaguered boy. "You can feed him
on the couch, or we'll have your *dat* do that while I heat
up the breakfast casserole and the sweet rolls I brought
along."

"The goat's milk's in the fridge—*gut* thing Leah brought
us a fresh batch yesterday," Billy Jay said. "If you warm it
on the stove, I can feed him. I was Mammi's best helper at
takin' care of the baby."

"I know you were, sweetie," Mamm said approvingly.

Sending her a grateful smile, Jeremiah went into the
front room in search of Glenn. Flat boxes on the coffee
table—with a few congealed slices of pizza still in them—
and the scattered toys and newspapers attested to the fact
that Elva hadn't been able to keep up with the clutter lately.
After he'd poked his head into all the downstairs rooms,
he started up the wooden steps.

"Glenn, it's Jeremiah," he called out. "Bet you could
use some breakfast, and Mamm'll have it ready in a few."

No reply.

From his times of meeting with the preachers before a
church service, he knew to turn left at the top of the stairs.

His friend stood at the window in the first bedroom, silhouetted against the brilliant pink clouds that glowed with the sunrise.

"I'm sorry you're having such a rough time of it these past few months, Glenn," Jeremiah said from the doorway. He hesitated to intrude upon his friend's privacy in this haven Glenn and Dorcas had shared when she was alive, so he focused on practicalities. "Your *dat* says you've called Griggs Mortuary. Can I make any other calls for you? Your sister, maybe?"

"Already called her. Sadie says her family can be here by Tuesday if they leave this afternoon." Glenn's voice sounded distant and hollow, as though he was speaking from inside a well. "Griggs should be here any time now to take Mamm's—ah, there's the hearse now, coming down the road."

Glenn's sigh could've been the wind riffling the cedar trees in the cemetery. "Mamm was the glue that held us together after Dorcas passed—the only person who kept me going from one day into the next," he remarked in a broken voice. "I don't know how we'll manage—"

"It's not the same as having your *mamm*, but the women will get together at church today and organize a schedule," Jeremiah assured him. "You'll have meals, and help with Levi and the laundry, and every other bit of assistance we can give you, Glenn. You'll not face this alone."

When Glenn turned, his face was haggard and his expression was harsh. "Easy for you to say, now that Lydianne's picked you instead of me," he muttered. "You have no idea how I'd counted on having her to help me raise my boys and get my life back on track."

His remark stabbed like a knife, even though Jeremiah knew that intense grief was partly responsible for the rancor behind it. And at least Glenn had pointed out that Lydianne had made her choice, rather than blaming Jeremiah for stealing her away from him.

"I'm sorry you feel that way," he said softly. "My mother should have some breakfast ready shortly, if you'd care for some after the hearse leaves."

As he descended the stairs, his mind was a whirlwind of mixed emotions. He nodded encouragement to Billy Jay, who sat patiently on the couch with his sleeping baby brother against his shoulder. Jeremiah grimaced when he saw the clock on the kitchen wall. "Church starts in twenty minutes—"

"I warmed you some of the casserole, and here's a pineapple cream cheese roll," his mother said, pointing toward a plate on the table. "You'll not get through the service very well without eating something—and under the circumstances, who's going to kick you out of church for not wearing your *gut* clothes today?"

Despite his misgivings, Jeremiah smiled. Wasn't it just like his mother to cut to the chase and point out the proper priorities? "Billy Jay has finished feeding the baby," he remarked softly. "The hearse is coming down the lane, so maybe you should sit with him while they do their business."

After Mamm nodded and went out to the front room, Jeremiah slipped his arm around Reuben's shoulders. "Griggs will be here in a minute. Where do you prefer to be while they take Elva's body?"

Reuben blinked with comprehension, wiping his eyes. "I'm fine right here. I—I've said my *gut*-bye until the funeral."

Nodding, Jeremiah went to the front door to greet the two men who got out of the hearse and unfolded a gurney.

He saw that his mother had taken Billy Jay into the back room with the baby, and when the men entered the house, he directed them upstairs. "Elva's son Glenn is up there. You might want to give him a minute with her," he suggested softly.

His breakfast awaited him when he returned to sit with Glenn's *dat*. "Better eat, Bishop," Reuben said. "I can tell you that Elva's real sorry she's caused all this commotion while you're getting ready for church—"

"Don't be concerned about that. The preachers can run things without me," Jeremiah put in softly. He slid the plate of warm rolls in front of his longtime friend to entice him with their fruity-sweet aroma. "Why don't you join me, Reuben? Better try these rolls before Billy Jay spots them. They're soft and sweet and melt-in-your-mouth *gut*."

Intrigued, Reuben slowly took a roll from the plate. After they prayed briefly, Jeremiah gratefully dug into his warm sausage and egg casserole while Reuben bit into a sweet roll. When he closed his eyes as he chewed, Jeremiah was pleased that he'd at least made Glenn's *dat* feel a little better this morning—even if Reuben's sense of satisfaction would last only as long as he kept eating.

A few minutes after the hearse left, Billy Jay joined his *dawdi* at the table, so Jeremiah took off for the Flauds'. They only lived about two miles farther down the gravel road that ran past the Detweiler place. As he turned onto the lane, which was lined with unhitched buggies, he could hear voices singing the first hymn in Martin's big front room. After he put his mare in the pasture with the other buggy horses, Jeremiah slipped in through the kitchen to go upstairs for the preachers' meeting. Then he noticed that Ammon, Clarence, and Saul were already seated on the preachers' bench between the men's and women's sides of the congregation, ready to begin the service.

Feeling very conspicuous in his brown broadfall trousers and tan shirt, Jeremiah walked down the center aisle just as folks finished singing the hymn. He turned to face them as they closed their hymnals.

"Friends, I've just come from the Detweiler place, and I'm sorry to announce that Elva went to meet her Maker around three this morning. She passed peacefully in her sleep with Reuben beside her," he said in a low voice. "My *mamm* is staying with Glenn, Reuben, and the boys this morning. I assured them we'd organize your help with chores, meals, and housekeeping after the service today."

Folks whispered among themselves, surprised and sorry about his news. When Jeremiah raised his hand, they fell silent again. "Shall we pray before we proceed with the service?" he suggested.

"Dear Lord and Father of us all, we thank You for the life of Elva Detweiler, who served as a shining example of servitude her whole life long," he intoned with his head bowed. "Inspire us to be the best friends her family could possibly have in their time of sadness and help us to live our lives in constant readiness for that glad day when You call each one of us home to You. Amen."

Chapter Twenty-Eight

As Lydianne raised her head at the end of the prayer, she could imagine how desperate the situation at the Detweiler house must be just by looking at Jeremiah's dear face. The lines bracketing his mouth and fanning around his soulful brown eyes were etched deeper—lines that added such character to his skin, which was bronzed and weathered by his farming. She recognized the clothes he'd worn on their date—perfectly acceptable for socializing, but she could tell Bishop Jeremiah felt out of place in them as he sat before God and the congregation on Sunday morning.

He got called to Glenn's place while he was getting ready for church. Isn't it just like Jeremiah to put the needs of a grieving family before his own? He must've been such a comfort to them.

As the service progressed, with Preachers Ammon and Clarence delivering lengthy sermons, however, Lydianne couldn't miss the profound sadness that shadowed Jeremiah's face. He seemed lost in thought, gazing at the floor most of the service instead of appearing engaged in it. Instinct told her he was feeling something more painful than the concerns of a bishop caring for a family that had just lost a vital member.

After church, Jeremiah called a brief Members Meeting. The women agreed to write up a schedule for providing meals and assistance to Glenn, Reuben, and the boys. The men chimed in with assurances that they'd take care of the livestock chores and repairs that needed to be made around the Detweiler place before winter set in. They knew Glenn wouldn't have the time or inclination for such things while he was raising his sons and grieving his *mamm* and his wife—not to mention looking after his father, whose physical and mental health seemed to be declining.

When the meeting broke up and the other women headed for Delores's kitchen to set out the common meal, Lydianne lingered behind. She waited for a few of the men to finish chatting with Jeremiah before catching his eye. As he made his way between the fellows who were setting up tables, his expression lightened a bit.

"*Gut* afternoon, Sunshine," he said quietly. "It was a fine thing to see your encouraging smiles during the service, after the way my day began."

"I can't imagine Glenn was doing very well this morning," Lydianne remarked. "And how's Reuben holding up?"

"Reuben's a trouper. I'm a lot more concerned about Glenn, because he's lost the woman who was holding his life together after Dorcas's passing." When Jeremiah rubbed his hand over his face, Lydianne noticed that he hadn't gotten to finish shaving this morning. "But I found it particularly distressing that he . . . Glenn's still very angry because you've chosen to be with me instead of with him."

"And he blamed *you*, didn't he?"

"Not in so many words, but—"

"I could see it on your face during the service," Lydianne whispered. She longed to grasp his hand, but thought better of it with other folks around them preparing for the meal. "He thinks his life would fall neatly into place—that all his problems would be solved—if I would marry him and raise his boys."

Jeremiah smiled wearily. "He has a point."

"No, he has it wrong," Lydianne countered, trying to keep her voice low. "Just because he came on like a house afire doesn't mean I'd ever come to love him—or fit into his fantasy about taking Dorcas's place. I'll find a way to clarify that for him again, so Glenn's not taking out his frustration on *you*, Jeremiah."

His embrace took her completely by surprise. Right in the center of the Flaud's crowded front room, Jeremiah wrapped his arms around Lydianne and lightly rested his head on top of hers. "*Denki* for understanding my difficult relationship with Glenn right now," he whispered as he held her close against his tall, sturdy body. "Be gentle with him, though. Any man who's lost you—and his wife and his *mamm* and his dreams—is going to feel mighty low. You're a *gut* woman to care about his feelings—and mine—Lydianne."

When they eased apart, everyone was watching them, wearing speculative expressions. Lydianne felt heat creeping into her cheeks, yet she suddenly didn't mind that these friends had witnessed the emotion Jeremiah had shared with her. With a parting smile for him, she went to the kitchen to help carry platters of food to the tables.

Regina grabbed her playfully by the sleeve. "Well now, I guess we know what that hug meant, ain't so?" she teased. "And I couldn't be happier for you."

"Puh! We saw this coming all along, didn't we?" Jo put in as she grinned at the Helfing twins. "Lydianne won't be a *maidel* much longer—"

"But you won't marry the bishop until school's out in the spring, *jah*?" Lucy Miller was holding a pitcher of water in each hand, sounding worried about her future schooling. Lorena Flaud stood wide-eyed beside her, as though she didn't know whether to laugh or to cry.

The kitchen fell silent as the other women, gripping utensils and platters, turned to hear Lydianne's answer. She saw happiness on their faces, yet the mothers of scholars also looked as concerned as Lucy had sounded.

"That's exactly right, Lucy," Lydianne replied as she slipped an arm around each of her two oldest students. "Nothing's to be gained by marrying in haste—and I believe in seeing my commitments through. I fully intend to watch you both complete your studies."

Lorena hugged her tightly and then began clapping. The rest of the ladies burst into applause, as well. It was the moment that marked the end of Lydianne's private relationship with Jeremiah and the beginning of her official journey toward becoming the bishop's wife.

Never mind that he hasn't asked me yet. That's between him and me—with God as our witness, she reminded herself with a smile.

Four days later, as the crowd of mourners stood around Elva Detweiler's open grave to bid her farewell, Lydianne prayed for the bereaved family—and for guidance. The gray day matched the congregation's somber mood as Jeremiah made a few closing remarks about Elva's service to her Lord, and how she stood as a shining example of a soul who'd devoted her time and energy to her family.

After the pallbearers lowered Elva's plain pine coffin into its final resting place, folks took turns tossing shovelfuls of soil into the grave. As they stepped up, they were careful not to trip over the five small, rounded headstones that marked the young Detweiler children who'd preceded their mother in death.

Lydianne stole a glance at Glenn's older sister, Sadie Shank. Sadie stood between her brother and her husband, Ivan, alongside Reuben and a very subdued Billy Jay. The Shanks's four older children stood huddled behind them, looking unsure of how to handle the rituals of death and burial. The birth of the twins that Sadie and Ivan held in basket carriers had kept the family from coming to Morning Star for Dorcas's funeral three and a half months ago—and because the Shanks lived in Indiana, Lydianne had only seen Sadie a few times. With her dark hair and eyebrows, she closely resembled Glenn, yet Lydianne was struck by the sense of determined purpose that had displaced the grief on Sadie's face.

As the graveside service ended, folks walked toward their parked buggies for the short trip to the Detweiler farm for lunch. Sadie, however, took her brother's arm to pull him out of the crowd. "Have you thought about what I said?" she asked in a low voice. "You know full well you should move east to be with us, Glenn. There's nothing here for you anymore, and you can't possibly manage Dat, as well as the boys—"

"I've already told you *no*," Glenn snapped, hugging baby Levi closer to the shoulder of his black coat. "I'm not pulling Billy Jay out of the school here—"

"We have a school right down the road. He could go

with his cousins!" Sadie insisted. "You can move your woodworking business into a new shop on our property, and I can tend to Dat while—"

"You and Dat have never seen eye to eye, so why will that be any different—especially now that you have two new babies to feed in addition to your other kids?" her brother shot back.

"But as Dat's mind slips further away from reality—"

"Why should he live someplace else? It'll only confuse him more." Glenn's sharp glare could've carved the letters into their mother's tombstone. "You have your life, and we have ours, Sadie. Just forget it, all right?"

As he stalked off to catch up to his father and Billy Jay, Lydianne was sorry she'd witnessed such a rift in his family. Sadie and Glenn were the only two Detweiler siblings who'd survived to adulthood, so it was sad that Sadie had moved so far away, and that they couldn't agree about Reuben's future home and care.

Was Glenn's *dat* really losing touch with reality? Lydianne had observed a few forgetful moments Reuben had experienced since Dorcas's death—but who didn't occasionally lose track of details, especially when they were stressed or grieving? As she walked toward the Fussners' double buggy with Jo, Drusilla, and the Helfing twins, she wondered how Reuben would fare in the coming days without his daughter-in-law or his wife.

"Sounds like Sadie's determined that everybody at Reuben's house should uproot themselves, just because she says so," Drusilla remarked as Jo drove the buggy down the road.

"Too bad she had to call Glenn on the carpet with everyone else looking on, too," Marietta said. "Poor man's got enough on his mind without her telling him he should change his entire life."

"Sadie was always better at dishing up instructions than she was at taking them," Molly put in with a shake of her head. "Glenn and his *dat* will probably be relieved when she heads back to Indiana—although that's a horrible thing to say. It's a shame Sadie and Glenn were never close, and now the strain of losing their *mamm* is driving them further apart."

At the Detweiler farm, neighbors had cleared the central area of the largest barn so long tables, benches, and chairs could accommodate folks for the funeral lunch. Many of the women from church had provided large pans of baked chicken, baked potatoes, and side dishes, which were arranged on a serving table with plates, napkins, and eating utensils. Martha Maude and Anne Hartzler had finished setting up the meal while the rest of the congregation had attended the graveside service. They were removing the foil from the steaming containers of food as the crowd emerged from the many buggies parked along both sides of the Detweilers' lane.

As members of the family filled their plates first, Lydianne and her friends took up the pitchers on a side table and began filling water glasses. Esther and Naomi Slabaugh were cutting pies at a table near the back of the eating area. Conversations soon filled the barn while the first shift of people ate their meal. When Glenn went over to choose a slice of pie, the Helfing twins spoke with him.

Lydianne sensed the usual exchange of condolences as Molly and Marietta squeezed Glenn's arm and he nodded in all the right places. When Jo approached him, Lydianne decided it might be a good time to express her own sorrow, while Glenn wasn't seated at a crowded table with Sadie and her family.

"Mamm and I will be over tomorrow with your supper and to redd up the house," Jo was saying. "If there's anything else you need, please let us know, all right?"

Glenn seemed preoccupied, probably overwhelmed by so many offers of help. It was clear that although Jo and the Helfing twins were his friends, he had no inclination to socialize with them—much less consider them as potential mates.

As Lydianne stepped up to him, however, Glenn's expression became wary. Maybe he was ready to return to the table with his pie, so she didn't want to detain him for long. "Glenn, I'm sorry you've lost your *mamm*—"

"*Sorry*," he muttered, as though the word tasted particularly foul. "I'm sick and tired of feeling sorry, and of hearing about it, and—and you could still change that, Lydianne, if you'd give me another chance!"

Glenn's sudden turnaround stunned her, as did the raw anguish in his expressive dark eyes.

"We could start again and take it at your speed," he pleaded, leaning closer to emphasize his words. "If I knew you'd be my wife, even if I had to wait awhile, I could make it from one day to the next. I'd have a *life* again—"

Lydianne shook her head, stepping away when he grabbed her upper arm—but he kept his hold on her. This escalating exchange was *not* what she'd had in mind when she'd told Jeremiah she would ease the pressure between him and Glenn, but there was no escaping him. "Glenn, I can't lie about my feelings—can't promise I'll ever love you enough to—"

"But Billy Jay adores you! I can give you a *gut* home and—and we can take our time about—"

"No, Glenn. It would never work." Lydianne regretted being so abrupt, so cruel to a grieving man who believed she was the answer to all his prayers, yet there seemed no other way to get through to him.

Glenn blinked, still gripping her arm. "Fine, then," he whispered starkly. "I had to give it one last try."

When he suddenly slipped his arm around her shoulders, his kiss tasted like angst and anguish, bruising her lips with his desperation. Lydianne was too stunned to respond, until she freed herself with a gasp.

Glenn tossed his plate of pie back onto the table and stalked out of the barn. Aware that everyone had been watching them—especially the Slabaugh sisters, who stood wide-eyed at the pie table—Lydianne left, too, heading in a different direction from the way Glenn had gone.

How could her well-intentioned chat have gone so wrong? Why was Glenn so fixated on *her*, when her single girlfriends might've welcomed his attention? Lydianne felt so flustered and embarrassed, she wished the ground would open up and swallow her. Since that wasn't going to happen—and walking home wasn't an option—it seemed best to duck behind the nearest outbuilding to pull herself together.

What with Glenn's impassioned plea and kiss, as well as the embrace she'd shared with Jeremiah Sunday after church, folks surely had to be buzzing about the school-teacher who seemed to be enticing various men beyond the bounds of appropriate public behavior. She'd given the Slabaugh sisters enough feed to keep them clucking for months about her moral state and her standing with the Lord. Deacon Saul and the other men on the school board might soon be calling for her to confess more than one secret sin of the flesh, after witnessing her behavior—

"Lydianne. Wait up, honey."

Jeremiah's low voice cut through her frantic thoughts as she reached the far side of the chicken house. "You have every reason to be upset by Glenn's behavior—"

"People will think I led him on!" she protested, turning to face him. "Saul and Clarence already suspect me of wayward behavior, and the Slabaugh sisters will surely— and after everyone saw you hug me on Sunday, they're all thinking I'm some sort of loose woman, leading the two of you on—"

"Whoa." When he gently framed her face between his large, warm hands, Lydianne was struck by the deep affection in his eyes.

"Everyone saw the way Glenn grabbed you, and how you backed away," Jeremiah pointed out. "And there was no mistaking your tone of voice when you told him his wishes were never going to come true."

Heat crept up her neck and into her cheeks. "So, every person in the barn heard every word we said. Oh, my."

"It's embarrassing, but this, too, shall pass, Sunshine," Jeremiah assured her. "We'll chalk up Glenn's last-ditch attempt to his grief and his staggering personal losses over the past few months. Take a deep breath, Lydianne."

She blinked. When she inhaled and let the air out, however, her body began to relax.

"I have no trouble understanding why he gave it one last try, because *I* wouldn't let you go without a struggle, either," Jeremiah murmured as a smile lit up his face. "You'd be the solution to Glenn's biggest problems, but I'm so glad you don't want to be. Besides that, it's too soon for him to hitch up with *anyone*—but he's hurting too bad to realize it."

Jeremiah's soothing voice settled Lydianne's nerves. He was talking her down from an emotional ledge simply by stating the way things were.

"And if you were trying to reconcile Glenn's bitter feelings toward me, *denki*—but we should probably leave that be for now," he suggested gently. "Glenn has a lot of healing to do, and a lot of immediate challenges. I suspect our best gifts to him will be our prayers, some meals and housekeeping, some help with his boys and Reuben, and our willingness to listen when he wants to talk."

Lydianne nodded. She couldn't deny the gentle wisdom behind the bishop's words.

"I'd kiss you, but sure as I did, somebody would come around the chicken house looking for us," he said with a chuckle. "Why don't we mosey on back to the barn and see if it's our turn to eat? I'd be delighted if you'd sit with me, Lydianne. We have nothing to hide, and I want everyone to know that our feelings for each other are honorable and appropriate and probably permanent—even though that pertinent question still hasn't been asked or answered," he added lightly.

When he waggled his dark eyebrows at her, Lydianne couldn't help laughing and swatting at him. "What question might that be, Bishop Jeremiah?" she shot back.

He took her hand as they started back to the barn. "One of these days you might just find out," he murmured. "God love me if you give me the same answer you gave Glenn today."

Chapter Twenty-Nine

Saturday morning felt crisp, and the wind whispered that winter was only weeks away. Jeremiah simmered with new ideas and a single-minded purpose as he rode Mitch up the Helfings' unpaved lane. He was glad to see Pete's old pickup parked behind one of the twins' *dawdi hauses*—and he laughed out loud when Riley bounded around the house, barking raucously.

"Nobody sneaks up on *you*, do they, fella?" he teased as the golden retriever ran around his horse in wide circles, still barking. By the time he'd dismounted to tie his Percheron to the hitching rail at the side of the house, however, he'd had enough of the dog's racket.

He pointed his finger at the ground. "Riley, sit," he instructed. "Be quiet."

Riley immediately plunked his butt down, gazing up at Jeremiah with his tongue lolling out in a lopsided, adoring grin.

"*Gut* boy," he said as he vigorously rubbed the dog's golden head. "Where's Pete?"

The dog took off around the house, so Jeremiah followed him. As he walked, he noticed that the Helfings' white farmhouse and red outbuildings had been painted in recent weeks, and that the roofs and fences seemed to be in better repair than when he'd last seen them. Behind the house and the two *dawdi hauses* stood the small white building the twins called their noodle factory. Jeremiah chuckled when he caught sight of his nephew kneeling beside the shop's exterior mechanical works with his rear end sticking up in the air.

"I'm finally seeing your better side, Pete!" he called out. "What's going on?"

Pete remained on his knees but straightened to look at Jeremiah. He wrapped a playful arm around Riley's neck—and then quickly moved his other arm when his dog tried to grab hold of the large, rubber belt he was holding.

"I'm getting us out of the doghouse—again," he added as he shook the golden's shoulders. "Riley took a notion to play with the belt that runs the girls' mixer yesterday—snapped it like a rubber band. Luckily, they'd finished with the big batch of dough they'd been making, so they didn't lose any production time."

Jeremiah nodded. He could understand why a playful dog would be fascinated by a stretchy rubber belt—and he could picture Marietta and Molly's expressions when they realized that Riley had broken it. The breezy way Pete had referred to them as "the girls" hadn't escaped him, either, but he let it pass for the moment.

"So, they've still got their mixer and roller rigged up with small gas engines out here, which operate shaft-and-belt systems to run the noodle-making equipment inside," Jeremiah observed. "Looks the same as I recall it when their *mamm* started up the business several years ago."

"The look of things is about to change," Pete remarked as he released his dog. He deftly fitted the new black belt onto the higher wheel of the shaft—which went through a small hole into the building—before stretching it over the lower wheel, which was powered by the gas engine. "My next carpentry project will be to expand this shed to allow more space for a second dough roller, another workable, and another section of shelves where the noodles dry on screens."

"Because thanks to The Marketplace sales on Saturdays, Molly and Marietta's business has increased enough that they need more production area," Jeremiah said. He wasn't surprised to learn of the expansion, but it made him curious. "In your opinion, Pete, are they still driving the noodle business, or is the noodle business driving them?"

His nephew smiled, framing a diplomatic answer. "With the second roller they're buying, they'll both be able to flatten dough at the same time, and the new table will allow them to cut and dry twice as many noodles at once," he replied. "When I quizzed them about the same thing you just asked, Molly informed me that it was only logical to double up on equipment because their workforce is twice what it was when Mrs. Helfing was the sole proprietor."

Jeremiah laughed out loud. In his mind, he could hear Molly giving Pete this answer in that no-nonsense way she had of expressing herself. "Maybe your renovation work should include a wire cage around the outside mechanical system, so Riley can't break any more belts," he suggested. "Now that he knows how much fun it is, it might become a habit when nobody's paying attention to him."

Pete's eyebrows shot up. "Not a bad idea. I could rig up a chicken-wire cage this morning, and it could be a surprise when the girls get home."

He rose to his feet with a fluid strength that Jeremiah

was beginning to envy as he got older. "So, what brings you here this morning, Uncle? Are you on one of your bishop's missions? Or," he added in a teasing tone, "have you come to me because you want to feather your nest, *lovebird* that you've become lately?"

Jeremiah's jaw dropped—yet why should Pete's question surprise him? His nephew had been at the Detweiler funeral and had surely seen that he and Lydianne were spending time together. "If you're going to smart off, I could offer the job to Glenn or—"

"Not a *gut* idea, and you know it. Glenn's in no condition to concentrate on such a project—especially not at *your* place," Pete pointed out. "Ain't so?"

Jeremiah shook his head, chuckling. "I was teasing you. And *jah*, you're right on both counts, concerning Glenn."

"So what've you got in mind? With Mammi already living in your *dawdi haus*, you and your new bride will have the rest of that big white house to yourselves."

When had his nephew become so astute about living conditions and peoples' changing needs? Was Pete paying more attention to such details because he, too, was considering marriage someday?

Rather than asking questions Pete probably wasn't ready to answer, Jeremiah gave him a straightforward reply. "Truth be told, the *dawdi haus* could use some fresh paint—and whatever else Mamm might want. Then I'd like you to give the main kitchen a total renovation—"

"As in new cabinets and flooring and appliances?" Pete let out a whistle. "When you want to impress a woman, you go all out, man!"

Jeremiah looked his nephew straight in the eye. "Like marriage, home renovation is an all-or-nothing commitment you don't make more than once or twice in your life.

Might as well do it up right, considering the place is just like it was when Priscilla and I first moved into it."

Pete grinned, reminding Jeremiah of the mischievous kid he used to be. "That means you'll also want new flooring and fixtures in the bathroom—"

"Right."

"—and your hardwood floors need refinishing—"

"*Jah.*"

"—and you'll want an all-over paint job, inside and out," Pete finished. "Anything else?"

Jeremiah knew the dollar signs were adding up in his nephew's mind—and that was quite all right. "Think you could do the exterior painting and replace the windows before the snow flies? Maybe I'm getting older and notice it more, but the place seems draftier now that the nights are cooling down."

Pete looked away to hide a knowing smile. "The sooner you marry Lydianne, the sooner your nights will heat up—"

"Don't think I haven't thought about that—a lot," Jeremiah admitted, punching him playfully on the shoulder. "But Lydianne wants to honor her teaching commitment for the rest of the year, and as the bishop—and a school board member—I agree with her. And besides, it's not a done deal yet."

"She hasn't said *jah*?" Pete blurted. "Are you nuts, spending all that money on remodeling before—? Or is *she* nuts, that she needs convincing?"

Jeremiah had expected such a reaction from this nephew, who'd shown no signs of settling down or joining the Old Order church. And maybe he was being over-confident, assuming Lydianne fully intended to marry him.

What if she's only teasing me, playing that little game about popping the Big Question? What if I ask and she shuts me down, the way she rejected Glenn?

Every now and again, these niggling thoughts had filled Jeremiah's mind when he'd wakened in the night lately—because he didn't have Lydianne's answer. They weren't engaged yet. And if he waited too long to ask, or she had a change of heart, he would indeed have spent a lot of money on home improvements without improving his life one iota.

If Lydianne didn't agree to marry him, Jeremiah suspected he might become as embittered and desperate and depressed as Glenn was, even if it was for totally different reasons. And he would look like a fool, because after the events of the past week, his friends and family already considered them a couple.

But he didn't express his doubts to Pete.

"Patience is a virtue," Jeremiah finally replied. "Lydianne hasn't been married before, as I have. She deserves some time to be courted, and to adjust to the idea of living in a different home—"

"With a mother-in-law," Pete said in a purposeful tone. "Lydianne might recall that when Uncle Jude was courting Leah last year, Margaret Shetler was *not* a happy woman. She made no bones about Leah being the wrong choice for Jude—to the point that she moved out of his place."

"And the rest of us could understand Mamm's concern, because we shared it," Jeremiah reminded him. "Leah was most at home with her cattle and other animals—to the point she hardly knew how to make coffee, much less cook or handle kids. Your *mammi* has come around to considering Leah the perfect wife for Jude, however—and she's *ecstatic* because I've finally taken her advice, and Lydianne has responded to my attention."

"*Jah*, Lydianne responded to Glenn's attention after his *mamm*'s funeral, too," Pete murmured as he began to pick up his tools. "But seriously, Unc, I hope it works out for you, and I'm happy to have these projects to work on this winter. I also appreciate the way you've been paying my rent since I left the pet food factory—"

"Maybe with this winter's income locked in, you can pay your own rent, ain't so?"

Pete raked his hand through his collar-length blond hair, mentally adjusting to the suggestion. "*Jah*, it would look better if I was taking charge of my own finances—and of my life, in general," he mused aloud.

"It would look even better if your *mammi* made you some Plain shirts and broadfall trousers, so you wouldn't be wearing those jeans with the big holes in them—"

"These jeans are all the fashion now!" Pete protested. "English folks pay big money to wear worn-out denim like I've been hanging around in for years—because it's what I can afford."

Jeremiah waited him out, to see if he'd respond to the deeper issue beneath his suggestion to wear Amish clothing. Pete was nearly twenty-nine—far past the acceptable age for remaining in *rumspringa*—but Jeremiah knew there was no pushing his nephew to conform. If Pete felt his uncle, the bishop, or his *mammi* was forcing him to fit into the religious mold of the Old Order, the young man was likely to flee Morning Star and never come back.

"Maybe someday," Pete hedged after a few moments. "For now, it's a big improvement that I'll be supporting myself, the way Molly and Marietta have been doing for years now, ain't so?"

Jeremiah clapped his nephew's shoulder as they started toward the front of the house. "It's a step in the right direction," he agreed. "And *denki* for saying you'll do my renovations, because your workmanship is the *best*, Pete."

His nephew smiled modestly. "I'll be over later today to measure for the new windows. When I go to place the order at the lumberyard on Monday, I'll need a down payment for them, you know."

"I'll be ready with that money, and I'll give you an advance on your pay, too," Jeremiah replied happily. "Come for supper tonight—bring *the girls*, if you'd like," he added with a wink. "I'm going to mosey past The Marketplace and invite Lydianne, too. We can talk about what she and Mamm might want in the way of those renovations."

Chapter Thirty

When Lydianne entered the large, homey Shetler kitchen ahead of Jeremiah, she inhaled the heavenly aromas of frying chicken and the golden cornbread muffins that were cooling on the countertop. The table was set for four with a clean blue tablecloth and what she suspected were the better-than-everyday dishes. Bowls of coleslaw, mashed potatoes, strawberry jam, and home-canned peach halves sat ready, and she assumed the lidded metal pan on the other counter held some sort of dessert.

"It's *gut* to have you here, Lydianne," Jeremiah's *mamm* called from the stove as she carefully took pieces of crispy chicken from her cast iron skillet. She drained most of the grease and poured in milk thickened with flour. "We're not having anything fancy for supper, understand—"

"Fancy doesn't matter," Lydianne replied. "After a busy day at The Marketplace, it's wonderful to have someone else cooking my supper. *Denki* for having me over, on what I suspect was spur-of-the-moment notice," she added with a wry nod in Jeremiah's direction.

Margaret waved off her remark as she scraped the bottom of her skillet with a metal spatula. "Never you mind about that! It's nice to have some company tonight—and you never know what Pete might add to the conversation. I suspect, because the Helfing twins have also been at The Marketplace all day, he wouldn't be getting much in the way of supper, either."

Jeremiah's expression suggested a secret as he hung his and Lydianne's jackets on pegs inside the mudroom door. "I'll give you two a hint before Pete arrives, so you can be thinking about your requests," he said, sounding extremely pleased with himself. "I've asked him to replace all the windows as well as to paint the outside of the house as soon as he can get to it. And this winter he'll be doing some extensive remodeling inside."

His *mamm* was so surprised she dropped her spatula. "What brought this on? Will this *extensive remodeling* mean we'll be living with construction mess for months on end?"

"*You* will be living in your *dawdi haus* rooms, away from most of the commotion," he reminded her kindly. "Although, if you want some improvements in the *dawdi haus*, besides the fresh paint I've already mentioned to Pete, just tell him what you'd like."

Lydianne's heart beat faster. Amish homes typically underwent renovation only when major changes happened in the family—such as adding rooms to accommodate a growing family or aging parents—or preparing for a new woman to take over the household.

"Otherwise," Jeremiah continued, gesturing at the kitchen walls around them, "I've asked him to build us new cabinets in here, and to paint all the rooms and refinish the hardwood floors, and to update the bathroom. Because Priscilla doesn't live here anymore, and I'm ready to start fresh."

The way he added those final words, in a voice that thrummed with emotion, told Lydianne that the big change he was making in his life hadn't come easily. Her heart went out to him, and she wasn't sure what to say.

Margaret gazed at her son for several moments. Her smile came on like an autumn sunset, with a slow glow that brightened her entire outlook. "*Gut* for you, Jeremiah, and thanks be to God," she murmured gratefully. "In that case, whatever commotion Pete causes while he works will be well worth it."

As though the word *commotion* had been his cue, Riley burst through the mudroom and ran an excited lap around the kitchen table, yipping gleefully.

"Riley! Whoa!" Pete called out as he, too, entered the kitchen. "Don't you dare grab hold of that tablecloth—"

"Riley," Jeremiah murmured, establishing eye contact with the dog. "Sit, boy."

Immediately the huge dog plunked himself on the floor at Jeremiah's feet, gazing up at him with a doggy grin as he leaned into his leg. It was such a funny, endearing thing, watching the bishop so effortlessly make Pete's retriever behave, that Lydianne almost laughed—but she sensed Margaret didn't find the dog's antics the least bit humorous.

"Pete, if that dog doesn't settle down, he's going outside," Jeremiah's *mamm* stated, crossing her arms. "We have a guest for dinner tonight and we don't want to scare her off."

Pete flashed Lydianne a wink. "I don't think we have a thing to worry about, Mammi," he replied. "Riley will settle down now that he's seen everybody. If he can't keep a lid on it, I'll put him out."

When Pete bussed his *mammi*'s cheek with a noisy

kiss, the stiffness went out of Margaret's shoulders. "I hear Jeremiah invited Molly and Marietta to join us tonight, but they declined his offer," she said as she turned off the stove burners. "You haven't been causing them any trouble, have you?"

Pete bit back a grin. "I suppose they decided to do something with Jo again tonight. Those *maidels* are as thick as thieves—present company excepted," he added quickly as he glanced at Lydianne.

Lydianne laughed and held the bowl steady as Margaret poured the steaming gravy into it. "After a busy day at The Marketplace, we like to unwind over a pizza uptown— and chat about what we sold and who was there. Business talk."

"Girl time," Margaret put in. "Nothing wrong with that on a Saturday night—but we're mighty glad you've joined us, dear. *Denki* for your help. We're ready to sit down and enjoy our meal now."

Lydianne didn't miss the way Jeremiah pulled out the chair to the left of his place at the head of the table— where his wife would normally sit. As Margaret took the seat to Lydianne's left and Pete sat down across the table from her, it felt more like a cozy family gathering she'd attended dozens of times, than a first dinner at the home of her potential husband . . . and mother-in-law.

Help me to say and do the right things, Lord, she prayed as they all bowed their heads for the silent grace. *After all the years of eating with my girlfriends, keeping the secret I believed would prevent me from ever marrying, it's such a blessing to be here in the Shetler home with the man who knows my past and loves me anyway.*

As Jeremiah took two pieces of golden fried chicken

and passed Lydianne the platter, his dark eyes glimmered with questions. "What does the ideal kitchen look like these days, Lydianne? What kind of cabinets are best—and how would they be arranged? And what sort of flooring would it include? Trends and products have changed over the years," he added in explanation, "and I haven't paid the least bit of attention to such stuff."

Lydianne gripped the platter so she wouldn't drop it. Jeremiah hadn't said anything about the kitchen being *hers*—nor had he teased about renovating the kitchen when and if he asked her to marry him.

"I've never had to think about that," she replied carefully, "because I moved into a rental house owned by an English landlord. And when I bought the place, I didn't have the money—or the inclination—to change it around."

His smile acknowledged her diplomatic dodge. "But if you did think about it, what would you choose?"

She took a chicken leg, not at all sure she could eat it. This conversation felt a lot like the open-ended essay quizzes she sometimes gave her older scholars, who were often hard-pressed to write the answers they thought Teacher Lydianne would consider correct. As she passed the platter to her left, she noticed that Margaret's expression remained unreadable—and Jeremiah's *mamm* didn't seem eager to mention her own ideas, either.

"I'd need some time to give a *gut* answer," Lydianne finally said. "The kitchen's the hub of a household, and it wouldn't do to make such decisions without considering the possibilities—or at least without spending time at a home improvement store to see what the options are. What do *you* think, Margaret?" she asked quickly.

The woman beside her let out a short laugh. "To me, a

kitchen's a kitchen, and as long as all the appliances work and the drain's not clogged, I'm happy. But Jeremiah didn't ask for my opinion," she pointed out as she handed the chicken across the table to Pete. "What might be just as important is what you'd choose to put *inside* those cabinets—how much of the old cookware you'd replace with something new. And I'm happy not to be making that decision, either."

Margaret's answers sounded as vague as her own— probably because her son hadn't yet announced that he and Lydianne were getting married. Even though their engagement would be welcome news, Jeremiah's unspoken proposal was like that proverbial elephant in the room— everyone knew it was there, but no one wanted to talk about it.

Lydianne nodded as she accepted the bowl of mashed potatoes from Jeremiah, who showed no sign of commenting. It would be a major decision for any woman he chose as his new wife—how many of Priscilla's pans, dishes, and appliances would remain—yet many Amish men wouldn't even consider it a choice. They would simply assume that everything in the kitchen was fine and that any woman would be satisfied with the way it was.

With a glimmer of mischief, Lydianne decided to use a favorite classroom tactic to shift the focus away from *her*. "Jeremiah, it's very *progressive* of you to solicit my opinion about what makes an ideal kitchen," she remarked, keeping a straight face as she passed the potatoes to his mother. "Why do you ask?"

Startled by her direct question, Jeremiah dropped the gravy bowl. Thick, golden goop splattered his shirt and the tablecloth as the heavy bowl's edge hit his dinner plate and broke it. Pete burst out laughing, which in turn made Riley jump up from his spot under the table to start barking as though a fire had broken out.

Lydianne sprang to her feet with her paper napkin, immediately sorry she'd caused such a ruckus. As she and Jeremiah hurried to wipe the gravy from his shirt before it dribbled down farther, she tried to think of an appropriate apology.

"I'm sorry," she murmured. "I didn't—"

"No, you're not," he said under his breath.

"—mean to come at you broadside with—"

"Yes, you did."

Lydianne blinked. She tossed her saturated napkin onto his broken plate, confused by his muttered responses—until she noticed the lines around his eyes crinkling with suppressed laughter. Still seated calmly, Margaret was also fighting a smile. Pete was laughing so hard he was wiping his eyes, and Riley's excited barking escalated into howls as he circled the table with his wagging tail held high.

Lydianne couldn't recall the last time she'd caused so much chaos—

Oh, but I upset the apple cart big-time when I confessed that Ella was my child. Jeremiah took that in stride, too—just as he's chuckling at the way I tried to flush out his real question.

Jeremiah pointed at Riley. "Sit."

The golden obeyed his quiet command immediately. The kitchen filled with welcome silence.

As the man beside her rose from his chair, he held Lydianne's gaze. "I'll deal with you later," he murmured with a smile. "You folks go ahead and eat while the food's hot. I'm changing my shirt."

When Jeremiah was out of earshot, his *mamm* went over to lift the overturned gravy bowl from the table.

Lydianne stood to pick up the two halves of the plate, careful to keep the gravy and Jeremiah's food on it. "Margaret, I'm sorry your pretty plate got broken—"

"All you did was ask the same question that was buzzing around in *my* mind," she put in lightly. "It was worth a broken dish to see you take Jeremiah by surprise."

"Got what he deserved," Pete said, scraping gravy from the tablecloth with his spoon. "And you gave him a reasonable answer, too, Lydianne, about going to the home improvement store to see what sorts of cabinets and flooring are available.

"Don't let him off easy, girl," he added with a laugh. "It's *gut* when somebody makes Jeremiah toe the line the same way he insists that folks at church—and me—live up to his expectations."

As he and Lydianne strolled down the lane toward the river, Jeremiah's emotions bubbled like a copper cauldron of the apple butter many folks were making as October came to a close. After getting through the rest of supper without further incident, he knew it was time to state his case—yet he still felt more jittery than a teenager asking a pretty girl to ride home from a Singing. Even though he and the lovely young woman walking beside him had teased each other about his proposal for quite a while, wording it just the right way was another matter altogether.

And now that Lydianne had called his bluff with her purposeful question, his proposal *really* had to measure up. Any woman who could make him drop a bowl of gravy deserved words as effective as hers had been. Lydianne was intelligent, with a sharper sense of timing and humor than any other woman he knew. Those attributes were among the many reasons he loved her—but what a challenge she was!

"It's a beautiful evening," Lydianne murmured as she slipped her small, sturdy hand into his. "These maples and sweet gum trees are the most colorful I've seen this fall, with their bright reds and oranges and golds."

But their beauty doesn't hold a candle to yours.

Jeremiah hesitated to voice that sentiment. Would it sound too sappy or old fashioned for a forward-thinking woman like Teacher Lydianne? Her true beauty was inside, after all. She was more than just a pretty face.

"This section of the farm is one of my favorites," Jeremiah responded, hoping he hadn't let too many seconds tick by. "From here, you can see the fields where my popcorn crop's been harvested, as well as the pasture where our horses graze—"

"And look at the way your house is shining in the last rays of the sunset," Lydianne murmured with awe in her voice. "The white walls seem to glow from the inside out, radiating all the love of the family who lives there."

Jeremiah's throat tightened with emotion. As he gazed at the house he'd looked at thousands of times in his years of living here, with and without Priscilla, his heart suddenly saw it in a whole new light—

And that light comes straight from Lydianne, from a heart so loving and dedicated, that I'm not sure I deserve her.

"What a fine sentiment. I wish I'd said that," he murmured. He certainly couldn't voice his doubts about deserving her, for fear she'd agree with him. "I—I'm really glad

Pete's going to paint it soon and freshen it up inside over the winter months, too. It's work that's long overdue—"

"And you really are being very generous, Jeremiah, asking my opinion about those renovations," Lydianne put in. "I—I didn't mean to put you on the spot at supper or—"

"You did, too!" he blurted as he pulled her close in a playful hug. "And I needed that—and I need *you*, Lydianne, and *please* will you marry me because you're making me so crazy I can't think straight and—and I love you so much," he blurted out. "Please say you will!"

He closed his eyes with an anguished sigh. He'd sounded like an absolute idiot who couldn't string three words together in a meaningful sentence. At this most important moment, when he'd intended to be every bit as eloquent as Lydianne, he'd fallen flat. He didn't dare turn her loose and let her walk away, yet he couldn't look at her, either.

As the silence stretched between them, he knew he was doomed.

"Oh, Jeremiah, I love you, too," Lydianne finally whispered in a trembling voice. "Of course, I'll—yes! *Yes*, I'll be your wife!"

His heart stood still. His soul soaked up the peace and grace—and joy!—that enveloped him, surely gifts from God Himself. When he opened his eyes, Lydianne's crystal-blue gaze unhinged him and he hugged her close. The tear dribbling down each of her velvety cheeks touched him deeply as he let her answer sink in.

She said yes! Lydianne has agreed to be my wife!

Jeremiah chuckled, mostly at himself. "You know, I've delivered dozens of sermons, depending upon the Lord to give me the right ideas and the words to express them.

Yet when I asked you to—well, I must've sounded like I didn't have a brain in my head—"

Lydianne placed a finger across his lips to silence him. "You sounded like a man who's in love—with *me*," she added in a whisper. "Since the moment I knew a baby was on the way—more than six years ago, after I'd lost Aden— I've believed no other man would have me. Yet you, a *bishop*, forgave my secret past and—"

"Do you have any idea what a sense of *hope* I've known since we've been together?" Jeremiah interrupted her gently. "I thought I'd never have another chance at a new family, but now—"

His heart felt so overwhelmed with emotion, he embraced Lydianne again, loving the way her arms encircled him as though she'd never let him go. "Now, as I think ahead to late spring, when we'll marry, I realize that by this time next year—"

"I could be carrying your child, Jeremiah," she finished in a whisper. "I can't wait!"

"Oh, don't say *that*!" he shot back with a desperate laugh. "You're way too tempting, Lydianne, and if we don't *wait*, we'll have to answer to—"

"I know. A bishop and his woman have to toe the line. I'll try to behave," she murmured. She looked him straight in the eye as color rose into her flawless cheeks. "But I want you, too."

Jeremiah sighed from the depth of his soul and eased away from her. "We'd better keep walking," he suggested as he took her hand again. "I'm all too aware of how long it's been since . . . a wife shared my bed."

As they followed the trail to his favorite place beside the river, he realized how much Lydianne had blessed his life by simply being her inimitable self. He could already imagine his mother's excitement when they returned to the house to share their news, but at this moment he wanted to savor Lydianne's company. Dry leaves rustled beneath their feet as the gurgling of the river's current called to Jeremiah as it always had—like the voice of God, ever moving forward, reminding him that life never stood still.

"Ohhh. Look at this place," Lydianne whispered. "See the way the last of the day's light plays on the leaves? Smell the dampness of the shoreline, and hear how the water sings as it flows along? And look!" she said, pointing upward. "There's an eagle!"

Indeed, a lone bird soared far above them, drifting effortlessly on the currents of wind beneath its wings.

"They nest a little farther down the river, on the bluffs," Jeremiah explained. "I come here when I need to think through a problem, or to let go of troubling thoughts—or when I just want to bask in the sunshine on top of that big flat boulder, and remind myself of all the gifts God's brought into my life. Like *you*, Lydianne."

Her smile made him shimmer all over. "Listen to you, saying all the right things the right way," she said softly. "May I join you in your spot?"

"I was hoping you would."

Before he could help her, Lydianne assessed the smaller rocks and nimbly clambered over them to the top of the boulder. As she sat down, her attentive gaze told Jeremiah that she was taking in the details of this place and appreciating them as deeply as he did. He lowered himself beside her, gently wrapping his arm around her slender shoulders.

"I . . . I've never sat here with anyone else."

"Not even Priscilla?" she whispered. Her eyes widened as she considered this.

Jeremiah shook his head. "She kept her distance from the river because the current scared her, and she couldn't swim. She understood that when I took my walks, I often came here to have some quiet time—not that she was noisy or intrusive," he added wistfully.

"This could still be your place, Jeremiah—your special getaway—"

"But if you'll share it with me, it'll be even more special, Lydianne." He drank in the sight of her soft skin and the blond hair pulled neatly beneath her fresh white *kapp*—and the blue eyes that sparkled with such a sense of promise. "I mostly wanted to show it to you because this is where I found Ella after we'd been searching for her all night. She was curled up right here on top of this rock, because it had retained the day's warmth."

Lydianne's eyes filled with tears of wonder. "She came here looking for God, and she heard His voice," she whispered. "As long as I live, I'll never forget the moment she said that—not because she's my child, but because she'd had such a holy moment."

"And she recognized it for what it was," Jeremiah put in. He reached for Lydianne's hand again as he recalled that moment of joy and relief, finding Ella in the spot where they were sitting. "She looked so peaceful and trusting, so sweet—like an angel taking a nap. And she looked exactly like you, Sunshine."

"Resemblance aside, Ella *is* the greatest gift I've received in my lifetime," she whispered. "And right now, you're running a pretty close second, Jeremiah."

When Lydianne rested her head against his shoulder, Jeremiah felt a deep sense of satisfaction—the certainty that this was the first evening of the rest of their lives, and that God had meant for them to find each other the way He'd led little Ella to this safe place.

"I feel we're sitting on hallowed ground, you and I," he murmured. "That's another reason I hope we can consider this spot by the river our place."

When she smiled at him, Jeremiah saw himself reflected in her crystal blue eyes—and he loved being there.

"Anyplace can be our place," Lydianne said. "As long as we're there together, *jah*?"

Once again, she'd left him speechless. Jeremiah smiled, knowing he'd better get used to that.

Please read on for an excerpt from the next novel in
The Maidels of Morning Star series, available soon!

Christmas Comes to Morning Star

By
Charlotte Hubbard

Chapter One

Warmed by the sunlight streaming through the window of the newly expanded noodle factory, Marietta Helfing stretched. She felt like a cat, limber and strong, soothed by the low rumble of the motors that ran the two cylindrical noodle presses. As she carefully arranged a thin length of pressed dough on her worktable, she caught her twin, Molly, gazing at her from beside the other table, where she was also preparing to cut a large rectangle of dough into long strips.

"Penny for your thoughts," Molly remarked as she picked up her sharp knife. "And you look like you have a lot of them."

Marietta smiled as she, too, began to cut her dough into long strips about four inches wide. "This time last year—the day after Thanksgiving—I was going in for my surgery, and I was frightened out of my mind," she recalled as her knife moved deftly through the dough. "It's such a blessing to be recovered and working at full steam again, after all that time I was wiped out from chemo."

"And I thank the Lord every day that you're back to normal," Molly put in as they worked. "I'm looking forward to a fine, fun Christmas, different from last year, when we had to spend so much time getting you to your cancer treatments. Another gift is being able to work side by side now that we've doubled our work space and equipment," she added with a lilt in her voice. "Mamm would be amazed at the way her little business has taken off like a shot, and that we're selling so many bags of noodles at The Marketplace each Saturday."

"Jah, she would." Marietta worked in silence for a while, letting a wave of wistful nostalgia run its course. She missed their mother even more than she missed the breasts she'd lost during her bilateral mastectomy, but she was determined to forge ahead—to meet the demands of the eager customers who thronged their noodle shop at The Marketplace each Saturday.

After today's noodles were cut and drying on screens, she and Molly would bag and label the dried noodles they'd made earlier in the week, so they could load the wagon this afternoon for the drive into town on Saturday morning. It was a steady yet demanding schedule they kept these days, but Marietta felt good about paying down the mountain of bills she'd accrued following her mastectomy and chemo treatments. She and Molly would soon be banking enough income to support themselves well into their later years—an important advantage, considering Marietta didn't intend to marry.

After all, what man could possibly want a woman who was both damaged goods and unable to bear him children?

When she glanced at her sister, who was placing the first strip of her noodle dough into the roller to flatten it again, Marietta noticed a flicker of emotion on Molly's face. What could've caused such a discontented expression?

"Penny for your thoughts, sister," Marietta said as she,

too, began feeding a strip of noodle dough through her roller.

Molly shrugged, guiding the thinner strip of pastry with her hands for several seconds before she responded. "Sure is quiet without Riley and Pete around."

Marietta's eyes widened at her sister's wistful remark. For several months, Pete Shetler and his golden retriever, Riley, had stayed in one of their two *dawdi hauses* because Bishop Jeremiah Shetler had thought it would be an improvement over his nephew's former living arrangements. During his stay, Pete had done some much-needed maintenance around their farm as well as remodeled their noodle factory—while his active young dog had mostly dug up Mamm's flower beds, chewed the belts on their noodle-making equipment, and found other trouble to get into.

Pete had moved into a room at his uncle's house, however, when Bishop Jeremiah had announced his engagement to Teacher Lydianne Christner. Both men had felt it would be more convenient for Pete to live at the Shetler farm during the winter months while he did some extensive remodeling on the bishop's place. Although Marietta appreciated the return to a quieter routine without their renter, she sensed that Molly had secretly adored the muscular blond carpenter and his rambunctious dog.

"Maybe you should pay Pete a visit," she suggested. "I bet he'd be tickled if you took over a pan of that noodle pudding he always—"

"Why would I do that?" Molly blurted. Her tone sounded playfully defiant, but her brow furrowed. "It's not as though anything would come of it—even if Pete took the hint and asked me out."

"Why not?" Marietta paused, almost hesitant to continue.

She didn't want to limit her twin's future, and yet . . . "Just because I'll never marry doesn't mean you should forfeit a potential romance with Pete. Sure, he's clueless most of the time, but he seems trainable. And he's awfully cute."

"Let's not forget that Pete refuses to join the Amish church, so a romance with him is pointless—even if he knew the meaning of the word," Molly shot back. "Truth be told, I like Riley a whole lot better than Pete, anyway. I intend to remain here on the farm with you, sister, as we've always agreed upon," she added quickly. "We're turning thirty-five next month, so why would I want to change my life—and my attitude—to accommodate a husband?"

Although Marietta still suspected her sister had feelings for Pete, she was relieved to hear Molly's vehement insistence upon staying at the home place. The two of them had spent very little time apart; how would she cope with life alone in their farmhouse if Molly married? Such a lonely life was something she didn't even want to think about.

"And besides," Molly continued as she fed another strip of her dough into the roller, "we *maidels* need to stick together to keep The Marketplace going, ain't so? With Regina married now and Lydianne engaged to the bishop, it'll soon just be us two and Jo running the place."

Marietta nodded. Jo Fussner had been the driving force behind creating The Marketplace from a dilapidated old stable nearly six months ago. It wouldn't be fair to saddle her with all the responsibility for managing Morning Star's very successful Amish market, especially when she'd planned that the business venture would be a project for her four *maidel* friends to share with her.

"Jah, that's a *gut* point. Having a husband or a fiancé has changed things for those two girls—and I really miss having Regina around on Saturdays," Marietta put in.

"Once Lydianne's married to Bishop Jeremiah, there'll be no working away from home for her, either."

"Not to mention what would happen if we acquired husbands and they felt they should be involved with running The Marketplace," Molly speculated aloud. "That would change everything, and we'd no longer have control over how business was done there."

"Wouldn't be fair to Jo if we married and left the management all on her shoulders, either," Marietta put in. "Her bakery keeps her so busy nowadays, I don't see how she'd have time to take over all of the bookkeeping, as well."

For a few moments the two of them worked in comfortable silence, feeding the remaining strips of dough into their separate rollers so they could cut them into noodles suitable for soups and casseroles.

"I'm hoping Lydianne will keep doing our accounting at home after she marries," Molly remarked after a bit. "Can you imagine the fuss Drusilla will make if Jo spends even more time doing all the organizing and accounting? She's already squawking about the extra effort the Christmas season will require, and it's not even December yet."

Marietta laughed out loud. Jo's *mamm* was known for always seeing the proverbial glass as half empty rather than half full—and indeed, Drusilla often seemed to believe she had no glass at all. "We shopkeepers will all be busier than usual, starting this weekend when—"

The backfiring and familiar rumble of a pickup truck made them look toward the window. Molly's face lit up. She quickly shut off her roller, washed her hands, and started toward the door of the shop, laughing at the sound of a golden retriever's raucous bark. She opened the door just wide enough to slip outside, preventing Riley from entering the noodle factory—and spoiling their morning's work if he plunked his huge front paws on a worktable covered with dough strips.

"Shetler, we were just talking about you!" Molly called out.

"Maybe that's why my ears were burning, *jah*?" Pete fired back. "Were you talking trash about me, or saying how much you miss Riley and me causing trouble all the time?"

Marietta shut off her roller and braced herself against her worktable. Molly could deny it until the cows came home, but she was sweet on Pete Shetler, and he liked Molly a lot more than he would admit, as well. Their banter continued outside for a few moments while Marietta tried to still the apprehensive fluttering of her heart.

This is all in Your hands, Lord, but you know how lonely I'd be if Molly married and left me here by myself—even if she deserves her happiness.

As the shop door opened, however, Marietta fixed a smile on her face. After all, if she'd battled cancer and won, she could face whatever changes Pete Shetler might bring into their lives—or whatever he'd come to tell them today.